ON A QUIET STREET

BOOKS BY CARLA KOVACH

What She Did

Find Me

The Houseshare

DETECTIVE GINA HARTE SERIES

The Next Girl

Her Final Hour

Her Pretty Bones

The Liar's House

Her Dark Heart

Her Last Mistake

Their Silent Graves

The Broken Ones

One Left Behind

Her Dying Wish

One Girl Missing

Her Deadly Promise

Their Cold Hearts

Her Hidden Shadow

Meet Me at Marmaris Castle

Whispers Beneath the Pines

To Let

Flame

ON A QUIET STREET

Carla Kovach

bookouture

Published by Bookouture in 2024

An imprint of Storyfire Ltd.
Carmelite House
50 Victoria Embankment
London EC4Y 0DZ

www.bookouture.com

ISBN: 978-1-83790-495-2
eBook ISBN: 978-1-83790-494-5

This book is dedicated to those who have lost or been affected by the loss of a baby. My deepest condolences go out to you. X

PROLOGUE

My family are the world to me and I will do all I can to protect them from a past that will destroy everything I've worked so hard for, from a present that fills me with fear, to a future that will be ruined if I don't act now. It is down to me to put those who are the most precious to me first.

The life I have right now is perfect. I shake my head. Actually, it's not, but it will be. I will make sure of it and if anyone gets in my way, they'll regret it. That's a promise. As I said, family is everything. No one would disagree with me.

I cling to the toilet bowl and heave, knowing I don't have much time to sort this mess out. Time is not a luxury I have, so here goes.

PART 1

LEAH

ONE

NOW

'Leah, Leah.'

While lying on her side facing the window, she felt his hot breath on the back of her neck as he got back into bed and spooned her. The smell of the toast he'd left on her bedside table sent her stomach turning, the thought that he was cheating on her again too much to bear.

'I made you some breakfast.' He leaned over her and kissed her bare neck. She loved his smile; she'd always loved it. It's what first attracted her to him but now, she didn't know what to think. Who was making him smile like that? She liked to think he was happy about being close to her, but she knew otherwise and she wondered if she'd ever really made him happy.

Leah knew she'd have to appear thankful for the toast, otherwise they'd end up arguing like they were last night; and she had no proof he was seeing that woman again. Alison. She turned to face him. Her gaze met his sad brown eyes as he lay on his pillow. 'Thanks. I'll eat it in a bit.' That was the best she could do. If she tried to eat it now, it would only stick in her throat. The more she looked at him, the more she wondered if her brain was joining up dots that didn't exist. He'd promised her that Alison was long gone.

He exhaled and ran a hand through his chestnut brown hair, the same hair she'd often enjoyed stroking while they lay in bed. 'I'm sorry, okay. I really am and I don't like it when you're upset. I shouldn't have said some of those things last night but you hurt me too. The constant accusations have to stop.'

She wondered if he'd come home later with flowers or chocolates. That's what he did after they had a row. Last night, it had all started with the rose perfume and the messages. She'd accused him of meeting up with Alison again, and he had shouted, saying that Leah was being paranoid and possessive, accusing her of trying to control him. She wondered if he'd cleaned up the pieces of fruit bowl that he'd flung at the wall in a temper.

As if sensing her thoughts, he spoke. 'I'll buy a new fruit bowl. Maybe you could look online and choose something better.' She didn't want anything better; she loved that bowl.

On feeling his body next to hers, she wanted nothing more than to forgive and believe him but it irked her that buying gifts was his answer to everything, like money could fix the problem. 'It's not about the fruit bowl.' It was about those messages and the fact that he smelled of perfume and came home late – again. 'Cain, please let me see the messages. You've cheated on me in the past and it still hurts.'

He flung the quilt back. Standing naked with his back to her, he began to pull up his boxer shorts. 'This again. I told you, there are no messages.'

'I heard your phone beeping all night. You're making out like I'm crazy.'

He raised his eyebrows and huffed. 'I'm not making out like you're crazy, you are. You hear things when there is nothing to hear and now you tell me to treat you like you're not crazy. Babe, this level of possessiveness, it's too much. I can't breathe in this relationship.' He grabbed his phone off the bedside table. 'Here, take a look. Go on.'

With trembling fingers, she took the phone off him. Opening his messages would be a huge breach of trust – and she didn't want to be the jealous wife – but right now, all she could think about was him and Alison together and it was breaking her heart.

He tilted his head. 'If you do open those messages, it will show me that you don't trust me, and how do you think that will make me feel? Horrible, that's how.' He paused, then asked: 'What's this really about, Leah? You don't seem yourself lately.'

'It's about you coming home late all the time smelling of perfume and never answering your phone. I sit here wondering if you're with her again.'

'Here we go, dredging up the past. I was with a client. I'm working on getting a huge contract at the moment, one that could change our lives, and I come home to an interrogation. I'm doing this to make a better life for you, for us.'

'But it was Sunday yesterday. She wanted to meet up with you about work on a Sunday? Really?'

'She has a job which means she works all week. Sundays and evenings are when she's free to discuss the project.' He paused again. 'It's not about the perfume or me having meetings on evenings or Sundays, is it? I know you didn't get on with your mother and you hide your feelings well. She died and I know you need to process that. Once your mother's house is sold, you'll be able to move on. We can move on and forget the past. There's so much to look forward to. You need to focus on that, and I need to focus on getting this contract.' He leaned on the bed, his gaze locking onto hers as he kissed her. 'One day soon, we're going to have our dream home. We can have it all. Just be patient with me, please. I love you and only you. Okay?'

She shrugged and allowed her tears to spill. Yes, the mother she hadn't spoken to for years had died just before Christmas.

She had left everything to Leah, but that didn't take away the fact that Cain was upsetting her. It was more than the perfume and the meetings; it was his behaviour. He'd barely touched her for weeks, and when they were alone at night, it was like he was somewhere else; and seeing him angrily throw that bowl had scared her. Maybe now wasn't the right time. 'You're right. I love you too.'

He pulled his trousers on and buttoned his shirt up. 'I'm going to need my phone for work.' Last night, he hadn't let her anywhere near his phone but now, suddenly, he'd handed it to her. That told her one thing. If there were any messages, he'd since deleted them. Or maybe he wasn't lying and there was no affair. She gave him his phone.

'I mean it when I say love you. I've never loved anyone else, not really loved.' He paused. 'I know I've hurt you in the past and I will always regret being so stupid. I was an idiot. I can't do any more than keep apologising, but your need to constantly check on me is suffocating. We need to move on. Right now, I'm dealing with a very needy client, that's all. She wears the most hideous fake smelling perfume. I'm sorry about that too. Please trust me.'

Trust him. She remembered that six-month fling he'd had with their previous neighbour, Alison, within a year of them getting together. He'd lied about that until she caught them red handed. Alison certainly hadn't popped by to borrow some milk. A few years later, there were all the business weekends away where he'd conveniently not answered his phone at all. She'd seen a message pop up from Alison. He'd been having an affair with her, again. After a lot of work, they'd recovered and he'd promised he'd never hurt her again. Trust had always been an issue between them. She'd been so young when they met. He was older with his own house and she'd been in a hurry to grow up and move in with him. They'd been in this house ever since.

'By the way, my client is coming for dinner on Saturday so

you'll get to meet her. We need to impress if I'm going to get to project manage this one. It's a two-million-pound build, so a lot depends on it. It could literally change our lives and buy us a better house, especially when we sell your mother's property too.'

As he continued to speak about his work, she got out of bed, her nightshirt dropping over her thighs. She walked over to the window and opened the curtains to let the April morning sun shine through. The mention of her mother took her back to late last year, when she'd received a letter from her asking if they could speak as Jean had *something of utmost importance she wished to discuss.* Jean Harrison didn't mention she was dying in the letter, so Leah had ignored it; the thought of speaking to her mother again had been too painful. She wished now that she had responded to the letter, despite what Jean did to her. Maybe now she'd have the closure she craved. From the outside Jean looked like a wonderful mother but people don't always see what is right in front of them. They didn't see the mental scars that Leah carried from all the name calling, or that she'd been starved of a few meals because she'd put a few pounds on one Christmas. Her mother aimed to show nothing but her warped view of perfection from them both to the outside world at whatever cost to Leah.

Glancing down at the road, she spotted three girls who looked to be in their late teens huddled together. Her neighbour, Zara, rode her mobility scooter up the path. She tugged her beagle, Molly's, lead then she stopped to talk to the girl with the curly hair. Leah glanced up the road a little and saw the two other girls watching on. She wondered if a new family had moved onto the road. Zara shook her head and took something from the girl before continuing towards her bungalow. The girl's dark eyes met Leah's, and a shiver ran down her spine. Then one of the other girls looked up at her. She grabbed the curtains, shutting the sun out. Something in that stare told her that the girl was sussing her out, but why? Leah carefully stepped back, away from the window.

'I can't find my tie, the blue one. Have you seen it?'

He went to slide open her side of the wardrobe. She sprinted across the room. He couldn't go in there searching for his tie. Heart banging, she stood between him and the sliding door. 'Look, I'm sorry too. I shouldn't have said all those things last night. It's just—'

'It's okay, you don't have to explain but we do need to sort things out.' He lifted his hand and stroked her shoulder-length dark brown hair, his fingers getting caught in a lug. For a moment she was with the man she'd met all those years ago. The kind, attentive man who spoke about the wonderful life they'd have. He'd talk enthusiastically of the children they'd have who'd share their dark hair and her dimpled cheeks. How had her life become such a cliché she'd never know. A big part of her still wanted it to work. She wanted to be enough for Cain.

'I think we should go to the doctor, find out if there's something wrong, find out why we're not conceiving. We've been trying for a couple of years now.'

'It's not that long, really. People try for a lot longer.'

'Come on, I'm sure all this is the stress of dealing with your mother's house. It will happen, we'll have our baby one day, and you'll never have to go back to that house again.'

She took a deep breath. It had been a hard decision but she decided she didn't want a baby, ever, and if he mooched through her wardrobe, he might come across the contraceptive injections she kept hidden under her jumpers. She was never going to have a baby; the very thought of giving birth gave her palpitations. Maybe she could work through her issues one day. Even if she did, she was never going to bring a baby into a relationship with zero trust; but she didn't have the energy for that argument, not today. A tear threatened to escape as she thought of never holding her own cute writhing baby in her arms. Confused, is how she felt. 'You're right. Let me look for your tie.' She pulled away from him and wiped her bare arm across her sodden face. Riffling through his tie rack, she parted the sea blue and aquamarine ties and found the one he was looking for, his so-called lucky tie.

'I don't know how I missed that.' Leah didn't either. The tie was in its exact colour order, just how he liked them. His phone beeped loudly.

She stared as he read the message and laughed. 'What? Don't go all jealous on me again, it's just a joke from one of the lads on site. See you at six. I'll get a good bottle of wine and we'll watch a film and get cosy together or maybe we could have an early night.' He smiled as he continued knotting his tie. 'Got to dash.'

She exhaled as he slammed the front door and left. The thought of him being all over the woman smelling of rose perfume later made her blood run cold. She walked over to the window and watched Cain tapping away on his phone, a smile pasted across his face before he drove off. She nudged the window open a touch, to try to get rid of the smell of the toast she wasn't going to be able to stomach. There wasn't any sign of the three girls. They must have gone.

Cain and the staring girl had unsettled her. He was having an affair, and she was going to prove it even though it would kill her to find out he'd cheated again.

TWO

Molly's barking made her flinch, that's when she saw Zara riding towards her front door.

Damn, Leah wasn't even dressed. She slipped a hoodie over her nightshirt. Hurrying down the stairs, she opened the door, letting the beagle tread its damp paws along the heated floor. Cain hated her dog coming into their pristine house. 'Come in. Shall I put the kettle on?' Had she just said that? There was probably smashed pieces of fruit bowl everywhere. Clenching her clammy fists in a tense ball at the thought of Cain losing his temper, she hoped that Zara was too busy to stop for a drink.

Zara shook her head and remained seated on her scooter. 'No. I can't stay. My sister is visiting in a bit with the nephews, and I really need to get back and throw the dog bed in the garden before she comes in fake-choking and claiming the kids can't breathe because Molly is so smelly. Such a drama queen.'

'I know I'm not due to clean yours today, but I'm more than happy to pop by and run the vacuum over if you need me to.' Leah had been cleaning Zara's for several years now. It was Zara's idea that she set up her home cleaning business. Zara had started working from home due to her worsening condition, so they were finding their way through self-employment together. She owed her friend so much for urging her to take the leap from cleaner to business owner.

'No. I can manage. The place isn't even that bad. It's just my stupid sister. She does whinge about exposing the kids to a few dog hairs. She won't even let them stroke Molly.' Zara huffed. 'I think those kids have more chance of giving Molly something. They're always picking their noses and scratching their heads, and both of them scream like the antichrist entering a church when it's bath time. They're right little soap dodgers.' Zara grinned.

Zara always made her chuckle, even at her lowest. 'No problem, I have to go to my mother's house anyway.'

'I'm so sorry, mate. How are you coping?'

'I feel like the jobs there are never ending but I'm getting there.'

'Losing her must have been hard enough, but dealing with a hoarder, that's something else. Have you decided what you'll do with the house when it's done?'

'I'm going to rent it out.' That house had to remain hers forever. She and her mother both knew that. Despite the fact they hadn't spoken for years, Leah would stick to the plan they made. She wondered if the plan had changed. Is that why her mother wanted to see her before she'd died? She'd never know now.

'Good for you.' Zara raised her brows and began twiddling the ends of her blonde hair. 'Anyway, I didn't pop by to keep you here talking at your door in your nightshirt.'

'And you don't need me to clean and you turned down my coffee, so to what do I owe this pleasure?'

'I spoke to a girl a few minutes ago and she said her name was Charlotte. I'd just finished walking Molly and she stopped me. There was something about her...' She cleared her throat.

'Ignore what I said, I'm being an idiot and I best go.' Zara reversed her scooter down Leah's front path.

'Zara, stop right there.' Leah ran to her. 'We're friends. Talk.'

'And I want us to stay friends, which is why I should keep my big trap shut and my silly thoughts to myself. Pop by when you get five and we'll have a coffee.'

'What were you going to say?'

Zara breathed out. 'The girl. She wasn't quite sure where the Joneses lived.' She scrunched her brows, her blue-eyed stare fixed on Leah as she pulled out a slip of paper from her pocket and passed it to Leah. 'Here's Charlotte's number. She said she was searching for her parents and she gave it to me, and the only Jones I know around here are you and Cain.' Zara grabbed her dog's lead and rode her scooter to the end of Leah's path as she headed towards her bungalow.

'Wait, Zara...' It was too late. Her friend had gone.

THREE

Leah pulled up outside her mother's house, in the village where she grew up. She glanced at the house next door. Jean Harrison had never been one to mix, but Elisabeth Pearson had been different. They'd moved in about the same time and had remained close friends. Leah wondered if Mrs Pearson had visited her dying mother towards the end.

She checked her phone. Cain still hadn't called her back though she'd left him a message. Reaching into her pocket, she pulled out the slip of paper. It was feasible that Cain had fathered another woman's child. She knew he'd had an affair and she suspected there had been others. Maybe she should call Charlotte. As she went to press the numbers, she stopped. No, she couldn't just call Charlotte because what would she say? Whatever happened in the past, it wasn't Charlotte's fault and she wouldn't punish the girl for what Cain had done.

The golden sun reflected in the windows that Leah had scrubbed. Stepping out of the car, she shivered. Sun didn't equal warmth and her mother's house was as cold as they got. Jean Harrison had never hugged Leah or smiled, ever the stern-looking professional with all the answers. When Leah met

Cain, she thought her life was going to be filled with the warmth and love she'd sought.

A few weeks ago, the house had looked tired. Time had battered the exterior. The once white framed windows were chipped to the wood, and the old front door had needed a fresh coat of paint, but the building was solid. It hadn't been easy but she'd made Larrison House presentable again. The regency blue door finished the frontage, bringing it as up-to-date as possible without buying a new one. Her mother had made a clear will, leaving everything to Leah. She swallowed as she glanced at the house opposite. Her heart began to bang as Elisabeth Pearson walked past the large bay window, not noticing Leah.

Hurrying through the creaky gate, Leah hoped Mrs Pearson wouldn't see her. If she came out, Leah would definitely get quizzed on why she hadn't been to visit her mother for years. The past needed to remain buried, forever, not reopened while making small talk with Mrs Pearson. As she approached the house, she wiped a smudge off the brass nameplate. Her great-grandfather, Leonard Harrison, had name the house Larrison House. It had remained in the family since. She placed the huge brass key in the rusting lock and turned it, hearing the creaks echoing through the cavernous hall. Only eight weeks ago, it had been piled high with old newspapers and empty food packages, a symptom of her mother's hoarding disorder. Jean had always collected things but never anything of value. Two months and a succession of skips mixed with hard labour had taken care of the mess. There was only the study left to tackle. Leah shivered at what she might find. The thought of something scurrying out from a pile of junk didn't bear thinking about. The maggots in the kitchen sink had freaked her out so much, she'd ended up having to call Cain to come from work and deal with them. Of course, he'd mocked her for not simply washing them down the plughole.

Leah opened the lounge door to her left. Even though the lounge now looked cosy, with its traditional inglenook fireplace and original ceiling rose, it was filled with memories of her mother telling her to get out of the house and never come back. She almost choked on a little sob.

As she left the lounge and went upstairs, she passed the stained-glass window midway. Blues and greens flooded her face as the sun's rays reached for her. She hurried past it to her childhood bedroom, where she opened the wardrobe, sad that her clothes had long gone. Considering her mother never got rid of a thing, Leah had no idea why her bedroom had been emptied. Maybe her mother had wanted to forget what had happened behind closed doors all those years ago. Leah glanced at the bed where her crocheted square blanket was still draped over it. Why had her mother kept that? She remembered, up until her twelfth birthday, her stuffed cat had always rested on her pillow when she'd made her bed. After that, Tinkerbell had been placed away on top of her wardrobe.

Floorboards creaked beneath her feet as she walked over to her old empty bookcase, the one which used to house her *Sweet Valley High* book collection before she truly knew that romance was a myth. Her phone buzzed.

I can't call you back now, I have meetings all morning then I have to rush to site. Love you and I can't wait to come home. I'll get some wine on my way back. You choose a film. XX

It was for the best that she hadn't managed to get through to Cain. She needed a bit more time to work out how to mention Charlotte. Tapping came from above. She really had to deal with the rats in the loft. As she glanced out the window onto the street, a pair of staring eyes met her gaze. Mrs Pearson stepped forward with her fingers held out, and Leah almost stumbled back. Leah pulled the curtain across. She held a hand over her palpitating heart. If only Mrs Pearson knew why she'd left all those years ago.

As she went into her mother's bedroom, she shivered. The mattress that her mother had died on had been skipped. A sliver of red paint left a line where the skirting board met the floor. Her mother had liked the deep burgundy paint that had cocooned her at night while she slept. Even though Jean had been cruel to her, Leah had felt awful erasing all the things her mother had loved. It just saddened Leah that Jean hadn't loved her.

The bed – she couldn't help fixing her gaze on it. The urge to run out of the house and never come back was as strong as ever, but in another breath, she wanted to curl up on it and cry. Breathing in and out, she willed her heart rate to return to normal as she willed the ghosts of her past to leave her alone. She hurried out of that room and took a few seconds to compose herself. Yes, upstairs all looked fine. It was fresh and clean.

After heading back downstairs and into her mother's study, she fell into the chair positioned in front of a large leather-topped desk that Jean used when she brought her legal work with her. Business law. Leah had never been enough for her high-achieving mother. Great-grandad Leonard was so proud she'd followed in the family footsteps in reading Law. But Jean had always gone on about Leah's failings. *She wasn't smart; she wasn't pretty. She was too dumpy; she was lazy; she was going to be a failure because she'd never won a race at school. Life only rewarded the winners. Second place is still a losing place.*

Her phone buzzed again with another message from Cain.

So sorry, love. Going to be late. Got a meeting and I don't know what time I'll be home. I'll make it up to you, I promise. And don't make any dinner for me. Just see to yourself or grab a takeaway. XX

So much for Cain being sorry. Instead, he was going to spend the evening with another woman. She had no doubts he'd bring a client home on Saturday for dinner, but it was probably going to be one of his friends off site, just keeping up the pretence and covering his lies. Leah scrunched her nose and sighed. She pictured him with Alison, all those years ago. The woman had the most beautiful glossy dark hair that fell down her back, just like Charlotte's. Back then, she'd suspected their affair for weeks but Cain had lied and lied. His new clothes, the new aftershave, the bounce in his step – they were all a give-away – and the worse thing about knowing that, was because he was acting the same way, right now. Leah didn't have to read his messages to know. Maybe he was in contact with Alison after all these years. She felt sick at the thought. She'd never get that image of catching him with Alison out of her thoughts: the one of her semi-naked husband tearing at Alison's underpants while pushing her up against their kitchen island. It didn't matter that this was years ago, it was still as fresh in her mind. And he wondered why Leah didn't trust anything he said. Alison had moved out within a week and put her house on the market. Had she been pregnant with Charlotte back then, before she moved?

Leah opened up one of her mother's many laptops and began typing in a succession of passwords. Her mother's name, surname, and date of birth, one to six, Tinkerbell. She missed that toy. Where it ended up was a mystery. She tried her own name and date of birth. Every attempt came with an *invalid password* notice flashing on the screen.

Banging her hands on the keyboard, she yelled: 'Why leave me with all these laptops and no way of getting into them?' She slammed the lid down. Getting rid of the general clutter had been easy, but Leah knew she had to go through each piece of paper with care when it came to the study. Piles of box folders stood taller than her, and the bursting filing cabinets reminded her that there was still so much work to do. She grimaced at the stringy spider webs that reached the dusty chandelier in the middle of the high-ceilinged room, and led from there to the old floral swag curtains that didn't quite fit the bay window properly.

* * *

Two hours passed and she'd barely tackled one pile of folders, each full to the brim with old newspaper clippings. Nothing of relevance had been found so far but Leah didn't know that until she'd been through every single page. She let out a breath, deciding she needed a coffee break. Leaving the study, she felt a cold draught and shivered. She grabbed her jacket and put it on. A flash of a memory took her back to a sunny June day, her mother clutching the home phone in the hallway as she collapsed at the news of her father's death. The back doors had been open and the breeze had caught her mother's wispy hair.

A lump formed in Leah's throat as she remembered the palliative care nurse calling her to tell her of her mother's passing. She too was in her hallway at home. Again, a pang of regret told Leah that she should have visited her mother. Maybe Jean had been as full of regret, too. Maybe she wanted to tell Leah how sorry she was.

Leah gasped as a loud bang came from the kitchen. Trembling, she crept through the kitchen and nudged the French doors. They'd been open and were now bouncing against the frame as the gust tickled them. As she nudged the doors, she held her phone in her other hand, ready to call the police if she heard someone outside. She stepped onto the garden slabs. 'Who's there?' she shouted. She'd definitely locked the French doors last time she was there. Running back into the kitchen, she slammed the doors and locked them before removing the key. Last time she was here, she had been clearing her throat a lot because of the paint fumes while she was glossing the skirting boards. She sighed. No one had broken anything. Glancing out at the garden, she noticed that the daffodils in the one corner had been trodden down. Heart hammering against her ribcage, she ran through the hallway and out of the front door. Someone had been there and they'd been watching her. She felt their presence.

Elisabeth Pearson crossed the road. Damn, Leah had no choice but to acknowledge her. She'd been lucky to avoid bumping into Mrs Pearson since working on the house. She couldn't drive away, as she'd stupidly run out without her car keys and the front door was still wide open. 'Mrs Pearson,' she mumbled with a quiver in her voice. It was as if she was sixteen all over again and Mrs Pearson was about to tell her off for drinking a can of cider with the other kids.

The woman stared at her, eyes stark and hands in a ball, shaking. 'Are you back for good? You can't be here, not now.'

'Mrs Pearson, are you okay?'

The woman scrunched her grey brows and stared at her feet, then at Leah. 'Do I know you? Are you who I think you are?'

'It's Leah, Mrs Pearson. Leah Harrison. Although, I'm married now but I used to be a Harrison. Should have stayed a Harrison.' She let out a nervous laugh.

'Oh, you used to be so skinny.'

Leah ignored her. Mrs Pearson seemed frail and confused. She glanced at the woman's house and wondered if she lived alone now. 'That's right. I was.' Leah paused, wondering if she should ask Mrs Pearson about the note. 'Do you know if anyone was visiting my mother before she died?'

'Poor Jean. Such a shame. I spent a lot of time with her. She did have a lot of visitors and her nurses.'

The mention of Jean having visitors surprised her. 'Do you know who those visitors were?'

Mrs Pearson shrugged and stared into thin air with her mouth open.

'Mrs Pearson?'

'Sorry, dear. I can't remember. I need to go. There were no visitors. I don't know where I got that from. It was just the nursing staff. Forget I said anything.'

Leah swallowed the lump in her throat. Her mother had visitors but who were they? Mrs Pearson was definitely trying to backtrack on what she said. The woman stepped closer, her nose almost touching Leah's. She could tell that Mrs Pearson wanted to say something else but the words weren't forming on her lips. Sweat began to pool at the nape of Leah's neck as Mrs Pearson leaned slightly and whispered in her ear, before leaving her standing alone in the road.

Mrs Pearson's words repeated in her mind. 'She told me everything.'

FOUR

Despite hiding from her past and leaving home, her very soul was etched into every crack and crevice; it made her shiver. How could her mother have told anyone their secrets? Leah ran back into the house and slammed the front door. After checking all the doors and windows, she settled back in the study. Forget coffee, she had no time for it now. All she wanted was to find a password to access the laptops. She began feeling along every edge and corner of the desk for a secret drawer. Her mother would have used email; she would have had a whole online life that Leah was missing, maybe even a Facebook or Twitter account. Grabbing a pen from the pot, she began to bite the plastic on the end, a habit that had annoyed her mother when Leah was a child, then she noticed that the end had been removed. There was something wedged inside the plastic pen tube. Had her mother pictured Leah sitting in her chair one day, annoyingly biting the end of a pen like she always did? Shaking it, she released the coil of paper. In spidery handwriting, Jean had noted four words: 'I don't trust them.' Gasping for breath, Leah grabbed her keys and ran. Between that note, the slamming door and Mrs Pear-

son's weird words, Leah needed to get out of the house –
now!

* * *

She sped off and hurried home with all those words on her
mind. What exactly had her mother been saying to people on
her deathbed? Leah had left that house at seventeen, on the
promise that they would never say a word to another living
human being; but her mother had done the opposite. At home,
she paced up and down the kitchen, staring out the window
into the dark garden, trying to fathom out what she should do.
Should she try to talk to Mrs Pearson again, ask her exactly
what she knew and beg her not to repeat it? Or would it be best
to stay away and hope that in her slightly confused state, she
might just forget everything? How could her mother do this
to her?

Leah read Cain's last message. She knew he was verging on
merry because of all the hearts and kisses, all to appease her
while he was out with someone else. Was he out with Alison
having dinner and drinking wine? She pictured him so drunk,
he'd come in and start another argument; and then he'd be so
sweet the next day. Her heart began to hum in anticipation.

She pulled her mother's note and Charlotte's number from
her pocket, questioning the former and worrying over the latter.
Could her husband really be the girl's father?

The ticking of the kitchen clock banged through her head.
Six. Six thirty. Six forty-five. Seven. He still wasn't home. How
drunk would he be? She grabbed a chunk of cheese from the
fridge and swallowed it as a paltry offering to her grumbling
stomach, even then she felt like heaving it up.

She bit her thumbnail, recalling Mrs Pearson's confused
expression in the rear-view mirror as she pulled away. As soon
as the house was rented out, she'd barely ever have to go back.

Gardening and general maintenance, that would be her only involvement, which meant all the hurtful memories could be left behind. She flinched as the edge of her skin bled from all the chewing.

Seven ten. Seven fifteen. Another nail chewed. More blood. The screams in her head. Charlotte. The house. Her anxiety. Cain's lies. Their arguments. Perfume woman or Alison. Seven twenty.

* * *

She stood rigid, holding her breath, as Cain fought to get his key in the lock, missing a couple of times before finally bursting through the door. There was no, 'honey, I'm home,' greeting like in American sitcoms. There was nothing funny or warm about Cain right now. With a gaping mouth and glassy eyes, he stumbled through the hallway towards her and leaned against the kitchen island, the smell of rose perfume wafting from his shirt.

'I'm starving.' He reached into the fridge and pulled out the same block of cheese she'd picked a chunk from.

'I thought you went out to eat with whoever you had a meeting with.' Now she knew he'd had no time to eat. She pictured them checking into a hotel room and ordering wine or even something bubbly to start the evening off. Dinner must have been the last thing on his mind. Leah pictured him writhing on top of Alison. Had they spoken about their daughter? Maybe they'd been plotting how they could all set up together once Charlotte had been told about her father.

'Why are you staring at me like that, Leah?' He bit into the cheese and threw the rest back into the fridge.

'Like what?'

'Like you don't trust me, again.'

'It's just, you promised we'd have a nice night in and watch a film and again you come home like this. You said you were having a meeting and there would be food, but you're hungry.'

He slammed the fridge door and walked off, leaving her standing alone. With no explanation, he obviously didn't want to say any more about it.

As he pounded up the stairs, she saw that he'd left his wallet on the worktop. Grabbing it, she flipped it open and began searching through the notes until her hand brushed on a credit card receipt. He'd spent eighty pounds at The Hollybush, a country inn with cheap rooms and pub grub. All that was on it was a total, not the itemised receipt he normally insisted on having so that he could put it through his business as an expense. This was purely personal. Seething, Leah took a photo of it on her phone with shaky hands, then she placed it back in his wallet. There's no way he'd take a business client that far out from Worcester. He'd purposely headed closer to Stratford-upon-Avon, to find a place where no one would recognise him and Alison.

She sat at the kitchen table wondering what to do. Why couldn't he just tell her it was over or admit his lies, then they would both be free? Instead, he kept up this pretence that he loved her, but his moods were all over the place. Thoughts of Charlotte wouldn't leave her mind. It was all too much. There was another question she had to ask. Why couldn't she just leave him? She had her mother's house, some money and a little business that was screaming out to be expanded. Her mother's money could take it to the next level.

She pulled her phone from her pocket, pressed the Face-book app and brought up Cain's profile. As usual, his wall was pretty bare but his friend list had increased by one. Leah clicked into his friends but the addition didn't show up. They weren't a mutual friend. Cain had changed his settings. She threw her phone to the table, furious, confused and hurt because she loved him so much.

'Are you coming to bed? I'm missing you,' Cain called out from upstairs.

It was still too early for sleep, but Cain had had a drink. She turned off the light and went upstairs, wondering if she should sleep in the spare room. She headed up, and he held the blankets open for her to slide in next to him.

'I'm sorry, babe. I really love you and I don't want to lose you. I'm feeling the pressure right now. Can you bear with me? I promise, it'll all be over soon and we can get back to normal. You know you mean everything to me?'

She got changed and slipped into bed beside him, where he spooned her and stroked her hair. It felt so good, she never wanted this moment to end.

She really did love him. Maybe there was an innocent reason for him having a hotel receipt or maybe not. She wondered if their love could survive the news about Charlotte when it broke.

FIVE

My chest tightens and I don't want to take another step, but I do. I have to. It's time and I'm more scared than I've ever been in my whole life. This can't be happening. I'm not prepared for what's next but my mother is waiting and I have to do as I'm told. She grabs my arm and drags me, forcing my heels to draw lines in the thick carpet. I don't want to go. Inwardly, I'm screaming but it makes no difference. Nothing I say makes a difference...

'Leah, are you still awake?' Cain's voice pierces her thoughts.

She hadn't managed to sleep at all. Every time she'd closed her eyes, her mind raced with disjointed memories and now her body was clammy from all the tossing and turning. She'd worked so hard to forget, but now it seemed forgetting was the last thing she could do. Those words that her mother had left for her to find in the pen wouldn't leave her mind. Who shouldn't she trust?

'Yes.' Leah wrestled with the quilt, needing to get it off her. She saw Cain's outline in the darkness as he reached closer and stroked her hair.

Cain rolled out of bed, turned on the side lamp and headed out of the bedroom. 'I'm getting a drink. Do you want one?'

'What time is it?'

'Two in the morning.'

She thought it would be much later than that. Her mother's house and Cain's secrets were literally driving her crazy.

Stepping out of bed, she shuffled across the carpet and rubbed her eyes, kicking Cain's jeans out the way as she made her way to the en-suite. She flicked the light on, removed her nightshirt and began flannelling her clammy body down with some soap and water. The reflection staring back at her was not that of a thirty-four-year-old woman. She'd aged. A line had formed at the ends of each eye, and her pores were gaping. She prodded the spot on the middle of her cheek and wondered if perfect Alison had ever had a spot. Charlotte had looked perfect with her beautiful clear skin, glossy hair and tall svelte figure. Leah hadn't even seen the girl up closely but she knew she'd be perfect, just like perfect-bloody-Alison.

'I poured you some juice. Didn't know what you'd want.'

She exited the bedroom and made her way to her chest of drawers to grab a T-shirt. She slipped the fresh garment over her head.

'Come here.' He reached out, took her arms and pulled her onto the bed. The smell of wine and now coffee seeped from his mouth every time he exhaled. 'I'm sorry, I mean really sorry. I hadn't intended to be late but you know this client?'

She nodded. She didn't really know anything. There used to be a time he'd excitedly talk about his work and his dreams for his company, but now, he brushed over it most of the time.

'The one you're always with. She smells lovely and you're always with her.'

'We can't keep doing this. I love you and I love only you, okay? I know I let you down last night. I didn't mean to drink as much as I did but what can I say? I'm an idiot. I want this contract more than anything and I need your support. Yes, I got carried away and ended up knocking back a bit of bubbly but I have to show these people I mean business.'

'Okay, tell me about it.' What she really wanted to say was that she knew he had a client, but she also knew he was seeing someone and she wanted to ask if he knew about Charlotte.

'It's worth two million in total and you know that means a good cut for us. The ship is about to sail and we've got a first-class cabin. Just stick with me and trust me, please?' He lay back and pulled her close to him as he kissed her.

She recoiled.

'What's up?'

'Nothing, I'm just tired.' She was more than tired but she couldn't tell Cain what was on her mind. In no way did she trust him enough to go there. She was scared of whoever had trampled all over the daffodils in her mother's garden, and she was scared of the memories that house held. She looked into Cain's dark eyes and for a moment she saw a flicker of something she couldn't fathom. It wasn't as if he was hiding something; it was as if he was trying to fathom her out.

'Are you sure, because you don't seem yourself. You look worried, scared even.'

'It's just my mother's house. It's a huge project and I'm finding it hard being back there.'

'I told you. I can get some of the contractors on it. They'd have it emptied out and fully painted throughout within a few days then you'd be free of it. We can sell it and it's money in the bank.'

She shook her head. 'No, I want to do it. I need to do it.'

'Okay. I'll support you in whatever you want to do.'

She remained silent while looking at him, seeking the next clue, and she wondered if he could have visited her mother's house, to scare her. A vision flashed through her mind. Her money in their joint bank account. Would he take it? No, that was ridiculous. She had rights; and Cain hadn't trampled the flowers in the garden. She was definitely being paranoid. 'I forgot to ask: did you go anywhere nice for your meeting?'

'No, just a wine bar in Worcester. I've left the car there so I'll get a taxi in the morning to the office.'

He couldn't tell her the truth if his life depended on it. Maybe he was hiding Charlotte's existence from her? There was that.

'You smell good.' He reached under her T-shirt and began touching her breasts.

She didn't want him to touch her. Thoughts of Alison ran through her mind again. It would be so easy to sink into him and feel loved, but she couldn't, not until she knew the truth and she didn't want to discuss anything with him now. 'I don't feel too good. I think I might be coming down with something.' She nudged him away, placed a hand on her hot head and grimaced before grabbing the glass of orange juice and taking a couple of sips. 'I think I just need to go to sleep.' As she turned away from him, he switched off the side lamp and lay there. She knew he'd be staring at the ceiling in the dark and she didn't care.

He hadn't been in Worcester; he'd been in Stratford. But if she said that, he'd know she'd been looking at his receipts.

Liar. She had caught him out.

SIX

'Come in. Kettle's on. You know I was lying about that drink, right? So, if you've come for wine, I suggest you find a more fun neighbour like, I don't know, handsome bloody Josh at number twenty. I bet he's fun in more ways than one.' Zara winked as she jostled with her sticks to let Leah in. 'God, I feel old. At my age I should be living it up with cocktails, not coffee, but hey, that's life. I'm only forty-one but I feel like I'm bloody seventy.'

Leah smiled, knowing that Zara wouldn't want to send herself dizzy with wine. Her multiple sclerosis with its many flare ups did that to her anyway. 'It's okay, I much prefer your bad coffee. At least it wakes me up even if the conversation is dull. In fact, I really only come for the coffee.'

'My coffee is the best. Molly, chill out, will you?' The dog barked a couple of times and ran into the kitchen where it began drinking water from a bowl on the floor.

'It would be if you didn't put three spoons in each cup, but it keeps me awake, so yes, you make the best coffee.'

'Well, don't keep me in suspense.'

Leah furrowed her brows. Zara placed one of her sticks

against the cupboard and made the coffees. Leah grabbed both cups and took them over to the kitchen table where Zara joined her. 'Suspense?'

'That number. I've been worried about you. It's fess-up time. I'm a nosy cow and I won't apologise, mostly because I can't help but hear you and Cain argue sometimes. So even if I buried my head under ten pillows, I'd still hear the muffled shouts coming from your house while I'm lying in bed. Were you arguing about the girl?'

Leah sighed, not in the least bit surprised that Zara had tried to listen in.

'I was hoping you'd text or call but I gave up in the end. My sister stayed for dinner and those two bloody kids just cried every time they heard poor Molly snuffling around in the living room. Never mind. Spill it all out. What did he say?'

Swallowing, Leah took a sip of the coffee. 'I didn't tell him.'

'Why the hell not? I'd have had it out with him as soon as he came home and then I'd have wedged his nuts in a vice. That man has treated you like dirt.'

'I know, I know. But what if I have it all wrong?'

Zara flicked a loose mascara-caked eyelash from her cheek. 'You haven't got it wrong. I remember buying this bungalow from Alison all those years ago. She knocked ten thousand pounds off the asking price just to make me buy this place and get the sale through as fast as I could. Obviously wanted to make a clean break before she started showing. I mean, from what you said, all the neighbours knew what was going on. I guess the gossip would have been rife had she stayed.' She sipped her coffee. 'That girl looks a bit like him, like them.'

Leah coughed and placed her cup on the table. She doubted she'd be able to swallow another sip anyway. Her eyes began to water.

'Come here.' Zara placed a cold hand over hers and linked

fingers with her friend. 'I'm here for you. You know that, don't you?'

Nodding, Leah used her free hand to wipe her eyes. 'Stupid, aren't I?'

'Not stupid. Hurt. It's him who's stupid. You are an amazing person, Leah Jones. I know you'll tackle the issue when you're ready and, if you sack him, you know you can crash here if you need to.'

Leah let out a laugh. 'At least I have you.' She pulled her hand away and picked her cup up. 'Here's to good friends.'

'Good friends.' They clinked cups.

'You know, it's not Alison's fault or anyone else's. Cain is the married man here. It's entirely his fault.'

Letting out a breath, Leah shrugged even though she disagreed. Alison knew they were married, and if he was seeing someone else, they probably did too.

'There's something else, isn't there?'

'What?'

'I can tell, Leah.'

'As if finding out your husband has a grown-up daughter, the result of an affair, isn't enough.' Leah exhaled and loosened the light jumper at her neck.

'Of course, it's enough.' Zara tilted her head to one side and pressed her lips together. 'But if there's more, I'm here to listen.'

Leah bit her bottom lip. 'You have so much on your plate. I should be listening to you.'

'Look, your drama helps me forget what's on my plate so help me out here. I need something else to think about other than balance sheets and profit and loss accounts today. The longer I can delay going into the back room to get my work out the better. Go on then, what else is eating you up? Give me the drama.'

'It's probably nothing.'

'Your face doesn't look like it's nothing. Even Molly isn't convinced.'

The dog licked Leah's hand, so she patted her head. 'I went to my mother's house yesterday, as you know.'

'Okay. And?'

'When I was sorting through her paperwork, I heard someone in the kitchen.'

Zara's eyes widened. 'You mean an intruder? Did you call the police?'

'No, I'd convinced myself I left the French doors open and it was just the wind. I'd been glossing the skirting boards last time I was there, and I had those doors open. Maybe I didn't close them properly. They're not the best.'

'But there's obviously more or you wouldn't be worried.'

Exhaling, Leah continued. 'When I closed the doors, I could see that the daffodils had been trampled on at the far end of the garden. Someone had been there and it scared me. It didn't help that I found this weird little secret note stuffed in the tube of a biro.'

'A note?'

'Something my mother must have done. All it said was "don't trust them". I have no idea what she meant and it freaked me out. I couldn't get out that house fast enough.' Her hands began to shake as she recalled that moment.

'Oh, love. That sounds as scary as hell. You should call the police, you know.'

'I'll see how it goes. No one was hurt. Nothing was taken. I think my head's just in a funny place. Anyway, it's getting on a bit. I have a big, big house to clean before I even get to my mother's place today.'

'Well call me if you get worried or need to talk.'

'Will do and I have you booked in tomorrow. The full works, bathrooms the lot.'

'I'll get the cakes in. And don't forget, your financial year end is due this month. I hope you've been keeping your receipts this time.'

'You've trained me well, Zara. I've turned into an accountant's dream. Must dash.'

As Leah left and walked out onto the damp path, she knew exactly where she was going and it wasn't to clean a house.

SEVEN

After parking up on the industrial estate, Leah locked her car and headed towards the snack bar. Seagulls squawked above, each one adding to the chorus. A swarm of them swooped and landed before fighting over a dropped bread roll.

'What can I get you?' the man asked.

'A latte, please.'

Drink in hand, she crossed back over and entered the business centre where Cain rented an office. He definitely wouldn't appreciate her just turning up, even bringing him a drink, but she needed to know he was there and not with another woman. Maybe he was telling the truth. Perfume woman might be a client. The not knowing anything for certain was killing her.

Soft music played, and a receptionist came from the back room.

'Hi, I'm Cain Jones's wife, just bringing him a drink. Can I have a fob to get through, please?'

'Of course. Just fill this in, please.'

She popped her registration and time of entry in the logbook on the side, and the man passed her a plastic pass key. She followed the corridor to the stairwell. It was only one floor.

The walk upstairs would give her time to calm her nerves. Stomach skipping, she wondered if it really had been a good idea to try and catch him out. He'd know instantly that was the only reason for her visit when she turned up with a drink. She knocked his office door, but there was no answer.

Leah glanced up and down the corridor and pulled his spare key card out of her pocket, the one he kept in his desk drawer at home, and she pressed it against the sensor. The door clicked and she nudged it open with her bottom. A musty smell filled the air, and the coating of dust on his keyboard told her that he hadn't used it for a while. A photo of them on their wedding day had a cobweb trailing from it to the corner of the desk. She glanced around for his laptop but it was nowhere to be seen. Placing the drink on his desk, she sat in his chair. She grabbed a sheet of paper from his top tray. It was a quote for a huge project management job, made out to a company. He wasn't lying about trying to impress a client. The amount on the quote made her gasp. When he mentioned the contract that could change their lives, he was telling the truth. Maybe she was wrong about all the entertainment he was doing.

She slid his top drawer open and peered in only to find a couple of cereal bars and a few cans of energy drinks. Pulling her phone out of her pocket, she sent him a message.

I slept in this morning and must have missed you. How's work? Shall I pop to the office and we could have lunch together? Maybe grab something from the snack bar? I've just finished cleaning a house close by. X

A message pinged back immediately.

Sounds lovely but I have so much on. I'm leaving the office in a few minutes to head to site in Birmingham to give the builders a nudge. I'm sorry I came home a bit tanked up last

night. I'll make it up to you when I get this contract. Maybe a
weekend away to celebrate??? See you later. Love you. XX

Any thoughts of him possibly being innocent of her accusations were soon dismissed.

After a few minutes rooting around his office, she closed the
door and hurried back down the stairs, signed out and got back
into her car. She opened up Facebook and headed straight to
Cain's profile. He'd taken a selfie, suited up for work and
wearing his sunglasses, and used it as his new profile picture.
He had several likes. She clicked on them and saw that two men
and a woman had liked it. She recognised the names of the men.
They mostly worked on the projects that Cain ran. There was
only one liker who caught her attention: the unknown calling
herself Lady Rose, and her profile picture was a pink rose. A
lump formed in her throat. The rose was beautiful? Was she
beautiful? She typed in *Alison Hunt* in the hope that Alison's
profile would come up, but no one looking like their old neighbour came up on her screen. She wondered if Alison was Lady
Rose.

A comment followed by a red heart appeared on his
Facebook.

Looking the business. See you shortly.

This was Cain's slip up. She clicked on the Lady Rose
profile, but there were no details available. Her profile was
locked. She threw her phone onto the passenger seat and
gripped the steering wheel. That's when she caught sight of a
girl. The girl went to enter the business centre but then stepped
back and removed her sunglasses. Her light brown hair fell in a
long plait down her back. She removed her denim jacket to
reveal a short floral dress with leggings underneath. She went to
enter the building again but once again stepped back and stood

by the wall outside. As the girl turned her way, Leah furrowed her brow as she concentrated on her delicate features. She had seen this girl before, with Charlotte, when she looked out of her bedroom window seeing the three girls. Was she sure it was the same girl?

Her hair was different. She'd been wearing it loose that day but her build, her features, Leah definitely recognised them. What was Cain's potential daughter's friend doing at his office? It was too much of a coincidence to ignore. The girl turned. Leah leaned back in her car, hoping that she wouldn't get spotted.

It was no good. She was going to have to speak to Charlotte before she mentioned her to Cain. She pulled the slip of paper from her pocket and began pressing the number, but all she got was a dead tone. There was no such number.

Leah pushed herself back up in her seat and peered out. The girl had her phone to her ear, then she began to run down the road before disappearing around a corner. There was something weird going on and, right now, she didn't trust Cain and she didn't trust Charlotte either. There had to be a reason the girls were hanging around making trouble. Maybe Leah really had got everything wrong, or maybe Cain was up to something far worse. No, that girl was far too young for him. Surely, he wouldn't be having some sort of relationship with someone that age. She glanced at the Lady Rose profile again and felt a tear slipping down her face. Cain had met Leah when she was about the same age as those girls. She'd never thought much of it at the time. At eighteen, she'd felt grown up but, looking back, she must have come across as immature at times.

Cain's car pulled into the car park and he hurried out with his phone to his ear. Shoulders dropping, he began to speak but he was too far away for her to hear anything. Leah remained stiff in her seat in the hope that he wouldn't look over. Had he planned to meet the girl? He ended his call and entered the building.

Leah waited a few more minutes. Cain didn't leave the building, and the girl never came back. Her phone beeped.

Sorry, I'm going to be late again tonight. XX

What the hell had she become? She pulled out of the car park hating herself. She'd turned into the type of woman she'd really hoped she never would: a woman who spies on her husband. It would be easy to walk away, but what if she had it all wrong? She knew about his affair with Alison, and if they did have a child, it would be cruel to stand in the way of him getting to know his daughter. Maybe everything was about Charlotte, nothing more. She needed to get to the bottom of everything without riling Cain: her sanity depended on it.

EIGHT

Leah gasped as the man in the car behind her beeped his horn. Holding a hand up to apologise, she pulled away and took the turn towards the edge of the village, where the two houses were separated by about a quarter of a mile from all the other dwellings. It had always been Jean and Mrs Pearson on the dark and quiet street called Oakmore Lane. The trees framing the backs of the houses, blocking out a lot of light.

Since leaving Cain's office, her mind had been all over the place, flitting to Charlotte, then to the other girl and Lady Rose or Alison. She'd even sat in her car for ages, trying to fathom out what to do next but hiding from the problem was getting her nowhere.

She turned onto the last lane that filtered into a single-track road for the next half a mile, swerving to avoid rolling over the dead fox in the road. After passing the bus stop, she pulled up and stepped out the car. She fumbled in her bag for the key, digging under her tissues, lip balm and painkillers. Gripping the metal, she entered Larrison House and leaned against the front door as she took a few deep breaths. She pressed Zara's number, but her phone went straight to voicemail, which was odd. Zara always answered, working or not. She ended the call, not leaving a message.

On entering her mother's study, she slammed her phone onto a pile of folders and wept into her hands. She pulled a tissue from the box on the desk and wiped her face dry. As she went to grab another tissue, something slid from one end to the other in the bottom of the box. She shook it and the object shifted back and forth. After tearing all the tissues out, she reached in further and further until her hand brushed on cold metal. It was a key, a tiny gold key.

A knock at the door made her jump. She stuffed all the tissues back in the box, popped the key in her jacket pocket and ran to the door. Elisabeth Pearson stood on the path, one hand gripping a sparkly handbag, the other holding her huge sunhat in place so that it didn't blow off her head in the breeze. Leah glanced up at the sky and the suffocating trees. Grey dappled shadows splayed across the road. It definitely wasn't the weather for a sunhat. 'Mrs Pearson.'

'Leah. How are you today?'

'I'm okay.' She hesitated. 'Do you want to come in? I can put the kettle on.' She hoped Mrs Pearson would say yes. Her parting words the previous day had left Leah a little concerned. She needed to know exactly what her mother had said in her final days. She felt a shiver run through her as Mrs Pearson stared at her with a forced smile on her face. 'Coffee?'

'Oh, yes. That would be lovely.' As the old woman stepped into the hallway, she gazed around. 'It looks so different. Bigger.'

'I had to get rid of all the newspapers and knick-knacks. I didn't realise my mother had collected so much stuff.'

Mrs Pearson shrugged. 'Well, you wouldn't. You haven't been here for years. That's what Jean said.'

Her mother had been right. Leah had left the house at seventeen and never come back. The pain too much to bear. She wondered if Mrs Pearson was judging her harshly for her absence, but she couldn't stay in the house that broke her heart. 'Come through.'

'Did you know she was dying?'

Leah shook her head. Her mother had sent her the letter but she hadn't mentioned how poorly she was. 'I only found out after. The nurse called me as soon as it happened.' A knot formed in Leah's throat. She hoped that Mrs Pearson couldn't tell she'd been crying, but by the way the woman looked her up and down, Leah guessed she knew.

'I remember you, when you were a girl. You'd always come to mine when you knew I'd made cherry cake. That used to be your favourite.'

'That's right. I used to love your cherry cake.' Leah cleared her throat. As she flicked the kettle on, she kept pondering how she should ask Mrs Pearson about what she'd said, then she wondered if she really wanted to hear the answer to that question.

The old woman began staring at the dresser at the far end of the room and smiling as if engaging with nothing, then a fly buzzed out of one of the floral cups. 'What was that about cake?' Mrs Pearson furrowed her brows. Had she forgot they were talking about cake in the moment it took her to look at the dresser?

Leah let out a long-drawn breath and placed a cup of coffee on the kitchen table, two sugars, just how Mrs Pearson used to take it all those years ago. 'Would you like to sit?'

'Ah, yes.' She placed her sparkly bag next to the cup and sat.

'What did you mean the other day when you said: "she told me everything?" Were you talking about something my mother said? I hope you don't mind me asking.'

Mrs Pearson frowned. 'I never said that. Why would I say something like that?'

Leah knew what she'd heard but it was clear that Mrs Pearson was having a few memory issues. Either that or she regretted saying those words. It was too important to Leah, not to ask again.

'You whispered it to me when I was outside, by my car.'

'Whispering is rude. Didn't your mother tell you that?' She sipped her coffee.

'Did my mother tell you something when she was poorly?'

'We talked. She told me how you always wanted her to buy you a pair of ruby slippers, like the ones Dorothy wore in *The Wizard of Oz.*'

It was clear that whatever train of thought Mrs Pearson had been having that day had long gone. 'Do you have any family at the house right now?' She swallowed as she waited for an answer, not quite wanting to know but feeling the need to enquire given how Mrs Pearson seemed. She wondered if her husband had died.

'I have Harry. We manage.'

'How about your children?' They would be a little older than Leah.

'We're all fine. You should come over and say hello. Harry would like that.'

The very thought sent her heart racing. It was hard enough, facing her fears and coming back to Larrison House, let alone greeting everyone like they all used to be best friends. Her chest began to tighten. 'I err, I have too much to do at the house. Maybe another time.' Another time wouldn't come. Once the house was done up, Leah would become a stranger to it.

'Actually, Harry wouldn't like that. I'm not meant to be here. I should go. Thank you for the coffee.' She grabbed her bag and shuffled out of the kitchen and along the hallway.

Leah got to the front door before Mrs Pearson and opened it. She glanced across the road to see if she could see Mr Pearson but she couldn't.

'It's okay, Harry has popped to the bookies. He goes every day without fail, but he'll be back soon. Hope the rest of your decorating and sorting goes well, then you can leave. That would be for the best. Oh, and you should sort out your back garden.'

She called after Mrs Pearson but the woman ignored her and continued into her house. So much for getting to the bottom of what her mother may or may not have said to her. Leah hoped Mrs Pearson's words were nothing more than the ramblings of a woman suffering with memory issues, but something inside her told her that Mrs Pearson knew exactly what she was saying and doing.

The smell of coffee was calling. Mrs Pearson may not have wanted to drink all of hers but Leah needed the caffeine. After the morning she'd had, she'd have preferred a stronger drink but coffee would have to do. Glancing out of the window, Leah could see exactly what Mrs Pearson had been looking at. It wasn't the cup on the dresser: it was the garden. Not only was there the patch of trodden daffodils, but the heads of the remaining flowers had been torn off and strewn onto the grass. Her mother's stone owl had rolled over.

Running to the French doors, she unlocked them. 'No,' she yelled, as she ran over to the patch and held a daffodil flower by its stem. Falling to the ground on her knees, she gathered the rest up and held them close to her heart, the pain reaching her core. It was as if the air had been sucked from her lungs. She fought for breath and then let out a scream, not caring if anyone heard. No one would understand, not Cain, not Zara, not anyone.

First Charlotte turned up and now this. It had to be connected, and her mother was to blame for telling the secret she'd made Leah keep against her will. Whoever did this had to have got in somehow. The French doors had been open yesterday. It would be easy to think she didn't lock the door after painting the kitchen, but that was unlikely. She stood and ran alongside the house towards the back gate. It was locked. There were no scuff marks on the fence panels and no other way in. Her mother would probably have given other people keys when she was ill; she'd have needed help. She grabbed the stone owl and placed it back at the edge of the garden.

Leah pulled the little gold key from her pocket. Her mother left it there for her, along with the note in the pen. There was a word engraved in the metal along the side of the key. Bingley. She had to find out what the key opened and what her mother was trying to tell her with that strange note.

NINE

A few specks of rain landed on Leah's nose as she ran down Zara's path and knocked.

Zara opened her door, and Molly began pulling her lead and barking. 'I thought you might fancy walking Molly with me then we can come back and have a hot chocolate and share the super fattening giant cookies I have in the cupboard. Actually no one fancies a walk in the rain, except Molly, and I love her so I'll suffer, and you can suffer with me. The things you do for love.' She rode down the ramp on her scooter.

Leah pulled her hood up and closed the front door for Zara.

'Do you want to hold her lead?'

She took the lead from Zara and allowed the dog to drag them towards the wooded area at the back of their row. After updating Zara with the details of her day, Zara reached down and unclipped the dog as soon as they were far enough away from the road.

'I can't believe he lied to you again. Well, I can believe it because he's a tosser, but it's not on. You really deserve better. And that woman, Mrs Pearson or whatever her name is, what a weirdo. Do you think she pulled all the flower heads off?'

'I don't know what to think. She could have a key, but why would she do that?'

'You tell me? Have you ever upset her?'

'No. Not as far as I know.' Although if her mother had told her things when she was dying, that could have upset her. 'She did say that it would be best if I leave, once I finished sorting the house out.'

'Why would she want you to leave? You have every right to be there.'

Leah shrugged. She knew exactly why, but she also knew that if Mrs Pearson had heard the truth, she only had one side of the story. A memory flashed through her mind: Mr Pearson grabbing her by the arm before throwing her T-shirt at her, calling her a slag under his breath. She gasped and held a hand over her chest as her vision prickled under the streetlamp. She'd tried so hard not to think about that night, but being back at her childhood home so often was making it hard to forget. It was as if the past was trying to swallow her up and take her to the dark place she'd spent so long avoiding.

'Leah, what's up?'

'Nothing.' She counted in her head as she breathed in and out a few times. 'There's just so much happening; and I also tried to call that number, the one Charlotte gave to you. Although I doubt that is even her name as that number is not even in use. After seeing the other girl today...' Was Charlotte's friend really the girl standing outside Cain's office building? 'I don't know. I'm just so confused with everything.'

Zara's phone beeped. Her friend turned the screen away so that Leah couldn't see it.

'Everything okay, Zara?'

Zara nodded. 'Yes, it's nothing. Just a client.'

'This time at night?'

'What can I say? Some of them don't understand boundaries.' Zara didn't laugh like she usually did. A branch snapped in the dark clump of trees ahead. 'Molly,' Zara called. 'Molly.' A rustling followed by more snapping twigs followed. Both women stared at the area the noise had come from.

The dog hurtled through the undergrowth, nowhere near the sound of the snapping branch. Zara glanced at Leah and shrugged. 'A fox maybe?'

'Who's there?' Leah called. She stepped forward and parted a couple of branches. Someone shuffled, then ran off. Heart hammering away, Leah bent over and clipped Molly's lead back on.

'Let's get back, quick. That definitely wasn't a fox.' Zara whizzed ahead and turned her scooter around. 'Pervert,' she shouted as they hurried back to the main road.

'What if someone is watching me, Zara? First the flowers, someone in my mother's house, Cain's odd behaviour, now this.'

'Who knows? Try not to scare yourself. It's more likely to be some kids hanging about. They probably know the house is unlived in.'

Leah wished she believed that but she didn't. Her head began to pound. 'I think I'm just going to head home. I don't feel so good. In fact, I think I have a migraine coming on.'

'I'll hold the cookies until tomorrow. If you're not up to cleaning my house in the morning, no worries. We can make it another time. I'll text you tomorrow, see if you're okay.'

'Thanks, Zara. See you tomorrow.'

Leah watched her friend ride the scooter into her bungalow and waved as she closed the door. She glanced up and down the silent road. Everyone had come home from work hours ago, and kids rarely ever hung around this area. Curtains were closed and people had huddled up and shut the drizzly dark night out. Shivering, she hurried into her house, slammed the door closed and turned on all the lights before checking all the rooms.

Someone had been there listening to everything they were saying. They'd been lurking and waiting, but why and to what end?

TEN

'Leah?' Cain was home.

She opened her eyes and threw the snuggle blanket off her body before sitting up on the sofa. 'I didn't hear you come in. What time is it?' She must have nodded off while reading. Her book had closed on the floor, losing her page. It didn't matter. She hadn't been able to concentrate on the story anyway with all that had been on her mind. But she had been tired.

'Only nine thirty.'

'I've only been asleep about twenty minutes. Did you have a good meeting or whatever it was?'

He shrugged. 'What do you mean? Of course, it was a meeting.'

She inhaled, trying to determine if he'd been with Lady Rose.

He stood there holding a takeaway coffee cup. 'What's this, Leah?'

Bolting up off the settee, she realised her mistake. She'd left the coffee she'd bought him from the snack bar on his desk.

'I don't know.' Leah instantly regretted saying that. Cain

wasn't stupid. 'Okay, I brought the coffee to your office. When I messaged you, I was already there.'

'And you would have seen that my car wasn't parked in the car park.'

'You said you were getting a taxi in and I didn't know if you got the taxi straight to work before collecting your car later.'

He paused, as if trying to weigh up her lie. Truth was, she'd forgotten that he'd taken a taxi that morning and she hadn't even checked for his car. She'd been so keen to catch him out, nothing else had mattered. And, she had caught him out.

'I texted you when I was there and you said you were just about to leave to go to site. You've barely been at the office. Where have you been going, Cain?'

'This is ridiculous.'

'What is? Me trying to work out why you're lying to me?'

'I left the office at one of the other sites I popped in on, which is why I told you I couldn't meet for lunch. I worked out of a portacabin. I've been doing that for months but you're so in a world of your own, you don't take any interest in my work or what I'm doing.'

'My mother died, Cain, and I've had all that stuff to deal with. Forgive me if I haven't taken in every word you've said.'

'Oh, we're doing that, are we?' He slammed the coffee on the table, and a blob of liquid flicked out of the sipping hole in the lid. 'You said you didn't care if you never saw or heard from your mother again, and you haven't shown any kind of upset. For heaven's sake. We didn't even stop for her wake. We left as soon as the funeral was over, as you said you couldn't bear to speak to the three people who turned up for her service. Maybe I did neglect to think that you were more upset than you've been making out. Are you?'

Her eyes began to well up. 'I don't know.'

'You don't know? That makes me feel close to you.'

'It's complicated.'

'So you say, but you've never told me why. Leah, I'm sorry that you had a bad relationship with your mother, and I respect that you don't want to talk about it. I trust you, totally, and I wish you'd trust me, too. This is all getting too much. I feel like I'm being spied on. When I saw that cup...' He clenched his fists and walked out of the room, into the kitchen.

She followed him and waited by the door, wondering if she was welcome. He put his phone on the island and turned on the light above the cooker, then he grabbed a bottle of water from the fridge and gulped half down.

'I'm sorry. I just wanted to see you.'

'You were spying. At least tell the truth. You took the spare key card from my desk here and you used it to get into the office. Now I know I can't trust you not to go through my things. Do you root through all my drawers looking for receipts for flowers, love notes, hidden phones? Is that what you do all day?'

'No.' She couldn't hold back her tears.

'I'm sleeping in the spare room tonight. I need a bit of time to unwind and think.'

Leah stood alone as he stormed out and stomped up the stairs. She hadn't even had chance to mention the girl who turned up just before he did and, in a way, she was glad. The argument over her simply going to his office had been bad enough. Maybe she had crossed a line. Cain was right.

She wished she could tell him about Charlotte and the thought that she was being watched, but the fuse for the evening had well and truly been lit and saying any more would only lead to an awful night. The best thing she could do was let him sleep off his mood in the spare room and hope that they could talk in the morning once he'd calmed down.

His phone flashed on the worktop, revealing a message. As he thundered back down the stairs, she took a quick look at the screen, just managing to read it before it went black again.

You bastard. You complete utter bastard! People like you love playing games. You don't care about ruined lives, you only care about yourself. I hate you. I HATE YOU!

She ran to the kitchen table, as far away from that phone as possible, the message confusing her more. Charlotte, Alison, Lady Rose, the girl at the office. Who had sent this message? Had Charlotte managed to contact him and had he denied she was his daughter? Had he dumped Alison yet again? She hated not knowing and that message on his phone was a snapshot in time, one she couldn't delve any deeper into. Soon he'd have his phone back, and she couldn't unlock it anyway. She wished she'd never seen it, as all it did was make things worse.

He entered the kitchen, scooped his phone up and dropped her box of contraceptive injections on the table. 'You thought I didn't know. All this time you accuse me of lying and you are the liar. You!'

She swallowed the lump in her throat and allowed her tears to fall. 'I'm sorry.'

'Why didn't you just say: Cain, I don't want your baby? Why make me think we were trying?' He activated his phone and began scrolling. 'Look, I don't want to talk about today again, okay? I know you don't believe that when I'm out at night, I'm schmoozing this bloody client but when we have the dinner on Saturday, you'll see that you have nothing to worry about. I just need you to bear with me and stop the spying and the lies. Please. It's wearing me down.'

She knew the message he'd just read was probably wearing him down more. Did he want her now that he'd just dumped his other woman? She was going to help him secure the contract because she had to know who she was dealing with. She'd make a great dinner and be as charming as possible, but after that it was over. In fact, tomorrow, she'd start looking at flats online just to see what was out there. The rental income from her mother's house would soon be able to pay for a flat and more.

They were all but over and she knew it.

'Will you come to bed now?'

'I thought you were sleeping in the spare room.'

He shrugged. 'I don't want to go to sleep on another argument. Can we just pretend it didn't happen? Can we go upstairs, agree that we've both been a bit distant? You've lied to me too and look, I'm not making a big song and dance about it. We'll talk about it like adults. Let's just get this week out the way.' He held his hand out. For a second she could see the man she fell for and she wanted nothing more than to snuggle up to him in bed. She had lied and he was here now, offering her an olive branch. They got through Alison once, maybe they could get through this. If things didn't improve over the week, then she'd think seriously about leaving him. She wiped her wet eyes and took his hand, wondering why she kept making the same mistake over and over again.

ELEVEN

Cain threw a heavy arm over her and his snores became a constant hum. He'd spent a few minutes lying next to her, stroking her arm and telling her how things were going to be when he secured the contract. She told him she was sorry about the injections, and he'd apologised too for shouting, then he'd held her close and told her how much he needed and loved her. Then he'd fallen into a deep sleep, despite that horrible message he'd received.

Leah reached for her phone. The cross words between them jumbled around in her mind followed by the tender way he held her after, making sleep impossible. She was never going to sleep with so many unanswered questions on her mind. There was one question she could address right now: What she needed to do was to get Cain's phone, use his thumb to open it up and find out who had sent him the horrible message.

His hand reached over her body as he let out a snore. Moving him too soon would wake him and the best thing all round was for him to continue sleeping.

She gently fed her hand under his arm and lifted it off her, hoping that he wouldn't stir. While holding her breath, she shuffled closer to the edge of the bed, grimacing as the mattress made crinkly sounds. She remained still and silent for several seconds, to make sure she hadn't woken him, then she rolled out of bed.

Creeping across the wooden floor, she went over to his bedside and picked his phone up. His right arm lay over his side. She pressed the phone to activate it and the thumb print security flashed straight up. He let out a snort, sending her heart rate into overdrive. She paused, ready to place the phone back where she found it and leave the room, but he continued to snore. Reaching for his hand, she lifted his thumb and held it in place. Bingo, she was in.

She stepped out onto the landing in her pyjamas and hurried downstairs in the dark with only the phone lighting everything up. She pressed the Message app, hoping not to send the phone to sleep again.

Just as she reached the hallway, the doorbell chimed. *No, no, no, no!* How could this happen? If Cain woke up, he would see that she had his phone and he'd go mad. After placing the phone on the console table, she opened the door without a thought as to who was at the other side, so that they couldn't ring the bell again and wake him. It was gone ten thirty. Who on earth would be visiting at this time? Her heart sank as she saw the light go off on his phone. All that effort had been for nothing.

'Leah Jones, was Harrison?' Charlotte, the skinny girl with the curly brown hair, stood on her doorstep, swaying like she was slightly tipsy. The same girl who'd given Zara a phone number that didn't exist. Leah took in her features, trying to work out if she looked anything like Alison or Cain. She had their dark hair and eyes.

'Yes. Who are you?' The other two girls glanced over from

the pavement, all dressed up in heels and short skirts. The girl she'd seen earlier at Cain's office building was definitely the girl on the left, except her plait was now long wavy hair.

'How could you not know me? I'm your daughter.'

TWELVE

'Can we come in?' Charlotte asked as she went to step into the hallway. She glanced at the phone on the console table and hiccupped.

Leah pulled the door to, gently, carefully guiding the girl back onto the step, words struggling to escape her gaping mouth. 'No. My husband's asleep.' She stepped out and took Charlotte's arm, gently leading her around the side of the house, while trying to ignore the other two girls who were holding each other up. This was absurd. Leah didn't have children. The girl had to be mistaken. Zara had specifically said that Charlotte was looking for her parents, so she had to be looking for Cain, which is why the other girl had turned up to his workplace. Maybe she was helping Charlotte to find things out about him. Thinking of Cain, if he were to come down now and see Leah with his phone, he'd go mad and then she'd have to try and explain what the girl claiming to be her daughter was doing here, and she had no idea herself.

'Are you okay? You're not saying much,' the girl asked.

'Yes, I mean no. Can you please speak quietly? I don't want to wake my husband.' Leah furrowed her brows and shivered as the breeze picked up. 'Look, I don't know who told you I'm your mother or what game you're playing, but you need to go now.'

'But I've only just found you.'

Shaking her head, Leah transferred her weight from one foot to the other. 'You've found the wrong person and I'm sorry to tell you that, I really am. You're wrong and whoever you're working with...' she paused, not knowing how to say what she needed to say. 'You're both playing a very cruel joke. Did she send you?'

'Who?'

'Alison.' That woman was obviously having an affair with Cain, and now she was playing with Leah's head. This was beyond wrong.

'I don't know an Alison.' The girl looked down at the pavement and hiccupped again. 'Your mother said she was sorry for what she did to you.'

Her mother's letter rang through her mind. She'd wanted to speak to her before she died about *something of the utmost importance*. No, Leah didn't have a child. It was impossible. Someone was orchestrating this and they were out to hurt her. 'How do you know my mother?'

The girl's constant glancing back at her friends emphasised her worry. 'Meet me the day after tomorrow at the Hibiscus Coffee Lounge in Worcester. I'll be there at twelve. Don't use that phone number I gave to your neighbour; it's fake as I didn't want to give my number to some random. Give me your phone. I'll put my real number in it.'

Charlotte's two friends huddled together, trying to keep warm. The girl Leah had recognised from earlier glanced over, and her friend seemed transfixed to the phone that lit her round face up. Leah's head screamed for her not to hand her phone over, but she needed to know how Charlotte knew her mother and what her delirious dying mother could have possibly told her. As the girl went to type her number into the phone, the bedroom light flooded the drive. She snatched it from Charlotte and looked at her with pleading eyes. 'I need that back, sorry. Go now. Please.'

'But I haven't finished.'

'What's going on down there?' Cain bellowed.

'Please, leave,' she pleaded. 'I'll be at the café.' Her bottom lip began to tremble. All three of them hurried across the road and walked off into the darkness, leaving Leah standing on the drive.

Stomping footsteps echoed through the hallway as Cain neared the bottom of the stairs. His phone sat on the console unit. She darted back into the house, snatched the phone and stuffed it up her pyjama sleeve. She gently closed the front door. He took the last step while rubbing his sleepy eyes. 'Why are you up?'

'I err, I needed some water.'

'From the front door?' His stare sent her knees into a jellied state. The last thing she needed was a row about his phone right now. He stared at her for several seconds, and all she could hear was blood whooshing through her body and the sound of her own pulse pounding.

'I thought I heard a noise. I was just checking outside.'

'You should have woken me. What if someone is out there and they hurt you? Go back up. I'll make sure everything is locked and I'll check out the garage.'

Hurrying towards the stairs, she exhaled as soon as she passed the halfway mark.

Leah listened intently from the landing and, moments later, a music channel on the television burst into life. She ran to the bed, popped Cain's phone on the floor between his bedside table and the bed, making sure it stuck out just a little so he'd find it easily. If he'd seen it missing, he might be convinced he could have knocked it off the table in his sleepy state. She sat on the edge of the bed, confused. Instead of finding her answers by looking through all of Cain's messages, she was left wondering what the hell was going on, and to top it all off, Charlotte was weirdly claiming to be her daughter. She bit the skin around her thumbnail as she replayed the last few minutes in her head.

If her mother had been sorry, why the hell hadn't she made contact and told Leah herself? All she ever wanted was for Jean Harrison to regret the things she'd done and apologise, and now Leah would never hear that for herself. If this was an attempt by her mother at a parting mind trick, it was a good one. Her cruelty had lasted beyond the grave.

Charlotte was not her child; it wasn't possible. Tears flooded down her cheeks as she felt the weight of the secret that lay buried inside her. It wasn't possible because her baby had been born dead when she was sixteen. She grabbed her pillow and hugged it, imaging it was Sophie, and she cried until she had no more tears left.

THIRTEEN

Leah scrubbed and scrubbed the screen in Zara's wet room until her arms throbbed. It would have been so easy to call in sick, but she knew Zara depended on her and she had to be there for her friend. Instead, she scrubbed while ruminating over everything.

'You're going to wear a hole in the glass if you're not careful.' Zara placed one of her sticks down, next to Leah's foot. 'I was just going to have a coffee break. Mr Patel's cash flow forecast can do one for an hour. Have you got time to stay for a bit, or are you heading to your mother's house again?'

Leah threw the cloth into the cleaning caddy and smiled. 'Yes, there's still lots to do there, and I'm hoping to get it on the rental market within a month now. I'll have one of your coffees. I need one after the night I had.'

'Was it your migraine?'

'I wish it was. It wasn't that bad. I went home and fell asleep on the settee until Cain got back. That's when everything went wrong.'

Zara raised her eyebrows. 'I'll get those cookies and cakes out. Pack your stuff up. You've done enough today.'

'But I haven't put Molly's bed in the wash.'

'Sod that. She likes her bed a bit smelly. It's not like my sister's coming over again today or even in the near future, thank goodness. I'll see you in the kitchen, in five.'

After packing her cleaning things into the boot of her car, Leah hurried back into Zara's kitchen, where the coffee and snacks were already laid out on the table. She glanced at the giant cookies and muffins. On any other day, she'd be eager to dive in and eat them with her friend, but today she already felt sick at the thought of meeting Charlotte tomorrow, especially after what the girl had said. All night, Leah had lain awake, staring at the bedroom ceiling in the dark while Cain slept on the settee. She must have nodded off at some point as she didn't hear Cain get dressed or leave for work. He hadn't even woken her to say bye. She swallowed, not meaning for Cain to find out that she was using the contraceptive injection behind his back. She'd allowed him to get swept up in the idea of a family but no, she could never give birth again. The first time had broken her and she had vowed there would never be another, but she couldn't exactly tell Cain all that.

'Dig in.' Zara bit into a giant cookie and a few crumbs dropped onto the table. 'So good.' She licked her lips. 'So, why were you trying to rub a hole in my shower screen?'

'You just wouldn't believe it, Zara.'

'Try me.'

'I don't know where to start.' And she didn't.

'You left me and went into your house. What next?'

Leah took a blueberry muffin, picked a bit off with her fingers and ate it. She placed the rest on the table. 'Cain came home, obviously.'

'Did he stink of Alison again?'

'I don't know, I don't think so. He came home angry. He knew I'd been to his office that day.'

Zara furrowed her brow and flicked her blonde hair from her face. 'How?'

'I stupidly left the coffee I bought him on his desk, and he just knew. Anyway, that was nothing. We argue about things like this a lot, lately. He went on that I was spying on him and I had a go at him too, then he walked off. A message flashed up on his phone, and I managed to see it before it went black again.'

'And?' Zara's brows were now raised. She placed her cookie on a side plate.

'I can't remember the exact words as they flashed up so fast. Something like, "you bastard, playing games, ruining lives," and it finished with, "I hate you".'

'What are you thinking?'

Leah pressed her lips together and paused for a second. 'Jilted lover. It screams it.' She shrugged and pushed the muffin away. 'I can't eat this.' She began to choke up.

'Whoever sent that message got one thing right. He is a bastard. He's cheating on you, and he drinks too much. Bloody men. They think it's okay to use women and treat them like shit.' She pulled a serviette from next to the cakes and passed it to Leah.

'Thank you.' She blew her nose and popped it in her pocket.

'That's not all? What else has he done?'

Leah used the sleeve of her hoodie to wipe her eyes dry. 'It's not Cain.'

'Okay.'

'The girl turned up at the door with her friends in tow. It was quite late. I think it must have been about eleven maybe, and they looked like they'd been out drinking.'

'The girl? You mean Charlotte?'

Leah nodded.

'Was she looking for Cain?'

'No, that's the worst of it. She wasn't looking for Cain; she was looking for me. Thankfully he didn't see her, as I don't know what I'd have said.'

'But...' A confused look spread across Zara's face. 'I don't get it.'

'She said I'm her mother.' With raised brows, Zara leaned in. 'I had a baby at sixteen. I held this little dot of a girl in my arms and she was dead. Someone is playing the sickest of jokes on me. I lost my baby. How could someone do this to me?' Tears fell in abundance down Leah's face. 'I think it's my mother. She said something before she died to Charlotte, and she thinks I'm her mother. I don't know what to do.' Huge tears plopped on the table.

Zara grabbed one of her sticks and used the table to come around. Molly ran over, let out a little cry and lay her head on Leah's lap. Zara perched on the edge of the table and held Leah while she cried it all out.

'I had no idea. I am so sorry. That's a horrible thing to go through.'

Leah's heart skipped a beat as she thought about the tiny pale baby she'd named Sophie; the lifeless little girl who never moved. She'd only held Sophie for the few seconds before she was snatched from Leah's arms. How could her mother have filled Charlotte's head with the idea that she was Leah's daughter? Jean wasn't sorry on her deathbed. What she'd done was commit yet another act of cruelty with which to ruin Leah's current life. Her mother had also made an innocent girl believe that she was Leah's daughter and that was unforgivable. Was Charlotte innocent? So many thoughts were jumbling around in Leah's mind.

Zara's phone flashed on the table, and Leah could see it was a Facebook friend request acceptance. Not only that, but the person was called Alison. 'Zara, who's Alison?'

Zara sat up a bit. 'What?'

'Your phone, you've just had a friend request accepted by Alison.'

'Oh that. She's just a client and she kept messaging me

through Facebook rather than emailing me. I thought it would be easier. You don't think...?'

Leah was being ridiculous. 'No, sorry. Ignore me.'

Time was clocking on. Leah had to put an end to this nonsense and there was only one way to do it. Sophie had died. She was going to prove it, and she was going to get to the bottom of her mother's game. The gold key. She had to find out what it opened. Her mother had left it in that tissue box on purpose. She wanted Leah to find that key all along. Now she had, and she had to work out what it opened.

FOURTEEN

After leaving Zara's, Leah headed straight to her mother's. The journey had been filled with her wondering who the Alison was on Zara's Facebook notification. She said she was a client, and Leah had searched again for the Alison but couldn't find her. She wondered if Alison had blocked her. She settled into the study and opened the dusty curtains.

She pulled the mysterious gold key from her pocket and tested it in the already open filing cabinets in her mother's office. It didn't fit. She glanced around. There was nothing else in the room that needed a key. Maybe there was a tin or a box in the shed. Hurrying back out into the garden, she stopped for a moment and stared at the daffodils. She cleared her throat and forced all sad thoughts from her mind. Now wasn't the time to break down. As far as she could see, there had been no more damage overnight. Exhaling with relief, she decided that the flowers were one less thing she had to worry about.

Who was she kidding? She stared at the flowers that represented rebirth and new beginnings. For her, they had represented so much more and someone had desecrated them. Her heart began to pound and she gasped for breath. What if she'd been lied to by the person who was meant to care for her the most? What if Sophie had lived? Leah allowed her thoughts to wander back to that night. Writhing around on her mother's bed suffering with wave after wave of excruciating contractions, she remembered screaming and pushing, but exhaustion had kicked in. Hours had passed and it must have been the middle of the night. A tear slipped out. She didn't even know the time her baby had been born. In the early stages of labour, all she remembered was Jean's voice, telling her what a mess she'd made of her life and that this was her pain to bear and it would serve as a reminder of her bad decisions. Her memories after that were vague then and they were still as vague now. The codeine-based painkillers her mother used for her bad back had been the best she had at hand, and Leah had helped herself to them and everything had seemed woozy. Blood, she remembered bleeding, a lot; her mother wide-eyed and pale as she kept bringing more towels; then there was a voice, another person, but who? Had it been a dream? As she thought back, everything was blurry and when Sophie was taken from her in the lamplit room, she'd cried herself to sleep, knowing her baby was gone. She'd wailed Sophie's name with all she had left until she had nothing more to give. What if? She dared to hope that Sophie hadn't died and that the girl who had sought her out was indeed her tiny baby, the little girl she'd held in her arms and had wanted more than life itself.

She grabbed her phone and clicked the internet app. If she ordered the maternity test now, it would arrive tomorrow – if she paid extra. She got her card out, the one she used for her cleaning business, and she inserted the number and placed the order. That way, Cain would never know what she'd bought. However hard she hoped and wanted her baby to have lived, she knew she'd held a dead baby in her arms. She had to at least prove to Charlotte that she wasn't her mother. Charlotte had seemed convinced but there was a flicker of something else, something Leah couldn't fathom. She had the night to work out how she'd convince Charlotte to allow her to take a cheek swab. It was the right thing to do, for both of them. Right now, she needed to find out what the key opened.

She hurried to the shed and opened it. There was nothing that resembled a tin anywhere. Her gaze fixed on one of the back corners. She'd lain there scared one night after her mother had punished her for coming in fifteen minutes late. The sound of the key locking her into the dark, spider-filled shed had made her sob and beg, but Jean hadn't cared. Reaching out, she scraped all the cobwebs away from her head and pushed the lawn mower to the side so she could reach the shelves at the back. Nothing. The key was still a mystery and one she had to crack quickly.

She left the shed and hurried back in, making sure she locked the French doors. She checked the garden one more time, just in case she'd missed anything but it was fine. The tiniest ray of sun shone through the cherry blossom tree, breaking up the dark wall of trees beyond the garden. Very soon, the tree would flower for the briefest of time before its petals turned to mulch on the dying lawn.

Twiddling the key between her fingers, she had to try upstairs again. Taking the stairs two at a time, she passed her bedroom and stood on the landing outside her mother's. That very spot was where she'd felt the first trickle down her legs after her waters broke. She remembered her heart racing and her legs shaking as she stumbled to her mother's bed. She took a deep breath. Ignoring her banging heart, she stepped in and started rooting through her mother's drawers which were now empty of all her clothes that had long gone to a charity shop. Leah pulled out the tiny collection of jewellery boxes, but the key didn't fit any of them. The spare room. She hadn't tried looking there yet.

Stepping in, she nudged the boxes aside. She'd personally

packed each one and labelled them, ready for their respective destinations. Newspapers – there were no boxes in there. Bathroom – she'd barely taken any notice of everything she'd stored in that box She scratched the edge of the packing tape and peeled it back before tugging the cardboard open. After digging to the bottom and throwing the toilet rolls and shampoos out, she soon found that there were no tiny boxes that needed a key.

Her bedroom was virtually empty but maybe she'd missed a drawer. She hadn't properly checked under her bed. She'd pulled out the rubbish her mother had crammed underneath it. Most of it had been supermarket middle aisle special buys and mail order rubbish that had never been opened. But had she missed something? Maybe a box pressed up against the wall. She ran to her childhood bedroom again and stopped dead.

Her heart threatened to burst out of her chest as its pounding choked her throat. The daffodil wasn't there yesterday. She'd checked the house. The window frame rattled as a gust of wind came from nowhere. It was as if the house was shouting: *run, before it's too late.* A tickle passed the back of her neck as she thought of the past. It was as if her mother was there with her, telling her that she'd never let her forget the past. Without a second thought, Leah darted out of the room and almost slipped down the second half of the steps as she grabbed her bag and left the house.

As she reached her car and fumbled for her keys, Mrs Pearson, stood still in her doorway, staring as if in a trance. She took a few steps down her path. 'You look like you've seen a ghost, Leah. Are you okay?'

A tear drizzled down her cheek. 'No.' She couldn't catch her breath.

'Go home, dear. You need your rest. The news about your mother has obviously hit you hard.'

As Mrs Pearson went to place a bony finger on her wrist, Leah shuddered. She gasped and glanced up at the house, taking in the fact that someone or something was trying to get her attention. The daffodil had been a clear message. She placed a hand on her chest.

'Leah, I think you need a doctor, maybe an ambulance. Is it your heart?'

Boom, boom, boom – her heart banged violently. She couldn't answer the woman or catch her breath. Getting into the car, she started the engine and drove away, leaving Mrs Pearson standing in the road. After filtering onto the single-track road, she inhaled sharply over and over again. She needed to call the police. She pulled over into a passing place. She could breathe again. All she needed was to get away from her past. Punching in the number, she waited for the operator. 'Someone has broken into my house. You need to come. They might even still be in there.'

FIFTEEN

After twenty minutes of waiting, Leah watched as the police passed her and drove towards Larrison House. She turned the car around and parked behind them. Two officers got out. Leah glanced up at the windows, searching for movement, but she couldn't see anyone.

'Hello, are you Mrs Jones?'

Leah nodded at the uniformed woman and man. 'Yes, call me Leah.'

'I'm PC Trim and this is PC Crawford.' The man smiled. 'You said on the call that there was no one living in the house at the moment.'

'That's right. It was my mother's house. She died a few months ago and I've been tidying it up, so I'm not here all the time.'

'Are there any signs of forced entry?'

Leah shook her head and answered PC Trim. 'No, all the doors were locked and the windows were closed.'

'Does anyone else have a key?'

'I don't know. My mother was very sick towards the end,

and I know she had a lot of help so any number of people could have had a key.'

'Did she tell you who she may have given keys to?'

'No, we hadn't spoken for years.' She wondered if she should mention Charlotte to the officer but decided not to. She knew that the girl had spoken to her mother, but would her mother really have given her a key? Maybe Mrs Pearson had one. As the thought struck her, the old woman opened her front door and glanced over.

'Mrs Pearson. Did my mother give you a key to her house?' she called out, hoping that she could hear.

'No, dear. Are you okay now? I was worried about you when you drove off.'

She nodded. 'Yes, sorry about that. It just scared me because someone has been in the house. I panicked. Have you seen anyone hanging around the house or trying to get in?'

The two officers waited for an answer, and PC Crawford began making notes in his little book.

'No. I don't see many people around here, but of course, I'm in bed early and I take my hearing aids out then, so I don't hear much either.'

'Thank you.'

'Can we go in the house and have a look?' PC Trim asked. 'PC Crawford will double check all the windows and doors, just in case one of them is broken, and you can show me the bedroom.'

Leah led the way up the path and unlocked the door. 'Don't you need forensics suits and should I be going in? I might contaminate the scene.' She'd heard those words when watching crime thrillers on the telly.

'It's okay. You've already been in the house today. We're just here to take a look. Has anything been taken?'

Leah cautiously stepped into the hallway and shivered. It

was definitely colder than when she'd been in the house an hour before. 'Not that I could tell.' Her mother's laptops were still piled up. The little jewellery boxes that she thought the gold key might open seemed to have everything in them, not that there were any real diamonds or any gold. In fact, for all the money her mother had left, she had very little in the way of valuable belongings. She never did like buying flashy things, as she called them. There was nothing a burglar would want. 'They left something.'

'Show me.'

Leah led PC Trim upstairs, the stained-glass sun picture glowing yellow on her body as she passed it. 'They left a daffodil. It's here, in my old room.' As Leah pushed the door and stepped in, she found herself lost for words. The daffodil was gone. She ran to the bed and fell onto her knees. Pushing her fingers between the mattress and bed, she couldn't feel a thing. She bent down and checked underneath, again there was no sign of the flower. 'It's gone. It was right here.' She stood and slammed her palm onto the bed.

'Are you sure? You've been under a lot of stress lately, with losing your mother.'

'I'm more than sure. Are you trying to insinuate that I'm going mad?'

'Of course not. That's not what I'm saying at all but this is a quiet area and the house is empty.'

'Look.' Leah pointed out the window. PC Trim hurried over. She went to tell the PC about someone coming into the garden and cutting the flower heads off and discarding them on the grass, but she stopped.

'What is it?'

Leah took a deep breath. 'Nothing. I must have been mistaken. I thought I saw something, that was all. I'm tired and I'm sorry. I really thought...' she glanced back at the bed.

PC Crawford knocked and stepped into the bedroom. 'I've checked every door and window. All secure.' He walked over to the window in Leah's bedroom. 'This one is secure too.'

Leah sat on the bed and bit her bottom lip, at a loss as to where the flower had gone. 'I'm so sorry. I'm under a lot of stress.'

'Is there anyone I can call for you?' PC Trim asked.

Leah shook her head. The last person she needed to alert was Cain, and she didn't want to interrupt Zara's work. 'I'll be okay.'

'In that case, my advice to you would be to get your locks changed, especially if other people could have a key.' PC Crawford's radio crackled and a voice came through. 'We have an urgent incident to attend to.' With that, the officers said their goodbyes and left.

Leah lay on her old bed, not knowing how that flower had disappeared. Maybe it had never been there in the first place. She gripped the over-blanket she'd made out of little knitted and crocheted squares when she was a child. Something in the air shifted, like the room was closing in on her and her throat felt tight. Hot, she was hot. It was as if the house was laughing at her, playing pranks, trying to send her insane with that daffodil. Or maybe she was going insane. She flinched as her phone beeped with an email.

At least something was going to plan. The email confirmed that the maternity test would be couriered to Larrison House the next morning by ten. Standing, she hurried down the stairs and out onto the front garden, leaving the house behind for the night until she came back in the morning to take the delivery. There was no way she'd have it delivered to her house where Cain might find it. As she locked up and ran back to her car, she watched as yellow petals danced along the path in the breeze. Reaching down, she caught one between her fingers and held it close to her heart. What did they mean? She glanced around knowing that someone out there was trying to tell her something, but who?

SIXTEEN

Leah jolted up in bed, sweat pooled under her breasts and armpits. Where was Sophie? For a moment, the vivid dream she'd just had felt so real, she'd heard her baby crying to be saved but she'd failed. She shook her head and tried to calm herself before she woke Cain up. The quilt next to her rose and fell in time with his deep breaths. She didn't want to wake him as he'd come home in a good mood. He'd been attentive and loving, all the things she craved from him every day. Still, she hadn't managed to speak to him about the things that were filling her head.

Gently slipping out of bed, she walked over to the window and cranked it open a touch. The moon was full, just like it had been in her dream. In the distance, she listened to the barking dog, then a tear slipped from her right eye as she fixated on the sounds of the baby crying across the road, taking her right back to the night where she should have heard Sophie crying. But Sophie had never cried.

Right up to the moment of Sophie's birth, Leah had lived in denial of the changes in her body, but nature doesn't wait for a person to accept a situation. Seasons come and go; time passes and the end comes to everyone. Leah was going to have a baby and, up to the time of the birth, she'd willed it away, hoped that it had all been a nightmare; that she'd wake up and her bump would be gone.

'I'm sorry I didn't want you to begin with, Sophie,' she whispered under her breath as Cain snored. The baby across the road cried again. She held a hand to her heart and tried to picture Sophie's tiny lips, her bluish hands and perfectly formed fingers, and a fragility that felt unreal. Was that how Sophie looked back then? Leah didn't even have a photo to remember her by. Her mother kept banging on that she was to forget Sophie. The codeine and the blurriness of that night... had she created an image of Sophie that didn't exist?

Leah wafted her bed shirt to get more cool air circulating around her body. Finally panic and confusion gave way to sadness. A whistle of wind filled the air, flapping the curtains, and the hairs on Leah's arms began to prickle as she felt like something was off. She couldn't put her finger on what it was, maybe it was the shadows of the trees dancing on the dark road every time the wind blew them past the streetlamps. Maybe it was the tapping of walking feet, too far away to see who they belonged to. No, it was the fact that the walking had stopped and Leah couldn't see anyone. A figure crept out from the trees and continued walking along the path. Leah stared out from the darkness of her bedroom as the figure stopped at the end of her drive before turning to face her. The baggy coat and black baseball cap concealed the person's face and build. She stepped back hoping that she hadn't been spotted, that's when she heard the strangest ringtone. The yodelling continued for several seconds, then the stranger ended the call. A shiver ran through her body as the mystery person looked up. It was as if the air had been sucked out of the room.

Snatching the curtains, she pulled them closed and held her breath. Someone was playing with her mind and it had to be the same person who was watching her while she was walking Molly with Zara.

She moved left and peered through the gap in the curtains. There was no one there. She heard a baby crying and, in the distance, a barking dog. Was the stranger real? She was beginning to doubt herself. Psychotic breaks were a thing; she'd read about them. Cain's cheating, her mother's death, Charlotte turning up; the other girl at Cain's workplace; all these things were sending her over the edge.

SEVENTEEN

As soon as Leah pulled up outside her mother's house, she saw the courier walking up the garden path. She ran and signed for her test, thanking him as she pushed the key in the lock. Her phone rang. 'Cain?'

'I just wondered, can we just do something nice, maybe meet for lunch? I could head into Worcester and meet you.'

There was no way she could meet him even though he was making an effort. She had to meet Charlotte in Worcester. 'I'm at the house and I have a million and one things to do. I'm waiting for a delivery and I have a house to clean after. I can't cancel. I wish I could though.'

'Well, it was worth a try.' He paused. 'I don't want to lose you, Leah, and I shouldn't have been angry at you coming to the office. I know we have a lot to talk about. Look, about trying for a baby. I've been thinking about it. Maybe we're not ready and it doesn't matter...' He paused again, and she knew this was one of the things they had to discuss at some point, and she knew it mattered, but then he asked: 'Oh, are you still okay for the dinner?'

'The dinner?' She had no idea what he meant.

'You know, the big contract we need to nail with one of your fancy dinners. I need you on board with this. I was wondering if we could do a practice run tonight with the food. It's too important to stuff up. There are two of them coming.'

She couldn't believe she'd forgotten. 'Yes, of course. The meal. I'll sort it.'

'Okay, love you loads and can't wait to see you later.'

She wondered if she could say it back. She had loved Cain so deeply, but she'd been unnaturally dependant on him for her happiness and that wasn't right. He'd cheated and now that he'd been dumped, he wanted to worm his way back in. Even though it felt good to have his love and attention, it wasn't healthy. It was hard, because she did love him and she'd only ever loved him. 'I love you too,' she replied.

'Will you be able to grab some food and maybe treat yourself to a new dress? We need to look the business on Saturday.'

'Yes. I've got to go. Delivery's arrived.' With that she ended the call. Great, on top of everything else she had to do, she'd now have to go to the supermarket. Her shoulders slumped. She sat at her mother's desk and slid open the top desk drawer, where she'd left the gold key. Running it through her fingers, she watched as the thin shaft of light from the bay window caught it. It was useless. It didn't seem to open anything. Flinging the key back in the drawer, she slammed it closed.

The package in front of her wasn't going to open itself. She removed the instruction sheet. After having a quick glance through it, she placed it on the desk. She checked that everything she needed was there. Two sample collection swab packs, two envelopes and the larger envelope to send the swabs back in. If she got the envelope to a priority postbox that afternoon, she could have the test results back the following evening, or the morning after at the latest. It had cost a lot for a fast service but she needed answers fast. She removed one of the swabs, brushed it against the inside of her cheek and packed it in the test sample envelope, ready to go back. Now all she had to do was convince Charlotte to do the same. Leah had held her life-less tiny baby in her arms all those years ago, so Charlotte must have got everything wrong. At least the results would allow Charlotte to eliminate her and look for her real mother. Leah was doing them both a favour.

She walked into the kitchen, checking that the doors and windows were locked. The garden looked exactly as it did the day before except some of the daffodil heads had blown across the grass during the night. In her mind, she could hear her baby crying again, just like she had in her dream. Her mind knew how to taunt her.

She ran upstairs and sat on the base of her mother's bedframe in the exact spot where she'd held Sophie in her arms. Closing her eyes, she tried to replay that night in her head in the hope of remembering if her baby had taken even the tiniest of breaths, but she couldn't recall that happening. All she remembered were the precious seconds she had with Sophie and her own cries as her mother heartlessly prised the little one from her arms, telling her that everything would be okay and that she could now go back to her normal life. Nothing was normal about what came next, nothing at all. There was definitely another voice coming from the landing back then. Someone else had been there, which meant someone else knew their secret.

Leah opened her eyes and stared at the floor. The days after melded into a blur, a feverish blur, just like the dream she'd had last night. She gripped one of the spindles at the head of the bed, the same spindle that she gripped as she pushed her daughter out.

Shaking her head, she left the room and closed the door, hoping to keep that ghost contained.

It was nearly time to meet Charlotte and, in that short time, she needed the swab. She also needed to ask Charlotte what she'd been doing at her mother's house in the run up to her death. Did Charlotte really believe that she was Leah's daughter, and who gave her that idea? Rushing back down, she pushed everything back into the DNA test box and ran out the door. She was about to get her answers.

EIGHTEEN

Leah picked up her pace and ran past the Edward Elgar statue in the middle of Worcester. The cathedral bells told her it was midday. On reaching the café, she glanced through the front window hoping to catch a glimpse of the girl claiming to be her daughter. Charlotte hadn't arrived yet, not that she could see, but there were other seats around the back. Maybe she was sitting in the tiny courtyard, waiting.

A bell above the door rang as she entered the coffee shop. The fragrant aroma of coffee beans immediately made Leah's mouth water.

'Can I help you?' the woman behind the counter asked.

Stomach rumbling, Leah perused the muffins and giant cookies on display. Eating might just calm her nerves, or maybe a cake would make her sick. No, with her stomach churning, it was best to stick to a drink. 'Can I just have a latte, please?'

The barista nodded and began to make her drink. She tapped her card on the machine and stared at the door, wondering when Charlotte was going to turn up. What if she didn't turn up? What if it was all some kind of prank? She definitely hadn't ruled that out. Leah checked her bag for the third time to make sure the DNA test box was still in its place. As the barista began heating the milk, Leah dashed to the end of the café and peered out into the courtyard. It was busy but Charlotte wasn't there. She hurried back, took her drink, and found a table behind the one near the front window. Three women with pushchairs and toddlers laughed behind her at some joke about the terrible twos. She smiled at an angelic-looking toddler who grinned while sucking on a carrot stick. An elderly man sitting in front of the counter with a crossword book glanced across at her before going back to his crossword. It seemed everyone was out for lunch except for the girl she'd arranged to meet.

Her muscles tensed as her phone beeped. It was Cain.

Grab a bottle of brandy. Buy a good one. We need to offer something special to our guests. Get some champagne too. No cheap stuff. Speak later. X

Noon soon passed and more people began to arrive for lunch. People in suits filled the place as they ordered and chatted through their lunch breaks, and still there was no sign of Charlotte. Leah wondered if she should order another drink. The barista glanced at her as if to say she needed the table for the lunch crowd.

Leah flinched as Charlotte tapped on the window and waved. She walked to the door with her two friends and took her smart jacket off to reveal a pair of baggy jeans and a striped T-shirt. Leah's shoulders slumped at the thought of the other two joining them for what was such a personal conversation. She took in the other girl who had been outside her husband's workplace. Her hair fell in waves over her shoulders, and her pinafore dress fell just above her knees. What had she been doing at the office?

The bell rang as they all entered. Charlotte went up to the

counter and bought three cans of cola, and they all ambled over. The third girl, who seemed to be glued to her phone, took the corner seat. 'This is Freya' – Charlotte pointed to her seated friend followed by the wavy-haired girl – 'and this is Angel.'

She now had a name. Angel had visited Cain's workplace, but why?

Angel furrowed her brows as if suspicious of Leah, then she pulled up a chair from the table behind and squeezed in opposite. Charlotte sat next to her; knees tensely pressed together.

'I was hoping we'd be able to talk alone.'

Charlotte picked up a wooden stirrer and began twiddling it. 'I don't really know you and I didn't want to come alone. Freya and Angel know everything, which is why they came to your house with me. We're best friends so we look out for each other.'

'Okay.' It looked like Leah had no option but to include them, which was going to be tough. The last thing she wanted was for Charlotte to feel uncomfortable, so it might work out better. Leah felt a pang of sadness. If only she'd had friends back then, people to talk to and confide in. After her mother sent her away from her childhood home, she'd lost touch with everyone. Actually, that wasn't true: she'd distanced herself from her friends as soon as she'd missed her second period and confirmed her pregnancy with a test. It had become the big secret and she'd hidden from everyone as she ignored her pregnancy, in the hope that it would vanish. 'Tell me a little about yourself.'

'I grew up in Bromsgrove. We're all from Bromsgrove so we had to get the bus, but it isn't far.'

Leah glanced at the girl's brown eyes, almond shaped, just like hers. Her oval face was more like her father's. She shut those thoughts away. No way should she get carried away and start thinking of Charlotte as her daughter. It was impossible to tell if they had any similar features under Charlotte's thick make-up. 'Why do you think I'm your mother?'

'Because you are.' Charlotte leaned back and bit a shred of loose black painted fingernail. The girl nervously tapped her feet on the floor.

Angel picked up a wooden stirrer and began bending it until it snapped. 'Sorry.' She dropped the two halves on the table and sipped from her can.

'How do you know I'm your mother?'

'Nan told me.'

This girl had been calling her mother Nan. Leah considered that if Charlotte had seen a dying woman craving a grand-daughter on her deathbed, maybe she hung around in the hope that the lonely old woman would give her some of the wealth she exuded. Her scam radar was back with a vengeance. Maybe her mother had met Charlotte while out and about and told the girl that her only daughter had no contact with her. Her mother had been sick; she'd have been alone. She could have said all sorts. Leah struggled to ever imagine her mother being vulner-able but maybe people change, especially if they know they're going to die. 'What did she tell you?'

'She sent me a message one day on Facebook. Of course, there was no picture and I thought it looked like a weirdo message. But then she sent another. Again, she said she was my grandmother and that she also knew who my real mother was. That's when she told me she was dying. It was a shock to me too. I had no idea I was adopted.' Charlotte looked away and blinked back a tear.

Leah swallowed. So, her mother had contacted Charlotte. That's how this all started. 'Do you still have these messages?'

Charlotte glanced at Angel. 'No, I deleted them.'

That red flag was telling Leah to get up and leave. Why would anyone delete messages of such significance?

'I didn't want my mother to read them, my adoptive mother,

I mean. That's why I got rid of them. I know she's read my messages before. I only have to leave my phone out while I go to the loo and she's checking it like I'm hiding some thirty-year-old boyfriend or something. But she loves me and, although it's a bit stifling, she cares.' Charlotte shrugged and continued. 'She and my dad have been everything I've ever known. If they knew I was here, talking to you, they'd be heartbroken. They have no idea I visited Nan.' Charlotte paused. 'I went to her house a few times. I was even there on the day she died.' Angel looked away and placed a hand on her friend's shoulder. 'The nurse let me stay with her. Nan was insistent that she died at home, and she found a nurse who would help her to the end. That's when she told me things. She told me where you lived. She managed to tell me the name of your road and I knew your name. I knew I'd be able to find you.' She paused again and stared into her hands. 'She told me to tell you how sorry she was, that she loved you so much and that she'd been wrong. She wished she could have spoken to you one more time, but she didn't have your number. I don't know what happened. I don't know why you gave me up—'

'I didn't give you up. I don't have any children. I can only think that my mother was delirious in the weeks running up to her death.' She thought of the letter and wondered if all this would not be happening if she'd only responded. What if her baby had lived? She quelled the sob that threatened to escape. Her tiny baby lay in her arms, motionless, and when her mother took the little one, Leah felt as though her heart had been torn out and stamped on. She felt in her bag for the DNA test kit. This was the only way to get to the truth. A part of her felt bad for asking. Charlotte seemed so convinced that she was her mother.

Freya stood with her vibrating phone in her hand. 'My mum's calling. I best take this, sorry.' She left Leah with Charlotte and Angel. Angel began scrolling through her phone as if ignoring them, but Leah knew she was taking every word in. For a moment, she tried to imagine Cain having an affair with someone so young, and she swallowed down the hurt she'd been containing. After all, Leah was eighteen when they met and Cain was twenty-six. Her mother had totally cut off all contact after hearing of their relationship. She glanced at Angel again and wondered if Cain had been spending time with her, but she pushed that thought away. She looked so young. He had to be sleeping with Alison and all of this was a huge mistake.

'Nan wasn't delirious. We played cards and she told jokes. We watched films together; she said her favourite was *The Wizard of Oz*; it reminded her of you when you were little. She said you used to watch it together.'

Leah remembered that film; it was her mother's go to when she needed to get some work done, but she did have some memories of sitting with Jean while they watched films. Charlotte had really got close to her mother from what she was saying, closer than Leah had ever been to her. 'I don't know how to ask you this...'

'It's okay, you can ask me anything.' Charlotte scraped her dark hair into a ponytail and leaned back.

A few people began to leave the café. The mothers were still engrossed in their jokes, and the man doing the crossword packed up and left. Leah leaned forward a little, not wanting the barista to hear her speak. She pulled the DNA test kit out. 'I think it would be good for both of us if we did this test. It will tell us if I am your mother, for definite.'

'I thought you said you didn't have a child.' Charlotte folded her arms in front of her chest.

'I had a baby once but my baby was born dead.' Saying that out loud stuck in Leah's throat. 'I held my lifeless baby in my arms. Her name was Sophie.' She took a deep breath. Charlotte looked at Angel again as if seeking reassurance. 'All you have to do is brush your cheek with the stick. I'll send it off and, very soon, we get the results. We'll both know for sure.'

Charlotte took the swab from Leah. She rubbed it across the inside of her cheek before passing it back. 'I've got to go.' Charlotte stood and pulled Angel by her arm. 'I have proof by the way. I'll bring it next time, to show you.' As Freya came back over, Charlotte grabbed her too and dragged her along with them.

'I should take your number,' Leah called, but Charlotte ignored her.

'I've got to go. I'll come to Nan's tomorrow lunchtime with the proof.' The three girls hurried outside.

Leah watched as they passed the front window. Charlotte's arms went up in the air, and Angel nudged past her, shaking her head. Were they arguing? Freya stormed out of view. Maybe Charlotte believed Jean's ramblings, and maybe the poor girl was as confused as Leah was. A minute or two later, they were gone. Leah finished her cold latte.

The three laughing mothers behind her got louder, then one of the babies began to cry. Her chest tightened and she inhaled sharply, the sound too painful for her. Placing her hands over her ears to block it out, she darted through the café door. As soon as she burst out into the fresh air, she headed over to a wall and gasped for breath, taking all that precious oxygen into her lungs. She glanced down the path at the shops. The girls had gone, but she caught someone familiar disappearing down a side street. No, it wasn't Cain, surely? It was her imagination in overdrive.

She ran as fast as she could to her car and sobbed until she'd reached exhaustion point. It was all too much but at least she had the swabs. All she had to do was post them right now and wait for the email to say the results were available to view.

Her mind kept whirring over what Charlotte had said. She had proof. What proof? Could Leah really be Charlotte's mother? The wringing in her heart wanted so much for the girl to be telling the truth. She'd have done anything to know that Sophie had lived, that her tiny baby had cried, had grown... If Charlotte was Sophie, Leah had missed out on being her mother and that hurt more than anything. How could Jean have done something so cruel?

NINETEEN

Leah grabbed the shopping bags and the dress from the car, knowing that she barely had any time to get dinner on. Cain would be home in two hours and, despite how up and down their relationship was, she didn't want him to lose the contract. She'd made sure that the swab had been sent back, and she'd got the shopping. The whole walk around the supermarket had passed in a haze. Charlotte had given her hope, but was it dangerous to hope? As she'd walked up and down the aisles, she kept telling herself not to get carried away. She shook that thought away. It was no good torturing herself with hope that could simply be dashed by the next evening when the test results came through. She gripped the bags until her knuckles went white. How would she tell Cain?

She dropped her bags on the kitchen island, pulled the wrap dress out and hung it on the back of the door. It looked better on the mannequin in the shop. She held it up against her body. It looked dowdy, but it would have to do.

Grabbing the sides of her hair in her fists and pulling, she roared with frustration. The not knowing was killing her and, in the meantime, she had to act as if all was fine. She was Leah, the wife who was preparing to entertain her cheating husband's clients. Right now, she had to concentrate on the things she could control. She was going to make salmon en croute and a dark chocolate mousse. It would help pass the time.

* * *

Two hours later, she pulled the salmon out of the oven. Cain was late and each time she called him his phone had gone straight to voicemail. She stared at the food displayed all over the island. All that effort had been for nothing as the food was spoiling. Her phone beeped.

> *Sorry, going to be late and don't know what time I'll be back. Can't answer phone, I'm in meetings. We'll be okay tomorrow with the food. Don't wait up for me. Love you and miss you loads. XX*

She checked the time. It was almost eight and he'd ignored all her calls. It was obvious he was with perfume woman. Her mind kept flitting between Angel and Alison. She grabbed a chocolate mousse in a ramekin and threw it at one of their white walls. Blobs of it slid down the wall onto the tiles below. She grabbed two puddings and stepped over the mess. Only Zara would understand the day she'd had.

* * *

Hours had passed and the mousse had been enjoyed by Zara at least. Molly lay her snout in Leah's lap as she cried to her friend on the couch. 'I'm so confused, Zara. I just don't know what's going on. I call the police about a break-in and the flower had gone. As for Cain, he's been an arse.' Sobbing, she grabbed a tissue and wiped her nose.

'You've been through a lot. I don't know how you're holding it together, love. Do you want to stay here tonight?'

Leah shook her head. 'I can't. I left the place in a mess. There's mousse all over the wall.'

'Let him clean it up. It's his fault after all.'

A little laugh escaped Leah's lips. 'No, I need to get back and I need to go to bed. Thank you for listening.'

Zara placed an arm around Leah. 'Anytime.'

'Are you okay? I haven't asked. I've been so wrapped up in myself. What a useless friend I am.'

'You are not useless. You do so much for me all the time. I'm glad I can be here for you for a change.'

'What do you think of it all?' Leah shuffled forward on the couch and perched on the edge.

'Which bit?'

'Charlotte mostly?'

'From what you've told me, I just don't know. I think if your mother told you Charlotte, sorry, Sophie was dead and she wasn't, it's unforgivable. You need the truth and you've done the right thing in getting this test. Very soon you'll have the answer and then you can take it from there. I can't think why the other one, Angel, would need to go to Cain's work place. That's odd. I can't think how they'd be connected. And I don't know why the three girls would argue outside the shop or why Charlotte looked a bit angry when she did the swab thingy.' Zara paused and tilted her head. 'Just don't get attached or too involved until you know what's going on. I'd be wary and I don't know why I'm saying that. It's just something doesn't seem right and I don't want to see my bestie getting hurt, okay?'

'I'm already hurt. What does it matter if I sink even lower. I'm beginning to think that nothing matters any more.'

'It just does. Besides, you can't fall apart, I need you.' Zara furrowed her brows as she checked her phone.

'Zara, is everything okay?'

'Just work.' She placed her phone in her pocket.

The words *fall apart* made her smirk slightly. She felt like her life was unravelling before her and there was nothing she could do about it. 'Anyway, I should go.'

Leah said her goodbyes and headed back to her silent house and began to wipe the chocolate mousse. She sent a text to Cain.

When will you be back? It's almost eleven.

Half an hour passed and he hadn't replied. She turned all the lights off and ambled up to bed. She went to close the curtains. That's when she saw the figure, again. But instead of being scared, Leah just felt angry. Opening the window, she called out. 'Who are you? What do you want?'

The figure turned away and disappeared into the darkness of the wooded area. The dog barked and the baby cried. Not only that, but the mother opened a window and shouted at Leah for waking her baby.

She held a hand up. 'Sorry.' Had she seen a figure or had it been as real as the daffodil on her bed? Right now, she had no idea and that scared her more than anything. She lay on her bed, hugging her pillow.

TWENTY

Leah prised her eyes open to the clattering sound coming from the kitchen. She hurried downstairs, rage building up inside her. Last time she checked the clock, it was about three in the morning, but soon after she'd fallen asleep. 'Where the hell were you last night? I was worried.'

About to bite into a piece of toast, Cain stopped and held it between his fingers. 'Car broke down, can you believe it? I had to call recovery and they took hours. You know what it's like. I'm hardly vulnerable or a priority so they left me there, in the middle of nowhere.'

'You didn't call. I messaged you.'

'I know and I only got the message when I walked through the door. I had no signal.'

'Well how did you call the recovery service?'

'Someone stopped to see if I was alright and let me use their phone. They were on a different network so they had a signal. God, I feel as though I'm under surveillance with you but that's nothing new, is it? I've had a terrible night and this is what I get.'

More lies. She got a little closer and she could definitely smell that revolting perfume again. 'Who is she, Cain? I just don't want you to treat me like I'm crazy. I can't do this any more. I can smell her all over you.'

'I'm the one lying, am I? I found those injections in your wardrobe. We're meant to be trying for a baby and you made me think it might happen every single month. Did you ever stop to think that it's your own lies sending you like this? As for last night, I had a meeting with a client. I told you.' He threw his toast at the plate. 'I seem to have lost my appetite.' He stared at the new dress she'd bought. 'What's that?'

'I bought it for the dinner.'

Heart banging, she hoped now that he'd just leave and go to work. He was right. She had lied too, but his lie had been going on for ages and, if she trusted him, she might not have been sneaking contraceptives behind his back and she might have opened up to him about her past. But that wasn't entirely true. The thought of giving birth again still scared her, but Cain had no idea what she'd been through and she didn't want to blurt it out mid-argument. There was too much at stake, especially if Charlotte was lying about who she was. Rather than caring about what she'd been through, he'd probably just judge her and she'd never hear the end of it. Or worse, he'd call the police.

'My grandmother wouldn't have been seen dead in that thing when she was alive. It looks like it belongs in a nursing home.' He stood and slammed his plate on the island as he walked out and went upstairs. 'I need to take a shower before work.'

His phone beeped.

Leah ran over to it, in the hope of seeing the message flash up.

I'm waiting. Are you still coming? Here's a little pic to get you in the mood.

Leah had made a decision during the long night. She was

going to stick around until she got the DNA results. Leaving him now would just add to her own stress, and she wasn't sure if she could stay at Larrison House with all that was going on. The idea sent chills through her. Although Zara had offered to put her up, she didn't want to impose. She was going to wait for the DNA results, but after that, she was going to tell Cain it was over. The way he'd just spoken to her had been the pits. Her mother's house was nearly ready to rent out, so she could live off the rental income and her cleaning work. Zara was right. She was too good for him, and with all that she was going through, she needed a husband she could trust, one she could tell everything to, and Cain wasn't that person. He'd definitely use her past against her and there was more, so much more, and she knew telling him everything could be her downfall, especially if he had someone else to run to.

Minutes later, he thundered down the stairs fully dressed. He snatched his phone from the worktop. Leah watched as he opened the message.

'Got to go. Look, I don't want to argue with you. All I'm asking is that you trust me when I say I was with a client.' With that, he left.

Leah threw the dress back into the bag it came in and grabbed everything she needed. Maybe she'd swap it for another, maybe she wouldn't. Today, she had more important things to deal with and the stupid dress and his stupid dinner were way down her list of priorities. She had to go straight to her mother's house and wait for Charlotte to arrive. The test results would be with her soon and she could decide what happened next. In the meantime, she needed to do some investigating of her own. There had to be a tin that the gold key opened, or maybe there was a trace of Charlotte in the house, if her mother had invited the girl in. She had to look harder and get through all that paperwork.

As soon as Cain sped off out of their road, she left. That's when she spotted the daffodil at the end of the path exactly where the figure had been standing. She shivered. Someone knew her secret and they were letting her know it. Only Leah and her mother were aware of the flower's significance. Hands shaking, she couldn't help but wonder if Jean had told Charlotte everything. She bent down and picked up the flower. The figure wasn't Charlotte: they had been taller. Her gaze landed on the wooded area, and she couldn't help but feel as though someone was there, now, watching and waiting.

TWENTY-ONE

Mrs Pearson left her house and scurried over in her slippers as Leah pulled up. She banged on the car window. Leah buzzed it down, not wanting to talk. 'You keep coming back.' The woman's brows furrowed and her pink cheeks and short sharp breaths told Leah she was flustered. 'You need to leave and never come back.' The tone in her voice was more concerned than angry, as if she was delivering a warning. Her straggly grey hair framed her round face.

Leah sighed, wondering if the woman needed some help. She wasn't herself. 'Is Mr Pearson around?' She wondered if he was looking out for her or if he'd even noticed that his wife wasn't in the house. From what Leah remembered, he spent all day watching reruns of *Columbo* and *Dad's Army*. He'd sit in his chair stinking while cracking open cans of cider.

'He's busy. He won't speak to you because he said that you ruin everything.' Mrs Pearson was matter-of-fact. A statement. Leah didn't quite know how to take it. She knew that Mr Pearson didn't like her but she didn't like him either, but ruin everything? that was harsh, especially after the way he'd treated her. Standing around with Mrs Pearson was eating into her precious time. She glanced up at the old woman's house, trying to work out if anyone was in, but she couldn't see a soul. She shivered and let out a sharp gasp under her breath before looking away. Sometimes the past was best left buried, and Mrs Pearson's house was a place she never wanted to enter ever again.

Leah stepped out of the car and walked past Mrs Pearson, holding the door keys in her hand. She turned to face the woman, who had followed her to her mother's front door, and took a deep breath to steady her nerves. Her grip on the key loosened and she dropped her hand to her side. 'What do you know of the girl who was visiting my mother in the weeks running up to her death?'

'What girl?'

'Shiny brown hair. You can't miss her if you've seen her. She has two friends that hang around with her. They all look to be in their late teens. They're called Charlotte, Angel and Freya.'

Mrs Pearson furrowed her brows. 'I don't know...' The woman shook her head over and over again as she slowly backed off down the path. 'Don't listen to her or them. They're liars. They're all liars. You need to leave, sell this place and never come back. Your mother was a liar too.'

'Why, Mrs Pearson. Why? What is going on?'

As the woman ran across the road, she turned back, eyes wide open as she shouted: 'Just go.'

'Did you ruin my daffodils?' Leah called out. She had to know if Mr or Mrs Pearson had been in her garden. Mrs Pearson slammed her front door. Maybe her mother had given Charlotte a key. They were friends as far as Leah knew. She shivered again, her gaze transfixed on their house. After the night Mr Pearson threw her out, things had never been the same. She turned away, knowing that if she thought too hard about it all, her chest would tighten and she'd be a mess.

Hurrying into her mother's house, she closed the door and took a few deep breaths, in and out, until she could feel her heartbeat return to normal.

She had an hour before Charlotte arrived. First, she checked the whole house, making sure that no one had been in since her last visit. The garden hadn't been touched again, and the back door was still locked. It was all as she'd left it. She pulled out the gold key from the desk drawer and placed it in her pocket, and started thumbing through another pile of folders in search of a password to the laptops. Another folder emptied and another one opened. She flicked through stacks of paperwork before sitting in the middle of the room so that she could arrange it into piles. She folded her arms and exhaled. Today's boxes and files contained old handwritten and printed recipes, along with shopping lists and to-do lists. She scooped up all the papers and placed them in a bin bag, ready to recycle. Sitting back at the desk, she leaned back, wondering what to tackle next. She grabbed the pad of Post-it notes and began to smooth down the crumpled piece on top but it remained lumpy. Brows furrowed, she lifted it up to find a squashed scrap of paper that looked like it had been rolled up at some point, just like the one she found in the pen.

Slowly, she smoothed it out, till she could read her mother's spidery handwriting: BINGLEY ↑ 7. What on earth did that mean? Opening one of the laptops, she tried to enter it as a password, but again it was rejected. She placed it on the desk next to the gold key. After scrunching her eyes and peering closely, she could make out a word on the gold key: it was definitely Bingley. It had to be a clue. Despite all that had happened between them, her mother had left something for her to find, and it had to be important given the effort she'd gone to. Jean knew that Leah would check every bit of paper. Adrenaline surged at the realisation: she could hear the blood whooshing in her ears. Bingley could be the make of key. She had to find out what it opened. The next thing she needed to decipher was the arrow. Did it mean north or up? She'd searched upstairs and the key didn't open anything there. Every crevice, every loose floorboard, every bit of chipped plaster; she'd looked everywhere while painting and tidying the place up. There were no hidden secrets to find in the house, no dug out bits of wall hidden behind pictures and no loose floorboards.

Leah checked her phone. It was only eleven thirty, giving her a bit of time to explore some more. She ran between the rooms, looking for something she'd missed. She turned away from the bed, not wanting to think about that night, all those years ago. The screaming walls were telling her to leave and never come back, but another voice, one tiny ray of hope, happily told it to shut up. Charlotte represented hope and, deep down, she wanted nothing more than the DNA test to show that her daughter had lived. She pulled the key out and clutched it so hard, the tip almost cut into her palm. Her head was telling her that none of that was possible. Births had to be registered. Adoptions came with a lot of checks and interventions from the authorities. Leah's little one had been stillborn, and Jean had taken care of things to protect herself from the shame of it all. Jean had given her no choice in the matter.

As Leah stepped onto the landing she looked up. 'You don't get any more up than a loft.' Snatching the pole from the airing cupboard, she began to wiggle the end into the gap to slide the catch. The hatch opened and she hooked the pole onto the ladders and pulled them down. Previously, she'd cleared out the Christmas tree and the old shoe boxes full of junk. There were no boards up there, just thick tufts of fibreglass and struts to step along. After carefully climbing up, she flicked the switch to turn on the strip light and waited as it buzzed into action, lighting up the confined space. If the arrow meant up, what could the seven mean? She counted the struts from the nearest wall and her gazed fixed on the seventh, noticing how her mother had numbered them. She stalled when she heard a rat scurrying. She really needed to call a pest controller and a locksmith as soon as possible.

Stepping carefully across each beam, one by one, she reached number seven and leaned down, pushing her hand under all the itchy insulation until her finger brushed on something cold. Heart pounding, she knew she'd found something that was going to give her answers. She gripped the small tin and wiped away the cobwebs. The key. She pulled it from her pocket and placed it in the intricate lock. The tin opened with a rusty creak. She gently pulled out the photos of baby Sophie wrapped in the blanket of knitted squares that she'd sewn together as a child, similar to the one on her bed. Underneath was a sealed envelope. She opened it. All that was written on the scrap of paper was an address.

Someone knocked the front door. She threw the photos and address back into the box and hurried out of the loft and down the stairs, before opening the door. Charlotte and Angel stood at the doorstep. Leah glanced down and almost stumbled backwards as she saw the tiny blanket from the photo in Charlotte's hand. Charlotte was her daughter. There was no question about it. But why had her mother lied? She reached forward and hugged the non-responsive girl, her heart bursting with love.

'I'm so sorry I doubted you.'

She let go, opened the box and passed Charlotte the photo. 'I don't know what happened. I'd never have let you go, ever. I thought you'd died.' Leah could barely get her words out as she let the girls in. She tilted her head and gazed at Charlotte's perfect nose and thick bottom lip. Her Sophie was right in front of her. She didn't need the test results to tell her what she could see. Her daughter had lived.

TWENTY-TWO

Angel and Charlotte followed Leah into the kitchen. 'We have so much to talk about. I want to know everything,' she said to Charlotte as she flicked the kettle on and grabbed the coffee. She wanted to know so much more, like how had this been allowed to happen? She couldn't hate her late mother more right now. 'I'm sorry, I don't have any cola.'

Charlotte shrugged. 'It's okay, I like coffee.' The girl paused, as she and her friend sat at the kitchen table, and then asked: 'Have you got the results back?'

'No, not yet. Shouldn't be long but it's ridiculous. I don't need them.'

Charlotte blew out a breath and glanced at Angel. Angel looked away. 'I used to make Nan a cup of tea while she watched the birds in the garden. She used to ask me to throw seeds out for them over the winter. There was this little robin that used to come up to the French doors and wait to be fed.'

Angel nodded. 'She seemed really nice.'

Leah couldn't envisage the Jean Harrison they were talking about. Her mother had been cold, uneasy to please and sharp tongued. 'You used to come too?'

Angel nodded. 'We took it in turns so she wasn't alone all the time. By we, I mean me and Charlotte. Freya didn't come. She spends most of her time with her boyfriend or in the pub.'

'How old are you both?' Leah placed the drinks on the table, alongside a bag of sugar and some powdered milk that she'd kept in the cupboard for when she'd been working. Maybe Charlotte would slip up on that question if she wasn't genuine.

'Eighteen,' Charlotte replied.

Sophie was born eighteen years ago.

'Same,' Angel said.

'Wow, so grown up.' Leah placed the baby photo on the table and nudged it towards Charlotte. 'This is the last time I saw you and' – she wiped the damp trail from her cheek – 'you weren't... I' – she sniffed and took a few seconds – 'When I held you in my arms you weren't breathing. My mother, Jean, took you from me and that was it. I never saw you again.'

'Where did you think I went?'

Leah shrugged. 'I don't know. I thought you were dead. I spent the first week in my mother's bed battling an infection. I don't remember much. All I remember is weird dreams, and being so hot I thought I was going to die. When I was awake, I couldn't stop shaking. I remember my mother trying to force me to swallow tablets, and...' She shook her head. Why would she remember Mrs Pearson? Mrs Pearson wasn't there. She couldn't have been. That voice she'd heard while giving birth had to have been a trick of the mind. Her mother had sworn her to secrecy. They were never to tell another living person what had happened, let alone Mrs Pearson.

'How old were you?' Charlotte stirred some creamer powder into her drink.

'Sixteen. I was younger than you. I was meant to take my GCSEs but I couldn't face going, so I told my mother I'd been and I hadn't. I hid in my room under baggy tops. Jean was so engrossed with her work – and that's not me knocking her working hard – but she didn't notice the morning sickness.' Leah remembered her mother being quite nasty to her, telling her she was getting fat and to stop eating so much. Her mother was rude and didn't mind hurting Leah, so when the girls described her as nice, it didn't seem like they were describing the same Jean. Maybe she'd changed. Leah regretted not visiting Jean after receiving the letter. At least she would have been able to lay their past to rest. 'I hid you well until near the end. My mother panicked. She told me I had to stay in so no one could see me.' Holding back her tears she continued. 'She wouldn't let me go out, kept going on about how shameful I was and that she'd sort everything. I didn't tell her, but I was going to keep you. I'd planned to run away with you in the hope that social services or the council would help. Then you were born and...' – Leah sniffed – 'I should have left earlier. Why did I listen to her?'

Charlotte looked into her hands. She glanced at Angel, then said to Leah: 'Nan didn't tell me who my dad was.'

Leah stood and walked towards the window and looked out. 'I can't talk about that.'

'But I need to know.'

Leah turned, knowing the pain of the truth. 'Why? You have a family who love you. I'd love to get to know you and, in my heart, I've always loved that little baby I held in my arms. As for the man who fathered you, please don't make me go there.' She couldn't do this right now. Going back to where it all began was too much.

Her phone rang. It was Cain. She stopped it ringing, and he sent a text instead.

I thought I'd pop to your mother's house with some lunch. I hated going to work on an argument. I'm really sorry. What I said was mean. See you in a short while. XX

'You have to leave. I'm sorry.' Leah snatched the cups from the girls and dropped them into the washing-up bowl.

'But I have so much I want to ask you.'

'Can I call you, later? My husband has just messaged to say he's on his way, and I haven't told him any of this. Can I have your number?' Leah passed her phone to Charlotte. That's when she saw Angel discreetly kick her friend, thinking that Leah hadn't noticed. Zara had warned her about moving too fast on this.

The girls stood, and Charlotte began to type her number in.

'I'm really sorry to rush you. Don't forget this.' She grabbed the baby blanket and gave it back to Charlotte, when all she wanted to do was hold it close to her face to see if there was any trace of her baby's scent on it. As Leah walked them to the door, she knew she had to ask Angel about being outside the business centre where her husband worked.

'Angel, what were you doing at the Business Centre on Blake Road the other day?'

'I err, I was meeting Freya in her lunch break and I got lost. She works for a company close by. Were you there?'

Leah nodded. 'I popped by to see my husband. He was out but I thought it was you.'

Charlotte grabbed her friend's arm. 'We best hurry. The bus is due any minute, otherwise we'll have to wait ages for the next one. Text me so I have your number.'

Just as the girls reached the end of the path, Cain drove around the corner. Leah quickly texted Charlotte so they now had each other's number. He pulled up behind her and watched as they walked towards the bus stop. Leah found herself watching him, to see if there was any recognition at all of Angel, but he wasn't giving anything away.

'I was just putting the kettle on. Do you want a coffee?' she asked as he walked up the path.

'No, I haven't got long. I just wanted to see you. I got us

sandwiches from the snack van. Veggie sausage for you and bacon for me. Who were the girls? It looked like they were just leaving.'

So, he had seen them. He glanced at the bus stop in the distance, and his gaze locked onto Angel's for a few seconds before he stepped into the hallway.

'Err, the girls, they popped by to collect a few things I put up online to give away. Just some free stationery. I didn't want to throw it in the bin as it was good quality. Obviously hard-up students.' She glanced across and saw that Charlotte had a bag large enough to accommodate some stationery. Her heart sank as she thought about the perfect little square blanket inside it. 'You best come in before the sandwiches go cold.'

Cain was checking up on her. He'd only been to her mother's twice and that was a few days after Jean had died, when the smell of death had been strong and clutter covered every bit of floor.

She shook her head. Something had shifted in him since breakfast. Maybe Lady Rose had stood him up. He glanced down at the three cups in the sink as he placed the sandwiches on the kitchen table. 'I'm sorry about earlier. What I said about your dress was horrible and as soon as I got in my car, I hated myself.' He drew her in and held her closely. 'I can see it's not a good time to try for a baby with all that's going on and I guess I feel like a bastard. I think it's this dinner party. So much depends on it and it's rattling my nerves. It could change our lives. When we get it, I promise I'm going to be a better person. I'll be home for dinner. We can go for that weekend away and do things together. I've been an idiot. Please say you forgive me? I can't lose you, Leah.'

As he held her, her phone beeped. She could just about see the subject flash up on the email. The DNA samples had been received. All she had to do was wait and soon she'd confirm what she now knew: Charlotte was her daughter.

'Are you okay? Are we okay?' Cain asked.

She pulled away slightly and nodded. They were far from okay but now wasn't the time to talk about that. She had tired of the nice Cain, horrible Cain merry-go-round.

'I have something for you. I was going to give it to you last night but that moment got ruined.' He pulled out an envelope.

She opened it and it contained a booking for a spa weekend at the end of the month.

'I love you so much and we're going to nail this contract together, then we'll have that weekend away to celebrate. Just you and me.'

She didn't have the heart to tell him she wouldn't be going, not while he was in such a good mood.

His phone beeped.

'I just have to make a call.'

He left her in the kitchen while he closed himself in her mother's study. She placed her ear to the door and listened to his mumbling, catching the tail end of what he was saying.

'I'll be there. I just have to pop to the office so I'll meet you in a couple of hours. Usual place.'

As he stepped out the room, Leah was already back in the kitchen.

'Got to go. Work problems.' He hurried out for Lady Rose, leaving his sandwich and leaving Leah alone, again. It looked like they'd definitely made up.

Standing in the dim and chilly kitchen she glanced out of the window at the daffodil patch. Charlotte was her daughter; she was sure of it. Although she said the results didn't matter, she wanted to give them to Charlotte. One question she did have to answer though: what lurked under the daffodil patch if not her poor deceased baby daughter?

TWENTY-THREE

There was something Leah needed to do and it couldn't wait. She popped the address from the box into her satnav system and began the short drive to Droitwich. Her mother had led her to it for a reason. Within twenty minutes, she pulled up on a side road heading towards the quaint spa town. She glanced at the terraced house that backed onto the River Salwarpe, and wondered why her mother would have kept this address in a box hidden in the loft. Charlotte said that she, Angel and Freya were from Bromsgrove. Should she knock and pretend to be doing a survey? Or maybe she could be looking for someone or even pretending to be a neighbour trying to locate a parcel? Anything to work out why her mother had kept this address in her secret box alongside a photo of baby Sophie.

A neighbour twitched their curtain. She'd been parked up for less than two minutes and the street was coming alive with curiosity. Maybe a neighbour with a lost parcel was the way to go. She opened the waist-height wooden gate and walked up the mossy path. Knocking, she waited for an answer. A tall, elegant woman, who looked to be in her mid to late thirties, with scooped back brown hair, opened the door. Make-up fresh, and coat at the ready, she looked like she was about to leave. She frowned at Leah. 'Can I help you?' Her long skirt bellowed in the wind as she said nothing and waited for Leah to speak.

Then it hit her: the smell of rose perfume. Leah's mouth began to dry up. What did Cain have to do with Charlotte? Did Cain know about Charlotte already? Maybe she'd approached him first and then he could have met her adoptive mother. Maybe that's how the affair started. She wondered if Charlotte thought that Cain was her father.

The woman sighed and folded her arms. 'Are you okay?'

'I, err, I'm trying to find my parcel. The courier said he left it at this address. We share the same house number. Sorry to bother you.' Leah popped her clammy hands into her pockets and smiled. She inhaled again and knew she wasn't mistaken about the perfume. It was definitely the same scent that Cain kept bringing home with him.

'A parcel.' The woman hesitated and pressed her lips together before continuing. 'I don't think anything has come here but I wasn't in this morning. I'll just check with my husband, see if he took a parcel in.' She left the door open and headed through the lounge, and that's when Leah lost sight of her.

She glanced into the hallway which led straight up the stairs. Several jackets had been thrown onto a row of pegs, some denim, others faux leather, and a large winter coat. Could they belong to Charlotte? Some could but they could equally belong to the woman who answered the door. She took in the row of shoes and stared at the trainers. Again, she couldn't be certain who they belonged to. A prospectus for Pershore College lay on the floor. It suggested someone of college age lived there, but even then, it was very little to go on.

'A parcel?' the man replied. 'Put the kettle on while I look to see if she brought a parcel in while we were at work. She didn't mention a parcel.'

Leah couldn't see the man, and she wondered who he was referring to. Could it be Charlotte and, if it was, how had they managed to take her in and become her parents? Shaking, Leah wanted to walk in there and shout and scream at them for taking her baby, but she held back and waited.

Then the man walked closer to her as he checked the lounge. That's when she recognised him. No, this couldn't be happening. How could she have not recognised his voice? She tried to breathe but her chest tightened. The urge to run away tempted every muscle in her body. Get in her car, drive off and pretend this wasn't happening. Instead, she stepped onto the garden and peered through the leaded window, straight through the cottage, and her gaze stopped on the man as he reached the kitchen table at the far end. It was definitely him. It looked like the couple were now whispering.

The grey sky began to swirl as she looked up, spinning, as her anxiety took hold. If she didn't get into her car and sit down, she'd fall. Gasping, she held on to the gate and prayed for the world to stop swaying.

'Are you sure you're okay?' The tall woman stood at the door.

'Yes,' Leah said with a squeak. 'Sorry, I have to go.'

'We don't have any parcels anyway. I asked my husband. Neither him nor my daughter have taken anything in today.'

'Thank you.'

Daughter. That word repeated in Leah's head as she stumbled into her car and slammed the door closed.

'She is not your daughter,' Leah yelled, as she hit the steering wheel.

She had to get as far away as possible. What she needed was her friend. She needed Zara. She had no idea how it happened but they'd stolen her daughter, and the very man who'd ruined her life was behind those doors, in that house, playing at being her father.

That man was a monster.

As she glanced back, he was staring at her. Without wasting another second, she pulled away and almost crashed into a car as she rejoined the traffic on the road.

TWENTY-FOUR

After parking on her drive, Leah headed straight to Zara's, apologising for interrupting her work. Her friend, as always, welcomed her in. 'It's okay. Work can wait. That's the joy of being my own boss, I can take breaks when I want. I'll make us a coffee and you can tell me all about it.'

With their drinks, they sat in Zara's conservatory, where Leah told her everything that had happened that day. Molly lay her head on Leah's feet and began to sleep. Leah gave her head a pat. 'I just don't know what to think any more.' She bit the skin around the edge of her thumb, a habit that came and went when she got stressed.

'You poor thing. I understand why you're confused. I'm definitely struggling to keep up. So, you think that Charlotte has grown up with her dad, that he knew and somehow got to keep her with this woman?' Zara looped her hair tie around her top knot, securing her stray hairs in place.

Leah nodded. 'It sounds ridiculous. Charlotte claims that my mother messaged her to tell her about me, but what if it was him? What if he decided to tell her himself and somehow everyone is lying to me?' She shook her head. 'No, it had to be my mother. Charlotte isn't like that. I don't know why I thought that at all. I didn't tell anyone about the baby, not even him. It was my mother.' Tears began to spill.

'You never told anyone else but your mother?'

'No, but I didn't tell her...' Had she told her mother more than she thought post birth?

'What didn't you tell her?'

Leah began to shake. 'I can't talk about it.'

Zara flexed her stiffening fingers before picking her drink up with trembling hands. A splash of liquid landed on her jeans. 'Did something happen, Leah?'

She wiped her eyes as she forced herself to think back to that night, the one she'd tried so hard to cast out of her mind. The word *slag* kept ringing through her mind, and all she could see was Mr Pearson's stern face as he bundled her out of his house. When they reached the hallway, he grabbed her arm so hard, she'd been left with a bruise for days. She choked for breath.

'Leah, what is it?'

She remembered his huge hand pinning her up against the wall, strangling her. He said if she told anyone what had happened that night, he'd kill her. Just as she'd been about to lose consciousness, he'd dropped her to the floor. Leah had then fumbled to get her T-shirt back on. Mrs Pearson had come back from her night out with friends, totally unaware of what had happened that night, only to see Leah leaving with her T-shirt inside out.

'Nothing.'

'It's not nothing.' Zara placed her drink on the coffee table and began rubbing her hand.

Leah could tell her friend wasn't doing as well as she made out. No way was she going to stress her out with the details.

Zara didn't need that right now. Besides, she didn't know if she could face telling anyone. *Slag* – that word sent her cheeks burning. She knew that Mr Pearson had felt no shame for what he'd done to her, and that her mother had felt no shame for giving her baby away to the monster who'd ruined her life.

'No, you're right.' Leah blew her nose on a tissue and gripped it. 'But I do need to stop guessing everything. I need to get those DNA results and discuss what to do next with Charlotte.' She forced out a laugh to cover the sadness. 'For once, Cain isn't my main problem. If only I'd known a few days ago how complicated my life was going to get.'

Zara placed a hand on her arm and gently squeezed it. 'He hurt you, didn't he? The man you saw today.'

Leah refused to let the sob in her throat escape, but her watery eyes were harder to hide. 'I can't talk about it, not now. It's just too much.'

'I'm here when you need me.' Zara's legs began to tremble. She pulled her tablets from her jeans pocket and popped one in her mouth before swallowing it down with a swig of coffee.

'Same.' Leah placed a hand over her friend's. She'd always be there for Zara, just like Zara had been for her. 'Are you tired?' Zara nodded. 'I'm going to head home, give you a chance to get some rest. Is there anything I can do for you before I go?'

'I'm good. I mean look at me. I'll be doing the Macarena later.' Zara put on her usual brave face. 'You have my key. If you need to, just come in but I'm heading to bed for a lie down.'

Zara's phone flashed. She grabbed it and turned it over. Leah knew she was hiding something, but Zara didn't want to talk about whatever it was. When this was all over, she was going to be there for her friend more.

* * *

After saying goodbye, Leah left Zara and headed back to her house. She popped her coat on the peg and kicked her shoes off, still trying to process what had happened. It was now gone five. Since Cain had left her at her mother's, Leah hadn't heard a thing from him. She thought of Lady Rose with her scooped up brown hair and sleek make-up. Was he still with her? She must have left as soon as Leah had driven off, where then she'd met Cain at their usual place, wherever that was. Her heart began to race as she thought of the man at the window, staring at her as she drove off. Were they both in on it together, setting out to destroy her? Why? Maybe Cain was merely a pawn in their game. Confused, she slammed the front door and hurried up the stairs, hoping that a shower would clear her head.

As she approached their bedroom door, she nudged it. She'd definitely closed it that morning, after she'd got up. The bed was still unmade and her hairdryer was where she'd left it, on the vanity table. Maybe she forgot to close the bedroom door, a habit she'd always had in the hope that it would keep spiders and insects out of the bedroom. She opened her top drawer, the one containing all her jewellery. Everything was still in place, including her gold bracelet. While checking the other side of the room, she spotted a few yellow petals on the floor, next to her side of the bed. She ran to the window, searching for the figure. Then she sprinted downstairs. No one had a key, only her and Cain, and Cain didn't know about the daffodils. Someone had been in their house and it wasn't her husband. The shiver in her body reached her knees. Only her mother knew about the daffodils.

Leah checked every window but they were all locked. Then she reached for the bifold door in the kitchen and opened it out to the patio. All day it had been unlocked. She glanced out at the garden, searching for footprints or some clue as to who had left those petals. Her phone beeped.

There's nothing like the smell of fresh flowers but they're easily trampled on and some die. Some deserve to die. How can you not see what's right under your nose?

The number was withheld, but she knew exactly who had sent the message. The phone slipped through her shaking fingers and landed on the doormat. She backed away from it, a hand over her mouth suppressing her need to scream. He had her number. Had he always had her number? She wondered how he would have got it. Charlotte could have messaged it to him. Why would he message now, after all these years? She knew exactly why. Charlotte was finding out too much, more than he wanted her to know. Leah was going to uncover the injustice that she'd suffered and she was going to blow his world apart. But that might blow Charlotte's world apart too. *Don't get too attached or involved.* Zara's advice was right. She had other people to think of. She couldn't bear to lose Charlotte now that she'd found her.

Everything whirred through her mind. Cain – his affair and his big contract, the dinner party. Her past – it was about to run her down with the ferocity of a high-speed train. Zara – Leah needed her but she also realised that Zara was struggling at the moment and there was something on her friend's mind. Charlotte – the baby she'd held in her arms had come back. More than anything, Leah knew she wanted the opportunity to be a part of her life in any way possible.

Her phone beeped again.

She reached down and picked it up.

Gasping, she stared as a dying weed GIF played out on her screen. He was coming for her. The daffodil had told her he could come into her world whenever he liked. He'd been watching her, and he'd been going into her mother's house too. She hadn't imagined that flower on her childhood bed. He was using them to taunt her.

Holding a hand to her chest to quell the rapid breathing, she thought of the levels of betrayal her mother had sunk to. All these years, Leah thought the secret was theirs. She had planted the daffodils, and they both knew what was underneath them; or, at least, Leah thought she knew. She ran into her own garden and began tearing up the daffodils she'd planted as a reminder along the border. No longer was he going to taunt her with them. They were all one big, fat lie and they needed to go, now.

One after another, she wrenched them out of the ground, taking up the whole plant as best she could. Back aching, she knelt and pulled up another, then another, until there were only two left. They all had to go. All these years, she'd tended to and loved those flowers in place of the ones at her mother's house. Each year, she'd cried over them as Sophie's birthdays came and went, all for nothing.

'Leah.' Cain stood on the patio. He placed his bag on the floor and furrowed his brows. 'What are you doing?'

'They have to go,' she cried as she pulled the last one up and sat on the wet grass while fighting to get her breath back.

'You've ruined the garden.'

'I don't care.' She held her head in her hands and sobbed.

He ran over and helped her up.

'Don't come near me, you cheating prick.'

As he came closer, she kicked out, catching his ankle.

Not deterred, he leaned over and helped her up. 'Not this again. What the hell has happened?'

She went to blurt everything out but only sobs escaped. How long could she contain all her secrets? She wanted to speak but she couldn't. All the pain of her past spilled out in tears and they weren't about to stop until she'd cried every last tear. *Slag*. That revolting word echoed through her mind. All she wanted was for it to go away and leave her in peace, but people like her didn't deserve peace.

She heard Cain's phone beeping. He checked the message

and a look of worry spread across his face. Hands gripping his phone tightly, he clenched his jaw and stuffed it in his pocket. She couldn't be sure but from the look on his face, it wasn't a message from Lady Rose or Alison.

Right now, all she knew was that she and Cain were toiling with something and neither of them wanted to tell the other what.

TWENTY-FIVE

Tears slip down her cheeks as he grunts on top of her. Tick, tick, tick. The sound of the carriage clock is counting the seconds. Frozen, all she can do is wait for it to be over as she lies there in the dark. Shadows from the crackling fire make shapes on the wall. She tries to focus on those as she escapes into her own world but a spark spits out, reaching her thigh, reminding her of the hell she's living in right now. She stares at another shadow that dances and grows before her. Its darkness spreads through the room, taking away the firelight so it's only him and her, in pitch blackness. 'You're hurting me, get off me. Please stop.' He doesn't listen even though she's asked him three times now. He heard, but she knows he's ignoring her – or did her words even come out right? Mumbling, that's what she's doing but it doesn't matter how hard she's trying, she can't say what she means, so all she does is weep and close her eyes in the hope that it will be over soon.

In her mind, she can see her mother, shaking her head. She hears Mrs Pearson telling her what a naughty girl she is as she holds a bunch of daffodils. Shame burns through her and she knows that she can never tell anyone or he will kill her.

The baby cries, making her jolt and the shadows withdraw.

* * *

Leah woke to the sound of an owl hooting. She reached over to Cain's side of the bed and felt the cold bedding. He hadn't been next to her for ages. 'Cain.' She stepped out and gently pushed the bedroom door without making a sound. As she reached the landing, she flinched at the sound of a step in the downstairs hallway. *There's nothing like the smell of fresh flowers but they're easily trampled on.* Those words were a warning and the dying weed GIF still made her shudder. While creeping down the stairs, Leah felt a change in the air, a slight breeze coming from what she imagined was their open front door. 'Cain,' she whispered, the hallway getting ever closer with each step she took.

A gentle whistle of wind tickled her bare feet. If Cain was up and couldn't sleep, he'd have the television or radio on, but only silence and darkness surrounded her. As she stepped into the hallway, the front door slammed closed, almost taking her breath away. Cain ran towards her as she screamed, and he turned on the light. 'It's okay, Leah. It's just me. I didn't know you were up.'

He held her and stroked her hair until the panic died down.

'What's going on?'

'I don't know.' He shook his head and walked back over to the front door. 'I heard a noise. It sounded like someone was on our drive, shuffling around. When I looked out of the window, I saw a shadow. I thought someone was trying to get into the house, so I came down to check.'

'And did you see anyone?' Leah forced the words out, not quite sure if she wanted to hear the answer.

'No, but I know someone was out there. I've checked the windows and doors. Whoever was there has gone. You should go back to bed.' He pulled his phone from the pocket of his dressing gown and stared at it for a few seconds.

'What's going on, Cain? Why are you checking your phone?'

He popped it back in his pocket. 'Nothing. I wasn't checking it. I just wanted to check the time. Go back to bed. I'll be up in a minute.'

She shivered as she thought of her stalker returning. As she climbed the stairs, she heard a loud bang as he hit the console table in the hallway. Leah had to know what was on his phone.

TWENTY-SIX

It had been a long day preparing for the meal. Leah checked her list. The dauphinoise potatoes were baking away in the oven. The salmon en croute was resting. Veggies were ready to steam and the butter sauce tasted delicious. The white wine sat in the chiller, while the red rested on the table in a crystal decanter, next to the brandy. The chocolate mousse needed nothing more than a few fresh raspberries adding to it. She ran over to the table and made sure the flickering candles in jars were all perfectly aligned, ready for their arriving guests. The champagne flutes were at the ready.

Cain walked in, his best suit looking pristine. He smiled at Leah and nervously blew a slow breath out. 'You look beautiful and the food looks and smells amazing. I'm so proud of you.'

As Cain leaned in to hug her, she stiffened. He rarely said anything that nice and she doubted he meant it. He'd been glued to his phone all day.

'I think we're ready.' She smiled, knowing that however she felt, she wasn't going to sabotage this potential contract. He'd never forgive her and, when she left him, she wanted the cleanest break ever, no more drama.

'I'm glad you wore that dress and not the new one.'

She brushed her hands over the black evening dress, the one he liked that never felt comfortable on her. Underneath she'd trussed herself up with shaping underwear to the point she was struggling to take in a full breath. He had won. Her wrap dress was waiting to be returned.

'I best check the potatoes. How long until they get here?' *Just get this over with, Leah.*

'Five minutes.'

He left the room and began pacing up and down the hallway while she remained in the kitchen. Leah's phone beeped. She glanced down, heart pounding as she hoped for an email with the DNA results, which were late. She'd paid a lot of extra money for the express service, and she'd been checking her messages all day. Sighing she clicked on the message from Zara.

Thinking of you tonight. Molly sends a woof for good luck. Hope you're okay after yesterday. Xxx

Leah sent a quick reply and checked her emails again. Nothing. She switched the fairy lights on so that the patio lit up. All day she'd been working on the house and clearing up her mess with the daffodils, and now the garden looked perfect again, albeit a touch bare on the one side. Leah had tried to bring the subject of the intruder up, but Cain had told her to forget it. He'd refused to say any more on the matter.

Cain's phone lit up on the worktop. Leah ran over and peered at it before the message disappeared. There was now a name at the top. The mystery woman had a name. She was called Rosie. It definitely wasn't Alison.

I just want you right now. I have to have you! X

Leah pulled the oven mitts on and removed the potatoes from the oven. She poked a fork in them. They were doing nicely, not like her. The urge to drop the dish on the floor and watch it shatter strengthened with each passing second. With shaky hands, she slid the dish back into the oven. The sound of the doorbell made her heart skip a beat. They were here. Right now, she had to forget that message. She had to paste on a fake smile and pretend that Cain was the perfect person to manage their humongous budget. After tonight, it was over. He was on his own.

Cain opened the front door. Leah removed her apron before quickly dropping it in a drawer.

'Hello, it's so lovely to see you both. Come in,' Cain said as Leah waited in the kitchen.

'Thank you for the invite. It's lovely that we get to meet you like this instead of at a restaurant or a pub. We just know you're going to be right for our project, don't we, darling?' the woman said.

Leah frowned. It sounded like the clients were a couple. Cain hadn't told her anything about the so-called clients. Where had she heard that voice before? The woman sounded so familiar.

'We certainly do, Rosie. We've talked non-stop about the plans and we love them. The architect says he likes working with you too, so I think we're onto a winner.'

Rosie, the name of the woman messaging Cain. Lady Rose was in her hallway. The man let out a nervous laugh, one that Leah couldn't fail to recognise. Leah's heart pounded, and she clenched her teeth as she fought the urge to run out of the back door and never come back. Not only did she now know who was sending Cain the messages, but she also knew who the woman's husband was. She'd been to their house yesterday and pretended to be looking for a parcel in her search for the truth about Charlotte.

'Leah, Leah. Where are you? I don't think she can hear over the sound of the extractor fan. Here, let me take your coats. Go through to the kitchen.'

Stilettos clipped on the stone kitchen floor, and the scent of roses hung in the air. Everything was about to come out, and Leah hadn't prepared for any of this. How could this be happening? She wanted to vanish and let herself into Zara's bungalow, where she could hide away forever.

'Mrs Jones, how lovely to finally meet you.'

Rosie's brown hair was tied up in an elegant knot, and her deep burgundy lipstick sparkled in the candles' flickering light. 'I'm surprised we've never met before considering we see so much of Cain, but it is lovely to finally put a name to a face. He showed us your wedding pictures. Isn't that charming of him?'

Rosie knew exactly who she was and the pretence was unreal.

Cain chatted to Rosie's husband in the hall.

'I saw you earlier.' That was all Leah could manage.

'No, I'm sure you're mistaken. We've never met.' Rosie subtly shook her head, a worried look on her face. 'Oh, I love your flooring, I so need these tiles, especially the mosaics. You have such good taste. Must add those to the mood board. My daughter is really hoping for a kitchen she can enjoy baking in. She's obsessed with pavlovas and brownies at the moment.'

The very mention of the word *daughter* sent Leah's eyes watery. Charlotte was her daughter, hers, and she was going to prove it as soon as that email turned up. She wanted nothing more than to scream at the woman who'd taken her life from her and the man who had hurt her, but Cain didn't know anything. Zara's caution spoke loud and clear in her head. *Don't get too involved until you know the truth.* Rosie was playing this game for a reason. For now, Leah had to play her part.

The conversation in the hallway died down and the two men entered.

'Leah, this is Derren. Derren, this is my lovely wife, Leah. I hope you're hungry.'

Derren looked just as Leah remembered him, but older. His cold blue eyes met hers, and it was as if a spell had been cast over her. He was taller than she remembered but still as strong looking.

'I'm absolutely ravenous and the food smells delicious,' he replied. 'You have a charming home, Leah, very charming, just as I imagined it would be.'

He reached out to shake her hand. She held hers back for as long as she could, but an angry glare from Cain ensured that she complied with his wishes and shook Derren's hand.

'Thank you.'

'No, thank you.'

Panic began to build as she remembered that night as the fireplace spat, as the shadows danced – the night that broke her – and she was reliving every moment in her head. His smile ebbed away from his eyes.

Leah jumped as the champagne cork hit the ceiling.

'I think we're all going to become great friends. Aren't we, Leah?'

TWENTY-SEVEN

'You've worked so hard. The food was amazing. You must give me the recipe for your potatoes.' Rosie leaned over and put her arm around Leah with a giggle. She grabbed the wine and topped up Derren's glass yet again before pouring herself another juice. 'I'm driving,' she said with a smile.

Cain laughed at something Derren had said, then he poured their guest another brandy, which they both downed in one. 'It's hot in here.' Cain stood and opened the bifold doors, allowing the background music to spill out. Leah felt her forehead crease with worry as she stressed, and Cain shot her a glance, a hint of anger in his glare. She forced a smile.

So far, Leah had managed to serve all the food and keep it together, but she didn't know how long she could keep it up if Derren kept on pressing his leg against hers under the table. The very thought of any of his body touching her turned her stomach, and he knew it.

'Where are you from, Leah?'

Now he was toying with her. She wondered if Rosie even knew about their past.

'Just local.'

'Local, where?' He held up another glass of brandy and leaned back while waiting.

'Erm, I think I just need to start the dishwasher before everything bakes onto the pans.' She stood.

'Leah,' Cain said as he tried to pull her back to the table. 'That can wait. I'll do it in the morning.'

She pressed her lips together as all three of them stopped talking. 'I don't want the food to bake onto the dishes.' From the look on Cain's face, she knew she'd just snapped at him. He glanced at their guests, his cheeks starting to redden with embarrassment. 'Sorry, I'm just a bit tired. It's okay, I'll do it now.'

Derren sighed, removed his napkin from his lap and stood too. 'It's definitely not okay. I'm going to help your good wife to stack the dishwasher.'

No, how could he do this to her? She scurried toward the island.

Cain waved a hand in approval and removed a pack of cigars from his pocket. 'Suit yourself. When you're done, maybe you can join me in one of these, that's unless you'd like to join me for one, Rosie.' Her husband winked at Rosie, and Leah knew they were slinking off to the garden, alone, to do more than have a cigar. In fact, Leah couldn't picture Rosie ever smoking a cigar, but what did she know?

Nothing about the whole situation made any sense and Leah knew that there was no contract to be had. Cain had just been Derren's way of getting to Leah, and he was using Rosie and Charlotte along the way. But why? Why now after all these years? Her mother contacting Charlotte had to be the start of it all. Leah hadn't managed to crack any of Jean's laptops to confirm that story, but she knew deep in her heart that Charlotte had told her the truth.

'Rosie?' Cain said, waiting for an answer.

'Sorry, what?'

'Cigar?'

'Why not. I don't normally smoke cigars but hey, live for the moment and all that. Let's do this,' Rosie replied as she glanced across at Leah.

Leah placed a pile of dessert plates on the island, watching as Cain held out a hand and led Rosie into the garden. Leah was sure there was a moment between them where Rosie gripped a bit too tight and her gaze met Cain's for a moment too long. Soon they were out of sight, leaving Leah alone with the monster from her past.

'So, Leah. What the hell is going on?'

She grabbed the plates and slammed them into the sink. No longer was she a scared sixteen-year-old. Anger brewed within. Seeing him yesterday had certainly been a shock, but she had to put that aside and think of Charlotte. 'You tell me. Why the hell have you been stalking me here and at my mother's house?'

'Stalking you? I've tried my best in life to stay out of your way. I moved away for years but Dad got ill, then he died and I had to come back.' Mr Pearson was dead. Elisabeth Pearson hadn't said anything to her when she'd asked her if her husband was in. Derren continued. 'If anyone is stalking anyone, it's you. What were you doing at my house yesterday?'

She shuddered as she thought back to the night when Mr Pearson threw her out of his house. Like father, like son. They were both evil to the core.

'I found an address amongst my mother's things. I didn't know it was yours.'

'So, you just turned up? I don't believe you. Pathetic, you were always all over me, just couldn't leave me alone and I thought we were friends.'

He had a nerve. Friends wouldn't do what he did to her. She pictured that night in her head. She'd had more than her fair share of cheap cider while Mr and Mrs Pearson had been out. Several other teenagers were there. The music had been loud, and two of them had been making out. They'd even used Mr and Mrs Pearson's bed at one point. She and Derren had been best friends and she'd trusted him. He'd been the person she confided in when her mother had been particularly cruel to her. He'd spoken about them leaving and renting a place together as soon as they'd finished school. They'd laughed together, tried to get into pubs while underage. They'd been there for each other when life got tough, but one night had put an end to that friendship. Tears pooled in the corners of her eyes. She grabbed a tea towel and wiped them away. The glassy-eyed look he gave her made her want to shrink and cry, but she wasn't going to. She was going to stand tall, for Charlotte.

'What you, your parents, and my mother did to me is unforgivable and I am going to make you pay. In fact, I'm coming for what's mine.'

He reached down and gripped her arm so hard, she almost buckled. He always was strong. Right then, she knew she had nothing to lose by stamping as hard as she could on his foot with her heel. She bore down, allowing it to pierce his shoe.

'Don't you dare touch me again or I swear, I will kill you.'

'Leah.' Cain walked in with an empty glass and he paused as he saw her clenched jaw and angry glare. 'Can we grab a dustpan and brush? Rosie has dropped her drink on the patio and there's glass everywhere. Is everything okay?' His slurred speech told Leah he was drunk.

She opened the cupboard underneath the sink and began to rummage for them. 'Couldn't be better.'

Cain glanced back at something Rosie was doing in the garden. He swayed for a moment and almost tripped out of the door. Once steady, Cain staggered past Leah to get to the sink. Standing between her and Derren, he ran the water and poured some into a glass. Leah saw that moment as her chance to get away from Derren.

She hurried out with the dustpan and brush. Rosie held an

unlit cigar between her fingers, smiling as she stood next to the smashed glass.

'I think your husband's had a fair bit to drink. I hope he's okay in the morning. I'll send him a text.'

'I think you both need to go.'

'Have we upset you? I thought we were having such a lovely evening.'

'Really, you think I don't know what's going on between you and my husband?'

Rosie tilted her head. 'Leah, nothing's going on, I promise. Look, we had a great time tonight. Let's leave it at that. I'm sure everything will seem clearer in the morning. I am so sorry about your glass. Right, I think I should get Derren home. It's late and you must be tired after all your hard work. Thank you for being so welcoming.' Rosie placed the cigar gently onto the patio table and went into the house, leaving Leah alone under the fairy lights.

Cain stumbled across the kitchen as he showed their guests to the door. Derren glanced back and shook his head before turning away from Leah.

Throwing the dustpan set onto the grass, she hurried back in and grabbed her phone. The results still hadn't come through. She scrolled up and down her emails then clicked into her spam folder.

Heart pounding, she listened to Cain chatting on the drive about what a good night they'd all had. She held her breath for a few seconds. The email was there. It had been there since four that afternoon and she'd failed to check her spam folder. She clicked on the link and logged in. The screen hung as the results loaded. As soon as she read the results, she ran back out to the garden. She found Charlotte's number in her phone and with fingers that could barely function, she typed out a message.

Why did you lie to me, Charlotte? How could you be so cruel?

Charlotte was not her daughter. She closed her eyes as she tried to remember how it had felt to hold Sophie that night, but there was nothing. She couldn't feel it; she couldn't feel anything. She thought of the blanket that Charlotte brought over. Sophie's blanket, she'd said: the one that had been buried with her little body, but it couldn't be the actual one, could it? The actual blanket was still safe, right where it should be. But Leah wanted it now. She needed it, and there was only one way to get to the blanket – and to the truth. She had to finally say goodbye to her baby girl.

TWENTY-EIGHT

'They rushed off a bit fast,' Cain mumbled in bed as they lay in the darkness, his back to her. 'Come to think of it, you were offish. On the most important night of my career, you had to look like you couldn't give a stuff.'

If Cain only knew that their guests were there to ruin her life, he'd think differently. She felt her jaw begin to tremble as she held back her emotions, and she clenched her teeth more tightly. Charlotte was not her daughter, and all Cain could do was moan about how Leah hadn't been the life and soul of the party. Then again, to be fair, he had no idea how her life had changed over the past few days and hours. Maybe it was time to say something. Derren was dangerous and Leah knew he'd do anything to keep her quiet. After all, his own father had said that if she told anyone, he'd kill her. Derren was just like him.

'Cain?'

He grunted and pulled the quilt up to his chin. 'Don't talk to me,' he slurred. 'Don't say a word.' A snore escaped his lips. Finally, he was falling asleep.

It was a blessing that she hadn't blurted everything out, because tomorrow she was leaving him. She'd speak to Cain tomorrow, tell him the bits he needed to know about Rosie and Derren, and she'd tell him that they were over. She was going to be brave and live at her mother's house. At least she could be close to Sophie, forever.

Charlotte's lie rang through Leah's head. To think, she'd almost said something to Derren about their daughter. Now, she was glad she hadn't since Charlotte wasn't hers. Charlotte was just a pawn in Derren's sick game. She was a girl who loved nothing more than making pavlovas and confusing innocent people. Leah stopped grinding her back teeth as soon as Cain started snoring loudly. If she was careful and quiet, he'd sleep like a log and wake up with the mother of all hangovers in the morning, ready for an argument about how she didn't try hard enough. But tonight was about finally learning the truth.

Slinking out of bed, she crept around towards Cain's phone and pressed the side button to wake it up. She was sick of everyone lying to her. He grunted as she placed the phone against his thumb and gently touched it against the screen, unlocking all of Cain's secrets. Hurrying out of the bedroom in the dark, she shut herself in the family bathroom, heart jittery as she clicked into his messages and selected *Rosie*.

I just want you right now. I have to have you! X

She stared, open-mouthed at the photo attached. It was a photo of a chaise longue covered in peacock feather patterns. Rosie hadn't sent anything more than a photo of a piece of furniture she was pretending to covet for her fake new mansion. She scrolled down further to see many messages but none of them were sexual.

I'm waiting. Are you still coming? Here's a little pic to get you in the mood.

Attached was a photo of Rosie and Derren holding a margarita and a mood board covered in shades of blue and green. She flinched as she saw a daffodil print cushion. Nothing good was coming of reading Cain's messages. How had she got it all so wrong? She clicked onto a string of messages from an anonymous sender, and she almost shrieked. The venom in them scared her.

> *You bastard. You compete utter bastard! People like you love playing games. You don't care about ruined lives, you only care about yourself. I hate you. I HATE YOU!*

There was one reply from Cain.

> *Don't you ever come near me or shout in my face again or I will end everything you care about in one conversation!*

Other messages came before. Who had sent such awful messages, and who had been shouting in his face and why? Maybe the sender was right and there was more to Cain than she knew. She read a few more.

> *Die, tosser!*

> *Where were you when you said you were at the office? I am going to ruin you!*

She glanced at the date. It was sent the day after Leah turned up at Cain's office and saw Angel standing outside. She shivered, knowing that Cain was lying about something so much bigger than having an affair. Charlotte had lied to her. Angel and maybe Freya were sending Cain horrible messages. Derren and Rosie were in their lives for a reason. She shook her head, more confused than ever.

A loud snort echoing across the landing made her jump slightly. After slowly opening the bathroom door in the dark, she listened as Cain whittered away in his sleep. She hurried to the bedroom and placed his phone back on his bedside table, grabbed her own along with her jeans and a sweater before creeping onto the landing. While scurrying down the stairs she pulled the top over her night shirt.

She stood by the front door and slipped her jeans on as she checked to see if Charlotte had answered. There was no reply and Leah hoped with all she had that the patchwork blanket had not been the one that her Sophie had been wrapped in. Had Leah even observed the different squares closely? It could have been any similar blanket, and if her dying mother had shown the photo hidden in her tin to Charlotte and her friends, they could have easily made something similar. Her thoughts flashed back to Rosie and Derren, then again to Charlotte, Angel and Freya; each one of them playing a cruel game but to what end? Her mother was behind everything. She had somehow started it and it wasn't going to end until Leah worked out what and why. The only way she was going to be able to do that was to go back to where it all began. She stepped out into the bitter night and hurried to her car.

* * *

'Leah.'

She flinched and turned. Her friend began to ride her scooter closer, and Molly followed.

'What are you doing out at this time of the night, Zara?'

Zara huffed out a laugh. 'I have a dog that wouldn't settle and I was up so thought I'd take her out for a little walk. Anyway, more to the point, what are you doing out?'

'Nothing. I just need to go to the garage. Indigestion after all that food tonight.' She knew Zara was too intelligent and definitely too outspoken to let that lie go.

Shaking her head, Zara began to scoot towards her. 'Leah Jones, I just don't believe you.'

Leah followed her behind the hedge just as she checked her bedroom window for signs of life, but Cain was probably still asleep.

Zara flashed the torch app at her. 'You have trails of mascara running down your cheeks and you're shaking. What's happening? Actually, don't answer that. Cain, Charlotte, everything else you don't want to talk about. Do you want to come in? I can put the kettle on.'

Tears began to slip down Leah's cheeks. She nodded as she followed her friend in and the dog trotted over to her basket.

'The business dinner. Cain's guests. The man, it was him, my baby's father. His wife is the woman I thought Cain was having an affair with, the one who stinks of that perfume.' She shuddered as she thought about the word father. Derren was nothing.

'I thought he was having an affair with Alison.'

Leah shook her head. 'Not this time.'

'Your baby's father, did you say? What was he doing there?'

'I don't know and I'm so confused, I just can't make sense of anything. I don't believe anything I see or hear. I don't know what's made up or what's real any more.' She grimaced and pressed her lips together for a couple of seconds as she thought about what to say next. 'I got the DNA results.'

'And?' Zara grabbed her sticks from the hall and began struggling from her scooter over towards her chair in the living room.

'She's not mine, Zara. I am not Charlotte's mum.'

'I'm so sorry, love. You weren't sure anyway but I can see how hurt you are. That was a horrible lie she told, especially as you lost your baby. I can't begin to understand the pain you're going through.' Zara slumped in her chair and got her breath back, her blonde plait falling down her back with a flop as she leaned forward. 'Where were you going? Were you leaving him without telling me?' Zara paused, and Leah didn't answer. 'I don't blame you if you were.'

Leah went to talk and all she could blurt out was, 'My baby...'

'It's over, Leah. It's hard but you can now move on and think about you. Put yourself first for a change.'

Leah sat on the couch next to Zara, and Zara placed a caring hand on her shoulder. 'If only it were that easy,' she said, blubbing uncontrollably.

'I'm here for you. You are a strong woman, Leah. You can get through this and I will help you.'

'You don't know everything.'

'I know enough. It's okay. It's all okay.'

'No, it's not okay.' Leah shook her friend off her and stood. Zara owed her nothing but here she was, being the perfect friend. Leah didn't deserve such love, not when Sophie's bones were buried in her mother's garden. Jean was so wrong. Sophie deserved to be remembered properly. The lie had to be exposed. At any time, Leah could have stood up and told Sophie's story, but Jean had scared her. Mr Pearson had threatened her. Jean's way was the only way. She said that Sophie was dead and nothing would bring her back. Jean didn't want the authorities involved; she didn't want the weight of shame that Leah would bring upon her so she cruelly took matters into her own hands, burying the truth and her baby's memory, saying that they had no option but to forget and move on. 'I tried to tell her.'

'Tell who?'

'My mother. I told her that he raped me. I was so scared and she didn't want to hear. I told her and it was like I'd never said anything then I kept wondering if I did. The fever I had after...'

'After what?'

'After the birth. It was like nothing I'd ever experienced in my life; I was so scared. My thoughts were jumbled. I even thought for a while that Sophie was alive in my arms, but when I came around, I knew she was dead and I felt that loss all over again. My mother said she never wanted to speak of it, and all I could do was tend to the garden, to...' Leah choked on her tears.

'To what?'

'The daffodils. Sophie's grave. No one else knew about the daffodils, only me and my mother.'

Zara's gaze met Leah's and her brows furrowed as she took in what Leah was saying.

'I deserve their punishment. Charlotte is here to make me pay. It's all my fault.'

Shaking her head, Zara grabbed her sticks and struggled to her feet. 'No, you were a scared child. What your mother did was unforgivable and you don't deserve to feel like this.'

'I have to go to the house. I need to see for myself if Sophie is in that grave.'

'Charlotte isn't yours. Is it a good idea to go digging and put yourself through all this?'

'I need the truth. I can't live like this any more.' Molly let out a slight yelp and lay her head on the side of her basket, her gorgeous chocolate eyes looking up at Leah.

'I'm sorry. You do need the truth.' Zara yawned, the dark bags under her eyes telling Leah that she was exhausted and had been struggling to sleep, no doubt because of the pain she suffered with. 'But I'm coming with you. You can't go alone.'

'Zara, no. You need to go to bed. I've got this. I promise I'll go and do what I have to do and come straight back here.'

'No, Leah. Forget me. Look at you.'

She wiped her eyes with her trembling hands; her legs threatening to disappear beneath her. She tucked her nightshirt into her jeans. 'I don't want to drag you into my problems.'

'Leah, someone has been watching you, they've been to

your mother's house, they've been to your house and you think you're safe there at two in the morning, alone? I would never forgive myself if anything happened to you. I'm coming and I'm driving, and that's that.' Leah went to speak but Zara interrupted. 'Besides, if you start your car up, it'll probably wake Cain and I'm guessing that as you're sneaking off in the night, you don't want him to know anything right now.'

Zara had a point. 'Okay, you win.'

'Come on then.'

Zara led the way to the door, getting breathless as she struggled with her sticks into her car. It looked like Leah had no option but to let Zara come along, and a part of her wanted a friend to be by her side when she found out the truth.

TWENTY-NINE

Zara hobbled out of her car breathlessly as she used her sticks to get to the front door. Leah placed the key in the lock and took a deep breath, dreading what she had to do next. They stepped inside Larrison House, and Leah used the torch on her phone to light up the hallway.

'Wow, what a house.' Zara glanced up the stairs and through the long hallway at the kitchen. 'Shall we turn the lights on?' She went to reach for the light switch, her stick dangling as she leaned up against the door frame.

'No.' No one except Zara could know what she was about to do. Leah blocked her hand from making contact with the light switch. Right now, she didn't trust anyone. She glanced across towards Mrs Pearson's house. It was all their fault. She shivered at what Derren had said. His father had died. All Leah could think was good riddance after he'd threatened to kill her.

'Why can't we turn the light on, Leah? This is your house. You're allowed to be here.'

Leah stared at the house opposite.

'What is it?'

'He used to live across the road. His mother still lives there, and I think she knows everything. I think she was a part of it all. She's been watching me and coming over. I think she vandalised the garden.'

'He, as in—?'

'Derren, her son. The one who raped me. Please, Zara, just follow me and leave the light off.'

She led her friend into the study and helped her into her mother's chair at the desk.

Her phone beeped. She snatched it from her pocket, wondering what Charlotte had to say for herself. As she opened the message, she almost fell against the wall. It wasn't Charlotte, unless she was using another phone.

I see you.

The three laughing clown emojis at the end of the message made her shudder. She ran to the door, peering up and down the road. There was no one around. She stared at each of Mrs Pearson's windows and not a movement or light came from that direction. The bushes rustled alongside the house.

'Who's there? Charlotte? Derren?' Her voice was barely a whisper. The last thing she wanted to do was needlessly alarm Zara.

No one answered. Her phone beeping again made her jump.

Poor little Leah. Can't find what she's looking for. Leah needs to die.

A twig snapped. Holding her breath, she shivered uncontrollably until her teeth chattered. She reached over and grabbed a dead branch from the grassy frontage and followed the sound, holding it in front of her. Whoever was out there wanted her dead.

Another message pinged. She let her breath out and read it.

Die Leah. There's a special place for you under the daffodils,
or what's left of them. Lying bitches deserve to die.

She went to shout for Zara but her friend wouldn't hear, not
from the study. The moonlight caught the leaves next to the
garden gate. It flapped wide open with a passing gust. Her
phone beeped again. She opened the photo; it was Sophie's
daffodil patch before it had been destroyed. Reaching over, she
closed the gate and sprinted back towards the front door.
Whoever had been watching her and taunting her knew she
was close to the truth, and they were close to her. They were
watching her right now from the bushes, taunting her. She shivered in the doorway, trying to catch her breath and calm her
banging heart. Just as she was about to slam the door, a fox scurried from the bushes and ran across the road. She pushed the
door closed and leaned against the wall, panting and holding a
hand to her heart. It was just a fox. No one knew she was here.
How could they?

'Leah, are you okay?' Zara called.

'Yes, I just got spooked by a fox.' She kept the messages to
herself. If she mentioned those to Zara, Zara would make her
call the police and then she'd have no chance of being able to
check Sophie's grave. First things first, she had to do what she
came to do. 'Are you okay?'

'Yes, sorry, I was just nosing.' Zara placed the laptop back
down and shone her phone torch at it. Zara's plait flopped
forward as her friend leaned over and furrowed her brows.
'DorothyOz 1939.'

'What?' Leah ran over.

'That's what's written in pen on the bottom of the laptop.'

Leah grabbed the other two and turned them over, and
again, the same words were written on the bottom of each of

them, in the corner. She knew that *The Wizard of Oz* had come out in 1939, as her mother had told her that many times. She grabbed the laptop from Zara and opened it. Once it came on, she entered her mother's words in the password box and the laptop came on. 'You're a genius.'

'I know that. I bet you're glad I came along now.'

She hugged her friend and stood over her, knowing that she had the key to her mother's world, all ready and waiting for her to explore. As soon as she'd done the deed in the garden, she was going to go through everything in each laptop. The truth was now hitting her in the face, all she had to do was look in its direction and piece together the puzzle. For now, she had to close the lid on it. They could look at the laptop later.

'Just wait here. I'm going in the garden.' Leah ran over and pulled the heavy curtains closed. Her phone beeped again.

Have you worked it out yet?

'Who's that?' Zara glanced up, shining her phone at Leah.

'It's nothing. Just a spam email.'

'Okay, well hurry up. This house is creepy. Nice but creepy.'

Leah agreed. The house had always been creepy but being devoid of love and laughter made it creepier. The ghosts that held the very foundations together were bursting to escape, and Leah wasn't going to stop them. 'I'll just shut this door, okay.'

'Why?'

Leah shrugged. 'As you said, the house is creepy.' She didn't want to tell Zara that some weirdo was messaging her. If the house was in darkness and Zara was shut in the study, maybe that made her safer.

'Okay.'

She could see the doubt in her friend's expression as she pulled the door closed.

Leah ran to the kitchen and grabbed a torch from under the sink. As she unlocked the French doors, she stood there for a moment, listening to the rustling of bushes as the breeze flapped them about. Without wasting another second, she almost tripped over the stone owl as she ran to the mauled daffodil patch, knelt on the grass and began shifting soil with her hands. As she ploughed through the earth, scoop by scoop, her stomach fluttered. Shadows danced on the back fence with her every movement.

She was so close now. She thought about the night she pushed Sophie out of her body. Her mother kept going on at her, shouting that it was her punishment for not keeping her legs shut. Leah had tried to tell her what had happened. There had been a party. She and Derren had been alone after the others had gone. She didn't want him to hurt her. Her mother had chosen to ignore the bits that were hard to hear. Tears slipped down her cheeks and mingled with the dirt from her hands.

It had happened fast, too fast. Before she knew it, the whole attack was over in no more than a few fast minutes. Her muscles had been weak from the cider and the room had swayed but she had tried to push him off. The glow from the fire licked the walls, and the crackling sounded like laughter as she lay there hurt, scared and humiliated. She'd whimpered *no* in his ear but he carried on, ignoring her pain. From the corner of her eye, she had spotted Mr Pearson watching from the lounge door. She pleaded with him to make it all stop as tears ran down her cheeks, but he closed the door.

Now, she flung a stone behind her back and heard it ping off the ornamental owl behind her. Her mother had buried Sophie. How deep, she didn't know. All she knew was that the patch of dug earth was in front of the tree base and that's where Leah had planted the daffodils, the joyful yellow flowers that symbolised rebirth, because in her heart she couldn't say goodbye to Sophie. She'd spent the latter month of her pregnancy wondering if she could love her baby and, near the end, when she'd felt her kicking and turning, she knew she never wanted to be parted from her. For so long she'd lived in denial. Derren had been sent to a residential private school, no doubt because of what Mr Pearson saw. Her mind went back to that night. As soon as Derren had finished, he discarded her like she was nothing. He laughed as he passed a comment on how they were just friends and how it had been a drunken mistake, then he staggered off and went to bed, leaving her lying in front of that fire with her skirt rolled up. Dead inside, that's how she'd felt, and she'd never recovered until Charlotte came into her life. Charlotte had given her hope only for it to be snatched away again, only for the betrayal to reach a whole new level.

Damp soil stuck in clumps to her fingers. She flicked the cold worm away, letting out a scream. After a few seconds of hyperventilation, she continued, digging deeper and deeper. She could have used a shovel but no, she didn't want to damage a single precious bone that belonged to her sleeping baby. She wanted to see that blanket and feel close to Sophie.

As she'd lain in her mother's bed on the bloodstained sheets, she held her baby and felt nothing but pure love. She had this mass in her arms but that mass was motionless.

The logical side of her mind told her that Sophie would be nothing more than bones now. She pounded her fists into the earth and cried while her heart broke, then she continued. Deeper and deeper, she dug but there was nothing until her fingernail brushed on something hard. Reaching in, she wiped the mud away to reveal a small white bone. All the time, Sophie had been buried in the garden, while she had dared to hope that her baby had lived. A primal cry came from deep within as her phone beeped again. She glanced at the message.

Got you!

A white-hot pain seared through her head, knocking her sick. As she went to turn her head, her mouth opened and closed. Unable to speak, she reached for her head. The metallic scent of her blood made her stomach lurch. The shadow on the fence got larger as her attacker neared. The stone owl rolled in front of her, smeared with her blood. It trickled down her face. She felt her attacker's warm breath on her neck, then in a whisper, her attacker said, 'I'm going to bury you with your past. I will not let you ruin everything I have worked so hard to build, Leah Jones.'

Another message popped up on her phone and she managed to read it through bleary eyes. It was Cain.

I saw you going out with Zara. You have to come back. We need to talk. You can't trust her.

She went to grab her phone but her attacker hit her again. That's when the world went black.

PART 2

THE GIRL

THIRTY

'How's the job hunting going, love? You know there are so many shops and restaurants looking for help in the run up to Christmas.'

I don't want to work in a shop or restaurant. If I have to tell that to my mum one more time, I think I'm going to explode. I know she means well and I know she wants me to start paying housekeeping, but I've had a succession of jobs I hate and they never last.

'I'm looking, okay. I'm just not sure what I want to do.'

My mother leans over and ruffles my messy hair before dropping a piece of toast onto a plate. 'You know something?' Mum sits at the table and I can tell she's about to lecture me, and I'm really not in the mood. 'I don't want to go to the office this morning and check through a million crappy purchase invoices. I've been doing that, day in, day out, since the day I left school thirty-seven years ago. I don't have the luxury of staying in bed all day thinking to myself, "I'm just not sure about this job. It's no fun and I'm bored, so I'll just stay in bed all day".'

She's trying to mimic my voice when I'm at my whiniest

and it is quite funny. I suppress the laugh that threatens to escape my lips. 'Okay, okay. I'll check out the shops, if you get off my back.' I smile and take a bite of the toast she made me. As soon as she leaves for work, I'm going back to bed.

'Thank you. I'll be home late but your dad should be back in a while.' She scrunches her eyes up to read our job share chart on the fridge. 'It's your day to run the vacuum around the house.'

'I know.' I roll my eyes. We have the same routine every week and today is my vacuuming day.

Mum grabs her handbag and car keys. Before I've managed to finish my toast, she's gone. I adjust my pyjama bottoms as I leave the kitchen and head back up to bed. Just as I've settled beneath my thick winter quilt, my phone buzzes. 'What now?' If it's Dad messaging to remind me about the vacuuming, I'm going to lose the will to live. I grab it and see a WhatsApp message pop up.

Hey bestie, wanna hang out later? I'm bored and I need to get my nails done. Mwah!

No, I don't want to go anywhere. Has she seen the rain and frost? I'm not leaving my bed, let alone this house. My fingers tap away as I WhatsApp her back.

My bed says no. I love you and all but I'm way too warm and cosy. Maybe tomorrow. We'll hang out then. We could watch a film if you're up for that? I haven't been to the cinema for ages.

As I wait for her reply, I check out Facebook. It's not a patch on TikTok, and even my mum has an account on Facebook, which is so uncool. But I do like to do a daily check, as some of my friends still use it. I go to bite my nail but remember I'm trying to grow them. It seems impossible but I am making an effort. It's annoying when my dad laughs and calls me Stubby Fingers. I have no messages but Facebook is insistent I have as it leaves the red notification up. Maybe it's that dreaded other inbox. I really don't like opening it. Last time I did, a man harassed me for days and I reported him when he sent me that revolting photo. I wish I could say it was the first time that happened but it seems to be a never-ending problem on social media.

I glance for a moment and see that the messenger doesn't have a profile picture. Rolling my eyes, I lie back and stare up at my artexed bedroom ceiling, knowing that whoever messaged me will just be another creep. My phone beeps again.

Okay, definitely cinema tomorrow. Don't you dare stand me up. Meet me in Worcester for 1. X

I reply with a string of random emojis and that tells her that I'll be there. Everyone's a winner. My mum will think I'm job hunting and I get to see a film. I click back into Facebook and wonder who Jean Harrison with no photo is. Her name sounds like she could be one of my mum's friends. Here goes. I open it up and read.

You don't know who I am but I know who you are. I've spent my whole life watching you. You were such a sweet little girl and you've grown up to be a lovely young woman.

Yuck, this is just weird. I'm not sure that I want to read on. I step out of bed and glance up and down my gloomy street. It's dark and dismal, not inviting at all. All I see is rain starting to fall and a grey mist in the distance as the road turns into fields after the junction. *I've spent my whole life watching you.* What a creepy thing to say. I should report it. I sit back on my bed and continue reading, just for laughs. No way am I going to reply to the weirdo.

I know this is going to shock you…

'No shit, Jean.' Actually, she won't. I think I'm pretty unshockable now. I've seen it all in my inbox. 'Go ahead, shock me, Jean.'

But I'm dying…

'Of course, you are.' She's dying and she somehow thinks I have money and I'll be able to send it immediately. Jean is out of luck. A – I'm not stupid. B – even if I was, I don't have any money. Okay, maybe I have enough to see a film with my bestie tomorrow but any more than that, I have to ask Mum. I let out a titter as I open my bedside drawer and pull out a packet of chocolate cookies and start crunching away.

I don't have long. It's more like weeks, maybe even a month if I'm lucky. No one will have told you this but your life isn't what it seems and you're now old enough to know the whole truth. I am the only person who can give it to you. I am your grandmother.

Not possible. I think of my dad's mother and my mother's mother. Neither of them would be sending me a message like this and playing a silly joke while calling themselves Jean. Why? Because they're dead. I don't have any room in my life for a made-up grandma or dare I think it, some rapist pretending to be a gran. What do I think? Sex offender or fraudster? Grandma Jean – I guess she's a fraudster.

I know at this point; you won't believe a word I say and I don't blame you. You have my blood in you which means you are an intelligent young lady but I beg of you to not dismiss me. Do one thing for me. Think hard. Have you ever seen your birth certificate? Maybe something has felt off all your life but you don't know what. How about family? Please don't upset your adoptive parents, they don't deserve it. They are good people and I hope with all my heart that you've had a happy life but please, I want to talk to you, just once. It's wrong of me to contact you out the blue like this, but my time is running out. Each day I get weaker and sicker so I know I don't have long. Please message me back so that we can arrange to talk.

My heart races. That's the end of the message. At least with men who send dirty messages, it's clear what's happening but with this message, she's asking for nothing except for me to dig into my life. My brows furrow as a thought enters my head. I remember asking why we'd never been on holiday abroad and I always got the same reply from my parents. Mum is scared of heights which makes her scared of flying. As for boats, they were a no go. My dad is seasick, so sick, he can't even go rowing on a still lake. As for the school trip to France a few years ago, that was a no too. My father said we didn't have the money but I know we did as he'd just bought a new car and unlocked some of his pension early. A friend also asked if I could go abroad with her and her family, they were even going to pay for me, but again, my parents said no. I still remember the argument and not speaking to them for a fortnight. Maybe Jean Harrison is telling the truth.

I grab the photo from my bedside table, the one of me and Mum and Dad, when we holidayed at Blackpool for the weekend. It was a treat for my fifteenth birthday. I'm in the middle eating a veggie burger, and ketchup had squeezed out of the side onto my T-shirt. The tower looms over us in the background. We had a lovely weekend. My mother had come with me on the big dipper and all the other rides, then we went to Madame Tussauds. My heart begins to thump in my chest. My mum, who claims to be terrified of heights, went on those huge rides with me. She lied. They lied. Who am I? I slam the photo down next to the cookies, frowning. I don't know what to do. I need my birth certificate to clear this up. All important documents are kept in my dad's office, the only room in the house I'm not allowed in.

I hurry out of my bedroom and down the stairs then I open the door to my dad's office. He has building quotes lying around everywhere, and his desk is adorned with smudges because he's never cleaned it. I almost trip over the hard hat on the floor as I head to the cupboard. I've always respected that this is my dad's space. Even my mum never ventures in, and she mostly calls it his hovel. Several cups sit on his desk, all with different amounts of mouldy black coffee in them. The smell of Deep Heat lingers in the air. He's always using it for his aches and pains. It really is a gross room. I open the cupboard door and, compared to the rest of his space, the inside of the floor-to-ceiling cupboard is tidy. He has piles of paper, envelopes, printer inks, pens. Everything has a place and seems to be labelled. I venture into the other cupboard and see boxes of files, all marked with project names, most of which I recognise as he goes on and on about them all. Then I see one marked 'house'. I slide it out and see a folder for utilities, council tax and the car. I continue to rummage until I find one that is marked: personal documents. Sitting on the dirty carpet, I open it up and see my mother's birth certificate and an old passport. There is the same for my dad. When I open their passports, I see stamps for Canada and South Africa. They've both travelled far and wide in the past. For a second, I can't swallow. My finger brushes their marriage certificate; but there is nothing of mine in here. Jean Harrison is right.

My heart is broken. What if my mum and dad aren't my biological parents? If they're not, who am I? Who gave birth to me? I slam the folder down and a photo falls out. It must have been almost wedged in at the back. It's a photo of me and I'm wrapped up in a white blanket in an incubator. See, I am theirs. This is me in the hospital where I was born. I let out a little sob. They never told me I was premature; in fact my mother said I was a large cuddly baby.

I have some huge decisions to make. Do I reply to Jean, and do I tell my parents about the message? Shaking my head, I know what I'm going to do. I don't have a choice.

THIRTY-ONE

I Facebook call Jean, then I change my mind and end the call. I'm still not sure if I've just got swept up in the message. Maybe there's a perfectly logical explanation as to why my birth certificate isn't in the folder with the other documents and why my parents never told me I was born prematurely. In my mind, I see my mum's lovely round face, always a smile on it, and I see my dad, big strong, grey-haired Dad, with bushy eyebrows, who has always been there for me and my heart swells with love for them. I can't bear the thought that Jean could be telling the truth. Pushing the folder back into the box, I hurry out of Dad's office, taking the photo with me.

I pull on my jeans and the warmest sweater I have in the hope that the heating kicks in soon. I'm under strict instructions not to mess with the thermostat. Ever since I turned it up to thirty degrees one day and went out, I've been told I'm not allowed to mess with it. I get back into bed, fully dressed, but definitely unable to have that lie-in I'd promised myself. The last thing I'm able to do is chill out. Maybe I should call my bestie and talk to her. She'd know what to do.

Facebook dings and it's a voice call. Jean's name flashes. My finger goes to press answer, but I can't do it. I don't know what to say, and it's only now I realise how much my hands are shaking. Jean ends the call, and I throw my phone onto my bed before pacing to the window and running my fingers through my tangled bed hair. It's no good. I need my friend so I call her. She answers almost immediately. I go to speak but my words come out confused and jumbled.

'Say that all again. I didn't catch any of it,' she says.

'Can you just come to mine? I need to show you something. Please.'

'I'm on my way. Who needs nice nails anyway?'

Within the hour, she's here and she too thinks the message might be genuine when I explain about the passports. 'Are you going to tell your mum?'

I shake my head. 'I can't. How can I?'

'Are you going to speak to this woman: Jean?'

I shrug, feeling sick inside. 'I don't know. I don't think I can. She called me but I couldn't answer.'

'Why not?'

'Why do you think?'

'Sorry.' My friend leans back against my headboard and crunches on one of my cookies. 'I understand. But don't you want to know what she has to say? If she's dying, you might not have much time. I mean, it might all be a big mistake. She might be mixing you up with someone else, but unless you speak to her, you'll never know.'

She's right but the thought of hurting my parents brings another tear to my eye. There's no way I can tell them about the message.

'It'll be okay. I'll help you. We can do this together. I'll call her if you want me to.' My friend goes to grab my phone, but I snatch it back.

'No, I should do it. If I agree to meet her, will you come with me?'

'Definitely. She might be a psycho. I can't let you go alone.'

I'm lucky to have such a good friend in Charlotte. Somehow, I think I'm going to need her. Where I fall short, she makes up. She's brave; I'm scared of my own shadow and I easily become tongue-tied and severely anxious when I don't know a person. If I'm going to get to the truth, I will definitely need Charlotte.

The front door rattles and Dad calls out as he enters. Right now, I feel slightly clammy. At some point, I'm going to have to open up to them about Jean Harrison, but right now, she's going to be my secret, one I'm only going to share with Charlotte.

'You okay?' Charlotte flashes me a concerned look, and I feel as though the colour has drained out of me.

I nod. Seconds later, my dad thunders up the stairs and knocks on my bedroom door.

'Come in.'

'Oh hello, Charlotte, I didn't know you were here.' His brows are furrowed and the veins in his temples pulsate slightly, which is a sign he's stressed. The creases around his eyes and across his forehead seem to have deepened lately, making him look closer to sixty, rather than in his mid-fifties. Charlotte smiles and he steps in, awkwardly glancing around my room as if looking for something but I don't know what. 'Do you mind waiting downstairs, Charlotte, just for a couple of minutes?'

'Course not. I'll wait in the kitchen.'

Charlotte leaves, and I want her to come back. My dad knows something and I don't want to hear what he has to say. I take a deep breath and struggle with the lump in my throat as he sits on my bed. I want to go back to when my mum was hassling me about getting a job, and I want to never have read the message from Jean Harrison.

He clears his throat and turns to face me. 'Have you been in my office?'

I shake my head but I know the word liar is spread across

my face. I've never been good at lying, but I can't hurt him by telling him what's going on, especially as it might all be a mistake.

'My office door was open and one of my cupboards had a folder jammed in it.'

'Maybe Mum went in there before she went to work.'

'Maybe.' He sighs and he bites his dry bottom lip. 'It's probably best you don't go in there, not with all my work stuff.'

He doesn't believe me. I can't believe I didn't glance back and check the room. If only I'd been careful enough to leave things as I found them. 'I won't, Dad. I wouldn't go in your office.'

'That's a girl.' He smiles and runs his hand through his receding hairline. 'Your mum and I love you so much. You know that, don't you?'

His behaviour is odd. My dad rarely talks about family and love. He just goes to work, makes dad jokes and rarely gets involved in matters of the heart, as my mum calls them. It's Mum who dishes out the hugs, and Dad who gives me the odd tenner before telling me to buzz off so he can watch football or programmes about people sifting through rubbish in sheds. That was unfair of me. He does hug me very occasionally and, when he does, I know it's genuine and he loves me. I don't know what to say to him. He knows it was me in his office. He knows I've been rooting through the folder, and I wonder if he's aware I have that baby photo. All I do is nod and it feels odd, but I say, 'I love you too, Dad.'

He leans in, pulling me into a big hug. It's so tight, I feel as though we're about to say goodbye forever, and I can feel his pounding heart through my sweater. He has to be my dad. Jean has to be wrong and she's fake. She's a scammer. She has to be because the man hugging me now is my dad. My phone rings again, and I see Jean's name pop up. My dad withdraws and glances over at it as it buzzes on my bedside table.

'Who's Jean?'

'No one important.' I end the call. 'It's about a job in a shop.'

'Shouldn't you answer it then?'

I shake my head. 'I don't want it because I have another interview lined up and I'd prefer to work there instead.'

This is the start of the biggest lie I've ever told and I don't know where it will end. All I know is that I can't speak to Jean and I can't come clean to my dad. He leaves, and I'm not convinced he believes anything I've just said. As he walks towards my bedroom door, his gaze falls back onto my phone. He opens and closes his mouth as if he's about to say something, then he shakes his head and leaves. It is right now I know my parents are hiding something. The name Jean just confirmed what he was thinking. He knows I know, but he won't say a word in case he's wrong.

Charlotte bounds back up the stairs. 'I was listening from down there, sorry.'

'What do I do, Charlotte?'

She rambles on for a few seconds, and my phone rings again. She answers it for me. I close my bedroom door and tell her to speak quietly. She speaks as if she's me and the lies tumble with ease from her lips. Before I can say anything, she's arranged for us to go and see Jean this weekend. I keep shaking my head as I mouth the word *no*. We don't know who this woman is, but the call has now ended.

'Keep Saturday free,' Charlotte says with a smile, as if she's pleased with herself.

It looks like I don't have a choice in the matter. On Saturday, I'm going to meet the woman who claims to be my grandmother, and I don't know if it's going to be the hugest mistake of my life.

THIRTY-TWO

It's Saturday and the rumbling of the bus makes me nauseous as it jumps through potholes. Charlotte hasn't said a word since we left mine, but she has stopped me picking my nails again. Every time, I go to pull another piece off, she gently touches my hand, raises her eyebrows and presses her lips together, giving me the look. As we turn into the village, I glance at the tightly packed terraced houses. There is only one shop in the village but it looks closed or maybe it's derelict. The windows are smeary and cobwebs cover the inside. This place really is the back of beyond. In fact, I didn't know this little village existed, but why would I?

'It's going to be okay.' Charlotte smiles. 'Stick to the plan and we'll be fine.'

The plan, it's ridiculous but I'm happy to go along with it. Actually, I'm not. I'm not happy with any of this. Since the other day, my mum and dad have been super nice to me. Mum said I don't have to take any job I don't want, and she didn't even moan at me for not doing the vacuuming. Dad gave me some money, and we had a lovely family meal and played board games, of all things. I want it to be like this forever. They didn't even moan when I asked if Dad could pick me and my friends up from a club next week, preferably around two in the morning. It was as if I could have anything I wanted, and I don't like it, not one bit.

I go to stand.

'It's not this stop.' Charlotte reaches for my arm to pull me back into the seat.

'I know. I can't do this.' The urge to get off the bus overwhelms me and I can feel my neck prickling.

'You can.'

The bus jerks as it pulls up at a stop, and I fall back into my seat. My heart bangs then the bus pulls off again. It's too late now. The next stop is our destination. I glance out the window, trying to push my nausea away but the sleet that is just starting to fall disorientates me as it escapes from the blanket of grey above. I shiver. Whether I like it or not, we are doing this.

Charlotte reaches over me and rings the bell.

'It's the next stop.' The bus slows down as the driver carefully navigates the narrow road before he pulls into the brick bus stop.

Charlotte nudges me. 'Hurry, or we'll miss it.'

With shaky legs I walk down the aisle then step onto the pavement. 'Where is it?'

The bus pulls away, leaving us on this gloomy isolated street, framed with large trees that block most of the light out. Charlotte frowns as she looks at her phone. 'It's a two-minute walk up this path and then it's on the right. I saw it on Google Earth. Jean has a nice house and, by nice, I mean big and old like something from a horror film.' She reaches over and pulls my hood up. 'It's going to be fine. We've got each other. Jean definitely sounded like a frail old lady. If she does turn out to be some psycho elderly woman, I'm sure we can defend ourselves.'

Charlotte chuckles but I can't laugh back. It's not her life that is about to be turned upside down. She has no idea what

I'm going through. Charlotte hurries ahead in her longline parka and chunky trainers, happily sloshing in icy puddles like a kid having a day out.

'Here it is.' She stops on the other side of the road and stares at the large house. It definitely reminds me of something I'd see in a horror film. Isolated, in the shadows, closed curtains and a huge front door that seems to be guarded by a spindly tree that climbs up the brickwork.

We step into the gutter to cross the road, feet sloshing in yet more cold brown water. I shiver as I hold my hood on my head, not wanting the wind to blow it off and ruin my hair. Someone opens the door, and I'm rendered motionless. Charlotte carries on. A lady carrying a sparkly bag hobbles out onto the step while battling to do up her dirty yellow rain coat.

'Jean Harrison?' Charlotte says as she stops at the end of the garden path.

The woman stares and wipes sleet from her face. Her gaze leaves Charlotte and lands on me as I stand in the middle of the road. Shivering, I don't know where to look. It's as if the woman is transfixed by me. She plods into the road in her wellies, where she stops right in front of me and stares.

'Go away and don't come back.' Her tone is more scared than angry. She takes in every feature on my face more than once. Her gnarly-knuckled index finger goes to grab my arm. The woman in front of me isn't Jean; I remember Jean's voice from the call. It's gravelly and breathless, and she speaks as if talking is a struggle. She coughs a lot too.

'Go away,' the woman shouts, then she hurries across the rest of the road and into the house opposite, where she's greeted by a person who I don't get a proper look at. They slam the door.

I can't get the old lady's stare out of my mind. Her stark look bored deep within me, but she's gone now, thank goodness. I can breathe again. A car horn toots. As I turn and see tyres screeching towards me, Charlotte yells and drags me onto the pavement.

'You nearly got yourself killed. What were you thinking just standing in the road like that? You were close to being flattened.'

I hope my banging heart will slow down soon. 'Did you hear that woman? She said to go away. I don't feel right about this.'

As I look up, Charlotte has already knocked. I'm about to meet Jean Harrison, whether I want to or not.

The sound of a key turning in a lock is followed by the large front door creaking open. A few specks of cracked paint fall to the floor. A woman in a nurse's uniform stands there, waiting for one of us to speak. Her huge glasses look large on her small round face, and her tight ponytail seems to stretch her skin, smoothing it out. Everyone around here stares. I'm glad I don't live in this creepy village.

'We're here to see Jean,' Charlotte says.

'Oh yes, she's been expecting you.' The nurse steps back and lets us both into the hallway. She closes the heavy door.

I have never seen so much junk. Newspapers and boxes full of random rubbish lean precariously against every inch of wall space. Dust motes dance in the air. Surely it can't be healthy to breathe in this much dust, especially if you sound as poorly as Jean does.

I feel as though my legs are about to buckle as I step further into the hallway. There's a smell of sickness in the air, like sweat and urine. The house doesn't feel like a home and, if Jean is right, I wonder if my birth mother grew up here and, if she did, did she find the house eerie and suffocating? A tinge of sadness hits me. I don't even know whether all this is a mistake, but if it isn't, I have to deal with the fact that my birth mother didn't want me and that thought chokes in my throat. I picture a woman giving birth to me and then turning her head as I'm taken away. Would she have even held or looked at me? Did she care and had she thought about me since or had she been glad to get me out of her life? I wonder if she was young or ill; or maybe she died in childbirth and my grandmother thought it was best I be adopted. All these thoughts run through my head and I don't know how I feel. I hear a choking noise followed by dry retching coming from above, and I'm scared of what I'm about to see. All I know for sure is that there's no going back now. I'm about to meet Jean Harrison and all I wish I could do right now, is run out that door and never come back.

THIRTY-THREE

As the nurse leads the way up the stairs, I take in the stained-glass window on the halfway landing. I peer at the picture of fields and the sun's rays, so much of it obscured by spider webs. The colours almost swirl in the middle of the sun. I lose my balance as I stare too hard into it so I look ahead. We continue walking up the rest of the stairs onto a dark landing, again dusty boxes are stacked up everywhere.

I can't let Charlotte continue the lie of pretending to be me, like she did on the phone. This is something I have to brave, even if I have to mumble my way through a conversation with her. The woman is definitely sick and she doesn't need us confusing her. I reach ahead and grab Charlotte's hand as it swings back. 'I'll talk to her, it's okay,' I say in a hushed voice so that the nurse doesn't hear. She's already halfway across the landing.

The nurse taps on a door just before she enters the room of the coughing woman. 'Jean, your visitors are here.'

'It's okay. I got this. You won't say everything you need to say and she's heard my voice.'

Charlotte is still going with the plan. I know it's for the best as Jean has already spoken to her. She'll recognise her voice. Why did I let her answer my call?

I flinch as Jean coughs again, and my stomach is churning. I'm sure I can smell vomit or bad food. My feet don't comply as I attempt to take another step. It's as if I'm frozen. I've never seen a really sick or dying person before and I'm not sure if I'm ready to see one now, or ever.

'Hey. Wakey, wakey.' Charlotte snaps her fingers at me and grins excitedly.

'I can't...' My voice is already giving out on me. 'She's been watching me all my life. She's seen my Facebook. She knows what I look like.'

'Shh. It's dark in there. It will be okay.' Charlotte ignores what I just said. She reaches for me and pulls me by my coat towards the open door.

The nurse talks to Jean and tells her that she needs to lift her pillows up so that she's more comfortable. Jean places her arm on a red pillow that lies beside her.

'You,' Jean says as she points at us and coughs again.

Charlotte drags me into view.

'It's me,' I say, but I'm so quiet, I'm not sure if she's heard. I can't pretend Charlotte is me, especially as Jean knows what I look like. I'm eighteen, an adult, but right now I feel as though I'm a scared little child. I have no idea how Charlotte is so unaffected by everything, but then again, it's not like her life is in tatters.

'Come, come,' Jean says. 'I can barely see you.' I wonder if she always has her thickly lined curtains closed. A lamp glows from the corner of the room but it's dim, leaving the other half in darkness.

I can see yet more boxes and a huge pile of old clothes and coats. The clutter is never ending, then I look at Jean, the woman claiming to be my grandmother. I'm not sure if we have the same shaped eyes that are quite close together. I can't help but stare. I know it's rude but her face is ashen, and the dark circles under her creased eyes are like nothing I've ever seen before. Her face is hollow, almost skeletal. Her sweat-drenched grey hair seems to be stuck to her forehead and ears. It's so thin, I can see most of her scalp and I have to remind myself that she has cancer. She must have had chemotherapy and I do know that patients can lose hair. A friend's mum had been through something similar, and I recall her telling me about it. With a shaky outstretched arm, Jean points a shaky finger at me and Charlotte, and then points to the black ottoman next to the bed. That's where she wants us to sit. Charlotte jabs me in the ribs, so I take a few steps in and head towards her bedside. I listen as the nurse walks down the stairs and I wish she'd come back up and stay with us. I don't like this one bit. Charlotte and I remove our wet coats. We place them on the floor and sit on the ottoman where I stiffly hug my knees.

'You came.' Without any introductions, Jean looks at me with scrunched eyes.

So many questions fill my head and I wonder if I'll manage to ask even one. It's as if my voice has gone. I don't know what to say.

'Yes, I've been—' Charlotte is about to continue ignoring what I said as she goes to tell Jean that she's been looking forward to meeting her, but I told her that I can't go along with the stupid plan. I nudge her in the ribs and hope she gets the hint this time. Jean is looking at me with familiarity. The woman is sick and I need to speak to her myself. I know Charlotte meant well when she answered my call from Jean. 'I've been looking forward to meeting you.'

'Your voice.' She coughs and places a liver-spotted hand over her chest.

I reach for her glass of water and hold it to her lips, where she takes a sip.

'It's okay, I can do it myself.' Jean takes it from me and has a couple of gulps before shakily placing the glass back on her bedside table. 'I spoke to you the other day.' Jean points to Charlotte.

'Sorry about that. This is my friend, Charlotte.'

'I don't like lies. There have been too many lies and I want to change that, which is why I'm glad you came.' Jean inhales sharply, clearly struggling to regulate her breathing as she speaks. A tear gathers at the corner of one of my eyes, and I hope she doesn't notice. The woman in front of me has a lot to cry about; my problems are miniscule in comparison.

'Are you sure you have the right person?'

She can't stop looking at me. 'I know I do. You looked, didn't you?'

'Looked?'

'For your birth certificate and let me guess you couldn't find it. You also feel it, don't you? You've always felt like something isn't right.' She pauses and wheezes. 'I bet you've never been abroad.'

I grunt an acknowledgement and that's all I can manage. Charlotte places an arm around my shoulder as if sensing my sadness. 'I looked for it, my birth certificate.' Tears begin to spill and I can't stop them. 'I love my mum and dad.'

'I'm sure you do.'

'Why did you have to tell me?'

Jean shrugs. 'I guess I'm selfish. I'm dying and I wanted to see you. You are my granddaughter, after all. Besides, someone will need to take this house over in the faraway future. It has been in my family forever.'

From what I've seen, I'd never want to live in this creepy house. 'Is my mother alive?' I almost stutter I'm so nervous.

Another wheezing fit consumes Jean. She drinks a little more water and gets her breath back. 'All in good time.'

I don't like her answer. It feels controlling, like she'll only release information on her terms. I need something concrete. 'Do you have proof?'

'What?'

As I thought, my voice was too quiet, but it's okay. I have Charlotte and I know she isn't about to hold back.

'We need to know if what you're saying is true. How can you prove that she's your granddaughter?'

'Like that, is it?' Jean says as she purses her thin dry lips for a few seconds. 'And who are you?'

'Charlotte. Her best friend.'

'Okay, I've worked in law all my life so evidence is important to me. I respect that.' She turns her attention back to me. 'Like I said, you're clever. You get that from me.'

I look down. The last thing I feel is clever with my cracking voice and nervous disposition. As my parents cross my mind, I think coming here was dumb and selfish.

'Okay. You had a cat toy, a lovely fluffy white one, that had a little ball inside that moved, making it sound like the cat was purring.'

My jaw drops and my chest tightens. I lost that toy when I was seven, leaving it on the beach when we had a family day trip to Weston-super-Mare, but I loved it so much. My heart broke when we got home and it wasn't in my bag. I nod.

'When you were adopted, your parents took that toy with you. I insisted they have it and they were so grateful, they said that you'd treasure it.' She clears her throat and winces as she sits up. 'Bloody hell, everything hurts.'

I'm struggling to catch my breath.

Jean continues. 'You have a blanket. Well, I hope you still do. It's made from knitted squares. Very mismatched in bright colours.'

Tears slip down my cheeks as I wait for her to say more. She's describing my baby blanket.

'It looks like this, doesn't it?'

She pulls out a photo from under her pillow and passes it to me. It's of a baby who is clearly bigger than the baby in the photo I found in my dad's office. I'm red and quite ugly. The blanket is wrapped around me and there is no doubt it's the blanket I keep under my bed, the same one I used to wrap my teddies in as a young child. I sob and Charlotte hugs me. She knows that blanket is mine too. We used to play teddy bear picnics together all those years ago when our mothers used to see each other for playdates. 'Please tell me about my birth mother.'

She huffs and looks away. 'Not yet. I have to do this my way. I have a proposition for you. A job.'

Is that why she brought me here, to work? 'I don't think so...'

'Hear me out. You come here every evening for four hours. We get to know each other, play cards and watch TV, and I pay you well. I know you need a job?'

'How?' I haven't mentioned needing a job.

'You young people don't care about your privacy. I read all your Facebook posts.'

Jean's right, I do need a job but not like this. It would feel as though I was taking advantage of a dying woman, despite the circumstances. 'I couldn't.'

'Look, I need a carer between six and ten, then I will get you a taxi home every night. I have a day nurse and a night nurse but there is a four-hour gap and I don't like being alone. I'll need someone to fetch me drinks and entertain me, a companion if you like. Don't fret, I won't ask you to bath me or help me to the toilet.' She stops to cough and splutter into a tissue. 'Besides, I have so much money, I barely know what to do with it and I'd like you to have it, so say yes.'

'No, I will come here to visit and I don't want anything.'

'In that case, don't come again. Our conversation is over. I'll call the nurse to let you out. Nurse,' she yells with a crackle in her throat.

There is so much more I need to know and Jean is calling the nurse to see me out. 'No, please. I need to see you again. My birth mother, who is she? Tell me.'

'No, you agree to my terms or I say nothing. Go back to your life, sweetheart.'

I wish I could say I like Jean, but I don't. Right now, I feel as though she's trying to manipulate me. 'Okay, okay. Only if I can come with a friend sometimes.' I don't want to be totally alone with her in this house, not yet. I want someone with me until I know I can fully trust her.

The nurse stands in the doorway.

Jean wipes a trail of spittle from the side of her mouth. 'Please arrange for this young lady to fill the six to ten shift. We don't need a carer from the agency, it's sorted. She's going to help me with drinks and entertainment, aren't you?'

I nod and wipe my red eyes. The nurse looks at me suspiciously.

Jean snaps. 'It's okay, she's family. I know what I'm doing. I'm sick, I haven't lost my marbles. Just go and sort out the paperwork and make it happen. I've had my solicitor draw up a contract. It's in my desk drawer.'

If she already has a contract drawn up for my employment, she planned all this. I find her rude but a part of me hopes that I will see another side to Jean Harrison. One benefit of coming here would be how happy it would make Mum to know I've found work. I won't tell her who I'm helping. All I need to do is tell her I'm working as a carer and it's every evening. She'll be thrilled for me.

Jean holds her hand over her mouth and yawns. She continues to talk about her routine and the house but her speech becomes a little slurred.

'She needs to sleep now. I'll show you around the house.' The nurse removes her glasses, rubs her eyes and puts them back on.

Charlotte and I follow her as she shows us around and gives me a set of keys. I don't know where this will lead, but I know I need to find out as much as possible about my birth mother before Jean passes and, from looking at her, I don't think it will be long.

THIRTY-FOUR

It's my fifth night and we're into December. I wanted to put a little Christmas tree up in Jean's room but she refused to let me get one. She said Christmas is a commercial waste of money and she doesn't condone it. I have to respect her wishes. It's also the first night I have come without Charlotte and I can't explain how alone I feel. Yesterday Charlotte brought some chocolate and we all watched a film together. It seemed strange that Jean had chosen *The Wizard of Oz* but we went with it. After that, we played cards which was quite fun. I've never played Rummy before. Jean is a shark when it comes to cards. I definitely wouldn't play her for money.

I watch as Jean's chest rises and falls, not smoothly but as if she's struggling. Now and again, she stops breathing but then gasps a little and other times, she lets out a little whistle as she exhales. A clump of yellow sleep has gathered at the corners of her eyes, and I resist the urge to reach out and clean it. The red pillow she normally rests her arm on has been cast aside. She still hasn't told me much about her cancer, but I'm guessing it's spread to her lungs as the cracking in her chest makes me wince.

'Jean,' I whisper, hoping that she'll respond.

'Huh?' She lets out a cry as she opens her eyes. 'You're still here and I'm still alive.'

I know more about her wishes now. She has refused hospital in any circumstance and has insisted that she come home to die. The nurses are privately hired, and Nurse Kayla has gone home now. The nurse explained what palliative care meant and that Jean was on morphine for the pain. I've learned so much these past few days but I haven't learned a single thing about my birth mother.

'Can we talk about my mother?'

Jean coughs so I pass her the box of tissues. I can't look as she spits into one so I turn away. As I turn back, I can see that she's deposited the tissue on her chest and is lying back down. 'She was nothing like you. She...' Jean pauses in thought.

Really? I can't believe that the woman who supposedly gave birth to me was nothing at all like me. Jean doesn't like me saying much and she snaps if I interrupt her. When I butted in, it wasn't intentional, I just wanted to know where I came from and I don't know why we're playing this game. I'm not her carer and she's not my client, but I'm forced to be here if I want to understand who I am. I'd welcome a job in a shop now.

Jean witters on and I listen as she tells me so much.

'Yes, your mother grew up in this house. My husband, your grandfather, died when she was little so she doesn't really remember him. It was just me and her. I had such high hopes for her. All that private tuition, down the pan.'

As she continues, I feel like I'm getting to know the woman who gave birth to me, and the urge to find out a name or an address overwhelms me. 'Does she live close by?'

Jean glances up at me and snaps. 'I said we'd get to that.'

'Sorry.'

'Now where was I?'

'School, you were talking about my birth mother at high school.'

'Ah yes, she went wild and I didn't know what to do. She'd lie about being at school and about where she was of an evening. I'd find out she'd been drinking on streets with some no-good boys and I tried my best to do what was right for her but I gave up. That's what I did. It became hard and I was working long hours at the time.'

No warmth comes from Jean, and I compare her to my parents. Mum hugs me a lot and she's always been there to listen to me. When Rory Tucker dumped me in senior school, she bought me chocolate cake and listened to me crying all night. That was love. When I lied to Mum and told her I was staying at Charlotte's, she forgave me, even though I threw up in her car when she drove me back from that night club, yet all Jean could say was how much of a liar her daughter was. Her daughter was being a teenager. I regret lying to my mum now. It must have hurt and worried her at the time.

'So, you were distant?'

Jean nods. 'We were like two strangers in this house. I didn't know her at all. And then, out of the blue I see her. After spending weeks in her bedroom, our paths barely crossing, I saw her swollen stomach and straight away I knew.'

She continues to tell me what happened next and my heart breaks for my birth mother. I don't know how she coped. She was younger than I am now and I can't imagine being pregnant. Not only that, but Jean paid for her to move out and live in a bedsit so she didn't have to see her again.

'What happened to me, after that? How did I end up with my parents?'

Jean's eyes widen and her jaw begins to tremble. Her stare is fixed on mine and I can't look away. Rain pelts against the window and it rattles. 'That's all for tonight.'

'No, please. I need to know who she is, if she's still alive and where she is.'

'You need to know and you also need to wait. Open my wardrobe.'

Jean never says please or thank you. I do as she says.

'Top shelf, at the back, there's a box with a key in it. Bring it to me.'

I begin to pull out all the moth-eaten blankets from the tiny space and I wonder how they ever fitted before. I also know I'm going to have to put them back, so I keep them as folded as possible. I grab one of Jean's plastic boxes full of tat and I stand on it, hoping that it won't crack under my weight. Jean was right. There is the tiniest of boxes tucked away in the corner. If I didn't know it was there, I'd never have spotted it. I reach in, straining as my finger touches it. I tap the side of it as hard as I can and it slides a little closer. I'm able to grab it now. I step off the box and go to pass it to Jean.

She holds out her hand to refuse it. 'Turn the key.'

Gently, I do as I'm told and open the box using the tiny gold key. To my disappointment, it's empty.

'You were hoping that all the answers to your questions would be in the box.' She smirks. 'Put these in the box.' She passes me the baby photo and a sealed envelope. Now, I want you to put these in the loft. I'll tell you how.'

'What?' Why does she want me to put her box in the loft? I also wanted that photo. It might not be much but it's precious and I feel I should have it. I glance at the baby in the photo one more time.

'Pass me the box.'

I pass it to her and she turns the key before removing it and placing it under her pillow. It's obvious she doesn't want me to take anything from the box or read what's in the envelope.

About forty minutes later, I find the stick that opens the loft and I'm sliding the catch to open it up.

'Be careful climbing the ladders,' Jean calls out from the bedroom.

I use the stick to hook the ladders and they come down with ease. It's not the first time I've been in a loft. I keep all my childhood toys and schoolwork in ours and I go up there to look through them regularly, but Jean's ceilings are high. I climb up until I'm peering into a dark void. She told me there was a light switch by the hatch, but I can't see it anywhere. I use the torch on my phone instead. I step onto the first wooden strut and flinch as I hear a squeak. Rats. My heart thrums.

'The struts are labelled,' she says.

'I know,' I reply.

'Number seven. Go to it.'

The number has been written on the wood, and I wonder if in the past Jean had stored things up here and used a number system to find things. As asked, I pull up the horrible itchy fluff and place the box within it. It can't hurt to take a look around. I shine my light over the other end and I see box after box marked Christmas so I know there has been fun in this house in the past. Carefully, I step over there and begin poking around a box of dusty red baubles. I dig a little deeper and find a folded piece of card with a picture of Santa on the front, so I open it. That's when I see the little girl standing next to Santa, holding a small wrapped present. I hold my torch closer. The little girl has two long brown plaits under a white woollen hat that dangle over each shoulder, and she has a cute button nose. I can see myself in her. If I found this photo in my dad's office, I'd think it was me. Actually, I wouldn't. This little girl is sad. She looks like she's about to burst into tears. This is all I have of my mother and I'm not even going to ask Jean if I can have it. I place it in the pocket of my jeans and hurry back down the ladders and pack them away. The night nurse will be arriving soon, and my taxi will be waiting outside to take me home.

As I walk back into Jean's bedroom, I see that she's still so I run over. She doesn't breathe or make a sound. 'Jean, Jean.' My hands shake. I'm trying to remember what Nurse Kayla said to me. She said it could happen at any time and I'm to call her so that she can come straight over. 'Jean,' I shout, tears streaming down my face. Just as I press Nurse Kayla's number on my phone, Jean sucks in a load of air and snorts.

'You're still here.'

I want to say, *and so are you*, but I think it's best that I don't upset her. 'I'm here.'

'Before you go, can you put this pen in my office? There's a pen pot on my desk, pop it in there. And this Post-it notepad, put that in or on the desk too.'

Really? The woman is dying and the house is a complete mess and she wants me to make sure I put her very average looking biro and Post-it pad away. I know it feels strange but it's obviously important to Jean. She reaches out and pulls me close, then she whispers in my ear. What she says chills me to the bone.

I say my goodbyes and hurry downstairs to put the pen and pad where she told me to. I see an address book on her desk so I flick through it. There are entries galore and I don't even know my birth mother's name. She could be any one of these people or none of these people. A key in the door makes me flinch so I hurry out and stand in the hallway, expecting to see the night nurse, but all I see is the strange woman who lives opposite. Her words ring through my head. *Go away.* She stares at me as if I shouldn't be here, but she is the one who shouldn't be here.

'Can I help you? I didn't know you had a key?'

'You don't know a lot of things.' She grins and lets out a laugh. 'It's lies, all lies.'

'What?'

She goes to shut the door but the night nurse stops her with his foot. 'It's a bit late for a social call, isn't it, Mrs Pearson, but I guess Jean won't mind.'

So that's her name. Mrs Pearson. The woman uncomfortably climbs the stairs, heaving herself up by the banister and panting as she reaches the middle landing.

'Don't mind Mrs Pearson, she's always visiting. It's nice when she brings visitors too.' He throws his coat on one of the hooks and leans his damp umbrella against the wall. 'How has she been tonight?'

'I err, I thought she died at one point but she took a deep breath and woke up.'

'Ah, that happens a lot. She told me last night how much she enjoys having you here. You played cards and watched a film, I hear?'

I nod, and then I hear my taxi driver toot his horn. 'I best go.' The truth is, I can't wait to get away from this house. Jean's whispered words hurt and before I even get into the back of the car, my sobs are coming thick and fast. All I can hear is Jean repeating them over and over again in my head. I've never felt unwanted in my whole life, until recently.

She didn't want you then and she doesn't want you now.

THIRTY-FIVE

Yesterday, Jean whispered those cruel words to me. Today, I pace up and down her landing, my legs feeling like they're about to give way. It finally happened. I had to make the call to Nurse Kayla and, true to her word, she came immediately. Soon after her, the doctor arrived. It seems that everyone is here. I call Charlotte. If ever there was a time I needed my best friend, it's now.

'What, Angel. I'm just about to get off with Si and he's as hot as hell. You know I was on a date tonight.'

I can't hold back my tears. Big snivelly cries escape my lips.

'What is it?'

'It's happened.'

'What?'

'Jean died and I was with her. I thought she was asleep and I was sitting on the ottoman, and... I must have fallen asleep as my head was on Jean's red pillow and she wasn't moving. I called her and placed my hand on her arm. I thought she'd gasp and wake up. She didn't wake up.'

'I'm on my way. I'm getting an Uber now. Hold tight, I'll be with you in a while. Have you called your mum?'

'No.' There was no way I'd call Mum and Dad. They think me caring for Jean is just a job. If they came here, something tells me that they'd know and they'd click. I can't let that happen. Tomorrow, I'll just tell them that the lady I was caring for has now been moved to a nursing home and I'm looking for another job. Besides, I don't want to talk about Jean to anyone, not yet. I need time to process everything she told me.

I walk down the stairs, leaving the chaos behind. That's when I bump into Mrs Pearson. Her wide eyes bear deep within me. I go to pass and she moves to stop me. 'She's gone, isn't she?'

I nod.

'Good. It was time. Certain things must die with certain people. Go home, little girl. Go home.' She goes to reach for a strand of hair that has escaped my clip, but I bat her hand out the way. Mrs Pearson scares me and I don't want her touching me. Not once has she made me feel welcome, and whenever she came to speak to Jean, they'd make me leave the house and stand on the path. I don't trust Mrs Pearson one bit. One good thing came of all this. I know my mother's name and the road she lives on, but for now, I can't bear to do a thing about it. I glance at the piece of paper Jean had written this information on. The house number is smudged so I can't tell what it is. Looking after Jean has taken everything out of me. I realise how much I love my parents, the people who actually brought me up. I can't just cast aside the memories of my mum reading bedtime stories to me or holding a cool flannel on my hot head when I had chicken pox. My dad took me camping, we laughed as it rained on the tent all night, and I even love him calling me Stubby Fingers. It'll be Christmas soon and all I want is to spend that time with them. I need normal. Mrs Pearson looks at me as if she knows what I'm thinking. Instead of saying another word, she steps aside and drags herself up those stairs by the handrail.

I gasp for breath and wipe my mascara-stained eyes. The garden beckons me. While all the commotion continues upstairs, I head through the kitchen and out of the French doors. The full moon shines down, highlighting the bony branches. I tear up again as I kneel in front of the patch that will turn into a carpet of daffodils in spring, and I think of my mother. Jean said this was her patch in the garden and that she tended to it. She didn't want me and it hurts my heart so much I can barely breathe. I wish I'd never met Jean Harrison. I might never find happiness again, ever. I stand and kick the hard soil to no avail.

'Hey.'

I turn to see Charlotte. She steps onto the cold icy grass in her ridiculously high shoes and starts to totter towards me, arms out at each side as if she's walking a tightrope.

'Thanks for coming.'

She almost runs the last couple of metres and falls into my arms. I catch her to stop her toppling over. The smell of tequila blasts my face as she blows a breath out.

'Sorry, I've had a couple of drinks.'

'No, I'm sorry. Maybe I shouldn't have called.'

Charlotte lets go of me and stands. 'You're my bestie and I'm here for you. Besties forever, remember? I changed my mind about Si anyway. He's a sloppy kisser. You saved me.'

I can't talk. Every time I go to say a word, a sob escapes.

'Shush. Everything will be okay.'

I want to shout at her, tell her it won't be. Meeting Jean was only the start of what's yet to come and I know things will get worse before they get better. As soon as I find the strength to do what I need to do, I'll do it. For now, I need to heal. All I know is, one day, I will meet my mother and I will confront her with everything, and I mean everything. Jean told me so many things but some didn't make sense. I have no idea what to believe any more.

'Did you find out any more about your biological mum?'

I shake my head. For now, I don't want Charlotte to know. If I tell her I have my birth mother's name and the name of the road she lives on, Charlotte will have me marching there right now and I'm not ready. All I'm ready for is my bed. I need to grieve for Jean, even though she was a pretty mean and snappy woman. I need to grieve for the life I once had that I know is a lie, and I need to grieve for myself as a tiny baby who wasn't wanted. People say that time heals. I hope it does because right now, I can't see a way forward. All I feel is this darkness pulling me in and I can't seem to bat it away.

Charlotte holds me tightly and rubs my back under the light of the moon. It escapes behind a cluster of clouds leaving us in darkness but I don't care. I just don't care any more.

THIRTY-SIX

'Alright, love. Charlotte's come to visit.'

My mum strokes my greasy hair but all I can do is pull my quilt over my head, shifting her hand off me. 'I don't want to see anyone,' I say in a muffled voice from under my bedding. I smell, I haven't changed pyjamas for days and I don't care. All I want is for everyone to go away and leave me alone. Christmas came and Christmas went. I didn't see my friends or get another job and, to my parents' despair, I've remained in my room moping for months. I'm so close to being frogmarched to the doctors. I keep hearing my parents mention the words, depression and hormones. I know they're worried about me but I don't know what to do to make them feel better. In fact, if I say anything, I will ruin their lives. All I want to do is scream and shout, ask them who I am, but I can't. I can't talk to them or anyone which is why I stopped answering my phone to Charlotte. It's not the first time she's visited and, each time, I've told my mum to tell her to go away and, right now, I'm going to tell her to go away again.

'I'll tell her to come up.' I can tell Mum is at the end of her tether by the tone in her voice.

I throw my quilt off my head. 'No, I'm not in the mood to talk to anyone.'

Mum tilts her head sympathetically and places her hair behind her ears. 'I know you're not, but I think it will help.' She pauses then goes on. 'I wish you'd talk to me. I know you keep saying nothing's happened and nothing's wrong but I know that's not true. I'm your mum and I can tell. Dad and I are worried.' Her hands are clenched, and I know she's hoping that I don't blurt out that I know I was adopted. Or does she want me to? Maybe she's ready for the truth to come out too. I can't tell.

If I agree to see Charlotte, my mum will leave me alone. 'Okay, I'll see her.'

'And you'll get up and have a shower.'

I nod and sit up. 'And I'll get up and have a shower.' I guess I've committed now so I will try to make an effort today.

Mum opens my curtains and lets the sun in. It's April. Jean is dead and I need to think about what I want to do next. Maybe I am ready to hear what Charlotte has to say about it all. Maybe I should go back to the house and lay my own ghosts to rest. Mum smiles before leaving my room and going back down to Charlotte.

I open my bedside drawer and, slipped inside a half-eaten box of biscuits, is that photo of my birth mother with Santa. I reach under my bed and drag my baby blanket to my chest and hold it close. It's all I have of her. She made it. I know that because Jean told me. Part of me hopes she made it for me. I need to feel wanted even though I know my mother wished I was dead. However kind and loving my parents are, I know I'm a reject.

'At last. Why have you been shutting me out? It's been forever.' Charlotte sits on my bed and passes me a milkshake. 'I got you this on my way. It's strawberry, your favourite.'

I take her offering and place it on my bedside. 'I'm so sorry.'

'Me and Freya have been really worried. She wants to see you too.'

'Really?'

Charlotte nods. 'Even though you messaged her to tell her to get lost and not try to call again. It'll take a lot more than that to get rid of Freya.'

'I... I didn't mean it. She just kept messaging and I didn't want to talk to anyone.' It was bad of me. Freya, Charlotte and I have been close for years but I didn't tell Freya about Jean. Hell, I've known Freya longer than Charlotte.

'I told her about Jean.' Charlotte looks away.

'What? You had no right.'

'She didn't know why you wouldn't talk to her. I had to say something.'

I close my eyes, not knowing how to reply to her. How could Charlotte have told my secret to someone else, even if it was only Freya? Her mum could talk to mine. Besides, it was my news to tell, if and when I wanted to tell it. I feel as though everything is snowballing again. I thought if I stayed in and didn't speak to anyone, it would all die down and I'd forget about Jean. All I want is to go back to the life I had before.

'Don't be mad at me, but she's on her way over.'

I grab the milkshake and go to pour it in her lap, but she snatches it off me.

'I know you're angry.'

'You do, do you?' She hasn't seen angry and even in my current frame of mind, I'm not sure I'll actually show her. I mean, I couldn't even pour a milkshake in her lap. I don't get angry; I withdraw.

'Look, we just want to help. We want our friend back. Let me help.'

Last time I let Charlotte help me, I ended up meeting Jean. Charlotte doesn't help: she hinders, big time. 'No, no and no. I just want you both to go away and leave me alone.'

Charlotte shakes her head. 'That would make me a terrible friend. Not going to happen.'

'You're already a terrible friend,' I snap. Instantly, I regret that comment. In my heart, I know Charlotte is trying her best. Even though I haven't answered her messages or calls, she's continued to try reaching out to me. She's never given up and she's here now. I feel my eyes watering, and she hugs me.

'It's okay.'

'It's not,' I cry. 'It's not okay until I find her.'

Charlotte hurries over to my bedroom door and checks that no one is around and she closes it. She holds a finger to her lips. 'Whisper, okay. I just heard your mum faffing with the coats at the bottom of the stairs.'

I nod and speak in a whisper. 'I thought I could just get on with things but I can't. I need to find her, but I don't think I can talk to her.'

'I said it was okay because it is. Whatever you want to do, Freya and I will help. We both love you and we'll do anything we can. I really think you need to find the truth then you can face it and move on. You can't carry on like this. We miss you. I miss you.'

I hug her, knowing that she's right. I really haven't got the strength to take the lead but Charlotte has. There is a knock at my bedroom door and Freya enters. My lovely friends have come to my rescue. I've spent months lying in this bed, wallowing in self-pity and grief, but I need to get up and do something before my whole life flashes by. There is strength in friendship and I know these two have my back even though they don't know the half of it. Some things I will never tell, not even to my best friends. My birth mother is a bad person and I'm going to make her realise what she's done.

THIRTY-SEVEN

I don't know how I let Freya and Charlotte talk me into confronting this but after not sleeping, I decided to get the bus to Jean's. I check my phone and see that I have no messages or missed calls, but why would I? It's seven in the morning and I'm meeting the others near my birth mother's house in two hours, which gives me a little time to come back to where it all started. Larrison House. I stare at the building and I feel as though it's looking at me. Two large windows, one each side of the over-sized door. They're like huge eyes and I feel them on me. I glance back at Mrs Pearson's house but the curtains are closed, thank goodness.

Shivering, I go to open the creaky gate but the postie stomps on the pavement from behind. Instead, I continue to walk slowly past until he's dropped what looks like a pizza flier through Jean's door. I can't go through the front; no one knows I still have my keys and I'd like to keep it that way. I sidle along the side of the fence between the panel and the dense trees and I reach a tree stump. Standing on it, I can see into Jean's garden. This is my way in. I know the gate will be locked. The nurses were careful when it came to security. Using all my strength I pull myself over the fence and I drop onto the thinning grass below. That's when my gaze catches that corner of the garden, the one that has haunted me since the night Jean died.

As I approach, I feel as though I can't breathe. The daffodils are beautiful but they were meant to conceal something so horrific I can't think about it. I try not to look as my heart begins to thud against my ribcage. I pick one and hold it close to my heart. My birth mother didn't want me. I drop the flower and trample on it. My phone rings. 'Alright, Charlotte.'

'Where are you? Freya and I are at yours.'

Damn, I said I'd meet them at Worcester for nine. They didn't say they were going to call at mine first. 'I, err, I'll tell you later. Just meet me where you said you would and tell my mum you made a mistake and you were meant to meet me in Worcester. Tell her you were meeting me after my job interview, for the early morning cleaning job.'

'Are you at a job interview?'

'No, but just say that, okay? I'll explain in a bit.' I know what an effort getting up this early would have been for Charlotte. She hates mornings with a passion at the best of times. I feel a twinge of sadness, as I told my mum I was leaving for an interview. She even asked me if my boots and leggings were a good choice of clothing, and I said they were okay as I was just going for a cleaning job. It got tense when she offered to drive me before starting work. I let her drop me off at the bus station to keep her happy.

'Yeah, will do. Don't be late, okay?'

'Won't be.'

Charlotte hangs up, and I find I'm still staring at those yellow flowers. I hurry to the French doors and open them. Sunshine glints off the shiny draining board. Someone has cleaned everything, and the place is virtually empty. I think back to the piles of clutter in the hall as I walk through and go up the stairs. I'm sure that very soon, the house will be sold and

I'll never be able to come here again. As I pass the stained-glass window and continue onto the landing, I stop and stare at Jean's bedroom door. Closing my eyes, I imagine I'm back there. I can hear her coughing and shouting at the nurse. With trembling hands, I push open the door, expecting the room to look the same as it was, but it too has been cleaned. I feel my hammering heart starting to calm down. I'm alone here. The mattress and all Jean's clothes have gone.

Walking around the house is different this time. I can amble, take in all its nooks and crannies as I imagine my birth mother growing up here. Her bedroom must have been the one at the back. I close Jean's bedroom door and open the other one. My gaze falls upon the bookshelf and the double bed, which is covered with a knitted square blanket, just like mine. I lie on the bed and pull the blanket close to my face and inhale. After a moment, my nose tickles and I sneeze. There is a cold dampness coming from the blanket but I can't stop hugging it. Why didn't my birth mother want me? Not only was I unwanted, but she wanted me dead and out the way. How could she? I hate this house and I hate her, and I hate those horrible flowers.

As I go to stand, I hear a key turn in the front door and there is a click as it unlocks. Someone is in the house. Did I close the French doors? I can't remember.

'Why did you come back?' Mrs Pearson yells, her voice carrying through the whole house.

I quickly creep into Jean's bedroom. There has to be somewhere to hide. She's coming up the stairs. The wardrobe, that's my only option. With all the clutter and most of the furniture gone, I step into the large wooden structure and pull the doors as closed as I can, leaving the slightest of gaps.

'I saw you. I saw you with my own eyes.' She hobbles into the bedroom, her hearing aid screeching. My heart pounds so hard, I'm sure she can hear it over the whistling, but she's looking at the bed and furrowing her brows. She glances my way so I hold my breath and sit back a little. Just as my phone beeps, her hearing aid whistles and she leaves the room. I almost hyperventilate. My stomach churns and I feel as though I might throw up. I've never done anything like this before and I know I'd get into big trouble if I'm caught here.

From the landing, Mrs Pearson yells again. 'Whatever you think you know, it's all lies. All of it. Jean was senile and sick. Go away and never come back.'

I peer through the gap again and I see that she's aiming her voice towards the loft. She thinks I'm hiding in there for some bizarre reason. As she starts to descend the stairs, I creep out of the wardrobe and wait the few minutes it takes her to finally leave. I need to get out of here, before she comes back.

I run as fast as I can until I reach the kitchen and burst through the French doors. The daffodils all look like they're facing me, laughing. I run over and trample on them with my huge black boots. All the hurt comes spilling out as another flower head is crushed under my boots. Once I've got my breath back, I check my phone. It's a message from Charlotte.

Just on the bus. Be there soon. X

I hurry over the back fence, snagging my hoodie slightly, and I run around the back of the garden and along the horse track so that Mrs Pearson doesn't see me. No doubt she's nosing through her window right now, waiting for me to leave.

The dense woodland behind the house feels like it's closing in on me. There's a good chance I'm going to see my birth mother today for the very first time and I don't know how I feel. Anger and hurt well up inside me. One day, when I have a child of my own, I'm going to make sure he or she always feels wanted and loved, and I would never hurt my child, ever. I don't know if I'll be able to say a word to my birth mother when I see her. I tried to look her up on Facebook but I couldn't find her. There were so many Joneses too. All this feels wrong. Maybe I should listen to Mrs Pearson. I should go home, call everything off and never look back. After what Jean said, I have a feeling that getting involved with the woman who gave birth to me is a big mistake. After months of toiling, I know I'm not in the right frame of mind for this, not yet. I need more time. I message Charlotte.

I've changed my mind.

She replies instantly.

No way. Not after how you've been the last few months. You're not alone in this, you have us and we are going to do this together. We can't lose you again. You don't know how hard it was for us when you wouldn't take our calls. Do this and you can move on with your life. Freya said to say we love you and hurry up.

I don't reply telling Charlotte I already know the truth and it's uglier than anything they can imagine. My hands are shaking at the thought of seeing my birth mother. A part of me hates Charlotte as much as I love her, because I know she will not stop going on until I do this. I guess I have no choice. She's right, I can't go on living the way I have been since just before Christmas. I need to face my birth mother.

THIRTY-EIGHT

'This is the road.' Charlotte takes us through a clearing in the trees and we come out onto a road full of richer people houses. Not like the one I live in, an ex-council house with a bath tap that drips all night. My dad has promised to fix it for months but he never does. He's always bone-tired when he finishes work.

Freya buttons her denim jacket up. Her harem pants blow as a gust of wind catches them. I fiddle with the tear in my hoodie as I glance up and down the road. The sick feeling in my stomach is still there from earlier and I feel bad for trampling on the flowers. I look up and down and there are so many houses. We know we have the right road but what we don't have is a number. 'It's useless, Charlotte. There's no way we can guess what number she lives at.' I glance at a house and see that we're up to number eighty-six and there are still more. 'We should go, maybe do some more research online.' I glance at the bit of paper with the very little information I have. Jean gave me her name and the name of this road. I know my mother is called Leah, but I haven't told Charlotte her first name as part of me wants us to fail at finding her, which is why I said I only had the name Jones to go on. Also, it feels odd to actually say her name out loud. I can't do it, not yet. I'm not ready for that. My heart begins to hammer. I shouldn't be here. 'It's getting a bit blustery. We should definitely go.'

Charlotte stops. 'Enough. It is not going to blow us to our deaths. Look up.' She waits for me to do as she says. 'It is a lovely spring day and you are just trying to get out of this.'

Too right I am. This is the last place I want to be. *Leah, Leah, Leah.* I say her name over and over in my head. It's on the tip of my tongue but I clamp my mouth shut.

'Remember what burying your head in the sand did to you for nearly four months.'

She's right but knowing that doesn't make what we're doing any easier. My legs are jelly-like and the more we head deeper into this road the more I feel as though I might collapse. 'I'm scared. I'm not ready. I won't be able to talk to her. I don't want to. I... I...' The words won't come out. I haven't seen her and I'm already dumbstruck. It's not like when I met Jean, this is bigger. Jean was cold but from what she said about my mother, I'm dealing with an arctic level iceberg of a woman.

Sighing, Charlotte places a hand on her hip. 'I'll do it for you. I am going to pretend to be you so you don't have to say a word. Just play along and if you like her and you want to get to know her, just say and we'll come clean.'

'But...' I want to say how silly her pretending to be me is, but she's right. Charlotte won't be upset if my birth mother is mean to her or rejects her, whereas I'll be devastated.

'Are we sorted?'

I nod. It's all I can do. I feel as though my tongue is fat in my mouth, and the words I'd want to say are a jumbled mess in my head.

'Where next?' Freya asks as she chews a lump of gum.

'Here.' Charlotte hurries over to a woman riding a mobility scooter while holding a beagle on a lead.

'Molly,' she calls as she gives the sniffing dog a gentle tug. 'Come on, girl.'

'Excuse me.' I watch as Charlotte runs up alongside her and pets the friendly dog.

The woman furrows her brows and glances back at me and Freya. 'Yes?'

'Erm, I'm looking for the Joneses. They live around here.'

I'm uneasy as the woman glances up at a house and hesitates. That's when I see another woman peering through the upstairs window. She has my hair colour, that much I can see. Although, I think mine may be lighter.

'And who are you?'

Charlotte looks down and frowns. 'I'm adopted and I think they might be my birth parents.'

'Oh, I see.' The woman rides a little further down and stops on the path outside a bungalow.

I can tell she doesn't believe Charlotte by the way she's looking her up and down. I glance back up at the woman in the window again. As I do, she steps back and drops the curtain. My throat is as dry as bone so I clear it. 'Tell her to hurry,' I croak.

Freya can see that I'm upset. She waves at Charlotte and points to her wrist. Not that she wears a watch but Charlotte knows what she means. Charlotte raises her brows and waves a hand to dismiss us. I can't quite hear what she's saying since they moved a little further up the path, but I watch as our friend writes something on a slip of paper and passes it to the woman on the scooter.

A man walks past the upstairs window and runs his hands through his hair. Could he be my father? Jean wouldn't talk about him no matter how hard I pressed. Maybe both of them didn't want me. I need to know who he is, who they are.

The woman on the scooter nods a couple of times, and as Charlotte walks back over, she glances up at the house next door again before scooting off down her own path and into her bungalow.

'What did you write?' I need to know what Charlotte said and did.

'Chill. I gave her your phone number and told her to tell Mrs Jones to get in touch.'

'What?' I'm horrified. I don't know what I'll do if she calls.

Charlotte breaks into a smile. 'Oh, Angel. Don't worry. She asked me for a contact number and said if she finds anyone by the name of Jones, she'll pass it on to them. All the while she was staring at the house next door. She couldn't have been more obvious. I gave her the wrong number so you don't need to worry. I think that's the house. We should knock.' She goes to walk towards the house.

I reach out, grab her arm and pull her back. 'No, not like this. I saw a man and a woman in the window.'

Charlotte shrugged. 'So, we get mum and dad in one go. Bingo.'

'He might not be my dad, and she might not want him to know. I could make everything worse. She didn't want me and she'll want me even less if I blow her life apart.'

'Okay, okay. Let's just walk past the house and check it out. But we're not dropping this.'

I nod, knowing that's the best we'll both agree on. As we slink past the car, I see a few business cards and building design brochures on the parcel shelf. After glancing up again, Charlotte drags me onto their drive while Freya stays back. 'Look, Angel. His name is Cain Jones. We've found the Joneses. And he has a mobile number and a business address.' She pulls her phone from her pocket and takes a quick photo of the card; and then we all run away, like we've done something terrible.

The woman I saw at the window is my birth mother. Leah Jones was Harrison. I didn't see any paperwork with that name in Jean's house. Something terrible must have happened between them if Jean cast her own daughter from her life and left not a trace of her existence in that house, except for that one photo I found in the loft. I'm not sure if I want to know what caused such a rift. The things I already know give me nightmares. I'm not sure I'm ready for more. When you know the woman who gave birth to you wanted you dead, you know you're walking a dangerous path if you insert yourself into her life. I'm scared, more scared than I've ever been.

THIRTY-NINE

Last night, I had the worst sleep ever. In fact, I'm not sure I slept. My mind raced with thoughts of the woman in the window. At one point I found myself clutching the photo of her as a child, my fingers were white and moments later I cried. That's when I decided I needed to spend the day on my own and where better to go than Mr Jones's place of work. It's not far from where Freya mum's business is, and Freya is helping her out this morning. I need to know if Cain Jones is my dad. I have his number and I am tempted to call and hang up, just so I can hear his voice. As I pass a loud factory on my left, I once again find I'm clutching my phone so hard my hand aches. He's no better than her. I refuse to believe what happened is all my birth mother's fault. He has to take some of the blame.

I'm struggling to find the business centre so I type the address into my Maps app and it tells me I'm at the back of the building. As I step towards the front of the building, the man in the snack bar gives me a little wave before tucking into a doorstep sandwich. The smell of bacon and grease hits my nostrils and my stomach goes queasy.

I stand outside the building and look at the signage, that's when I spot that his office is number 215. All I have to do is walk in, head to 215 and take a peek. As I step through the door and head in the only direction I can go in, I hope that the receptionist doesn't stop me – but they do.

'Can I help you?'

'I... I...' I can't speak. I tug on the edges of my denim jacket and suddenly my legs feel too hot in my tights. 'No.'

I run out, my plait swishing and hitting my back with every step. As I stand on the pavement, I take a few deep breaths, glad of the breeze to cool me down. That didn't go as planned but then again, it was stupid to think I could just breeze into a business centre, no questions asked. I glance ahead and frown. The silver car parked up is the same car that was parked behind Cain Jones's yesterday. My birth mother is here. I need to leave this area, fast. As I grab my phone, I see a head wavering low through the windscreen. She's in her car. Maybe she's looking for something in the footwell. I'm not going to hang around to find out. I grab my phone and press Freya's number. Right now, I need a friend.

'Hi, Angel,' she says.

'Can you get ten minutes off? I'm just round the corner.'

'Err, hang on. Mum, can I have a break?'

I listen as Freya's mum chats to her daughter.

'Mum said head over. I'll just finish what I'm doing and we'll go and grab a drink.'

She ends the call, so I hurry along the road towards the party supply outlet, where I ring the buzzer.

Freya opens the door. 'I'll just be five. Come in.'

I head into the main room and there are boxes and plastic wrapped costumes and wigs everywhere.

'I just have to get this order labelled and I'm all yours.'

Freya tears off some tape and continues. Her mum comes in and smiles, her blouse tucked into a pair of tailored black trousers. 'Hello, Angel. We haven't seen you for ages. How's things? What are you girls up to?'

I smile. Freya's mum has always been kind to me but I definitely don't want to share with her what's going on. It would get back to my mum before I could take my next breath. 'I'm going for this job and I just wanted to talk to Freya about it.'

'Ooh, what doing?'

Damn, I haven't thought that far ahead. 'Care work.'

Freya's mum tilts her head in sympathy. Everyone thinks my episode happened because the woman I cared for died, and that bit is true.

'Well, I think it's very brave of you to go back into care work and it's lovely that you want to help people. You're such a kind girl, Angel.'

'How are you?' I ask, trying to get the conversation off me.

Freya's mum shrugs. 'Well, I'll be happier once the morning sickness stops. It's been a godsend having Freya here to pick up the slack. She's taking over when I have maternity leave.' She places her hand on her barely pregnant stomach and smiles. She already loves her baby and it probably isn't any larger than my thumbnail right now. I know she's wanted another child for such a long time. After having Freya at such a young age, she'd struggled to conceive again so I'm happy for them all. 'I'm feeling blessed though. We already love little bean, don't we, Freya?'

Freya places the parcel into the box. 'We do. I am so hoping for a little brother. I've been hoping for years so I'm mega excited.' She walks over to her mother and kisses her on the cheek. 'See you in a bit, Mum. Won't be long.'

As soon as we're outside, I break down. Just that tender act of a mother loving the life growing inside her has started me off again.

'Angel.' Freya pulls me towards her and hugs me. 'What is it?'

'She didn't want me. Jean said she wanted me dead. My birth mother hated me.'

She rubs my back and I nearly choke on her hair as I bury my head into her.

'I'm sure she didn't. How do you even know Jean was telling the truth?'

Freya is right. I have no idea. All I know is when I went back to Jean's yesterday, all I felt was a pain and sickness. It seemed to ooze from the fabric of the house. The atmosphere was that of unloved and unwanted. Was the shame so bad that my birth mother wanted me dead? I hesitate. Jean saved me. If it wasn't for Jean, I'd be buried under those daffodils in the back garden. Heart hammering, I have an urge and I know I need to indulge it or I'll explode. Right now, I want to hurt something or someone so badly my fingers ache with tension. There is a bus due and I need to be on it. 'I have to go.' I pull away from Freya.

'Wait. Where are you going?'

I ignore her and run. The less she knows, the better.

FORTY

I went to the house again this evening, and I stared at those daffodils for what seemed like hours. It wasn't hours though; it was more like minutes. I still can't believe I pulled all the flower heads off earlier but the rage within had taken over. The very thought of those flowers chill me to the bone. I also went back to the Joneses' house. I can't keep away since we went there. This is consuming my every thought. After getting an Uber back home, I managed to quickly get changed into the first dress I find and now I wait. The doorbell rings and my mum calls. Closing my bedroom door, I hurry down the stairs. Mum gives me a little hug and waves me off as I climb into the back of Freya's mum's car. The smell of perfume coming from Freya and Charlotte makes me want to gag. Going out to a club is the last thing I fancy tonight but my friends insisted. Again, Charlotte wouldn't take no for an answer.

'Worcester, here we come,' Charlotte shouts.

Freya chats to her mum in the front, and I look out the window until we get there. Loud beats come from the club. The road is narrow and another car waits behind us.

'Hurry up,' Freya's mum says as we unclip our belts and step out.

The buildings are mostly black and white Tudor style, and in between the pubs and clubs, there are closed tea rooms and art shops. I normally love Worcester's nightlife where masses of students fill the bars, but right now, I wish I was back at home in bed, not wading through a cloud of smoke and vape mist.

Before I know it, I've been dragged into a dark room and I can barely hear Charlotte and Freya as I feel the thudding music pound through my feet. An hour has passed. I've had four cocktails on the cheap, taking advantage of the student specials. The several shots I've also drunk makes the blue one I hold in my hand all the more nauseating. Charlotte told me I needed them. They've danced, and I've stared into space for the past couple of hours. A lanky lad asks me if I want to dance. I shake my head.

'Angel?' Charlotte slams the blue drink down her neck in one go.

'What?'

'We're going,' she yells in my ear. Thank goodness for that. I want to go home.

As we walk into the chilly night, I follow my friends. Freya waits by the side of the road and, a few seconds later, an Uber has turned up. I almost fall into the back; my feet unsteady in my heels after drinking a bit too much. 'Can I get dropped off first?'

'Don't be daft, Angel. We're not going home yet. The night is still young.'

'Where are we going?' My head is fuzzy as she explains what we're doing, and I don't like it one bit. 'I don't want to go there. Turn back. Take me home.'

Charlotte turns to face me while Freya sits in the front. 'It'll be fine. I promise. We have to do this.'

I don't want to do whatever 'this' is. I get the gist of her plan and it's wrong. 'It's not the right time.'

Shaking her head, Charlotte takes my hand. 'It's never going to be the right time. We've had a few drinks, a bit of Dutch courage. I'll handle it, okay? All you have to do is say nothing and stand back. It couldn't be any easier. We can do this?'

I hiccup and hold a hand over my mouth, trying to keep the contents of my stomach down as we go over a few speed bumps. 'We can do this,' I say in a whisper, not believing in the words on my tongue.

'Do we have a first name yet?'

I nod. 'Leah.'

* * *

After we pay and get out, the Uber leaves and we're all standing outside my birth mother's house, in the dark. I hear a baby crying in the distance and I want to hold it and take away its distress. With all my heart I hope that little baby is loved and wanted. I go to grab Charlotte as she walks past the cars and rings the bell. Why am I going along with this? I burp and acid rises in my throat, leaving a sour taste at the back of my mouth. Just as the door is opened, I grab my phone and pretend to be scrolling and uninterested as I listen on.

'Leah Jones, was Harrison?' Charlotte says.

'Do I know you?'

I glance over, hoping that my birth mother won't make eye contact and she doesn't. I flick my hair out of my face and pull my short dress down slightly. For some reason I feel exposed, like everyone's looking at me which is silly as no one is. Freya can sense my unease so she places my hand through her arm and huddles close to me. I know she can feel me trembling.

'How could you not know me? I'm your daughter,' Charlotte says. I don't feel comfortable with this lie at all but the other part of me is intrigued as to how this conversation is going to go. 'Can we come in?' Charlotte asks. She goes to step in, but my birth mother stands in her way. Good. I don't want to go in the house. This is all too weird. A few more words are mumbled and I don't catch them until the woman speaks in a loud whisper aimed at us all.

'Can you please keep your voice down? I don't want to wake my husband up. Look, I don't know who told you I'm your mother or what game you're playing, but you need to go now.' I can't hear again as the voices are hushed, but then she raises her whisper again. 'You're both playing a very cruel joke. Did she send you?'

'Who?' Charlotte asks. I wonder if my birth mother means Jean.

'Alison.'

Who the hell is Alison? That took me by surprise.

'Your mother said she was sorry for what she did to you.' Oh hell. I can't believe Charlotte said that. I stare at my phone, not daring to look at them. 'Meet me the day after tomorrow at the Hibiscus Coffee Lounge in Worcester. I'll be there at twelve. Don't use that phone number I gave to your neighbour; it's fake as I didn't want to give my number to some random. Give me your phone. I'll put my real number in it.'

Freya and I continue to huddle. I wonder if my chattering teeth are giving me away as my birth mother glances at me, her brows furrowed as if trying to figure me out. She recognises herself in me, I'm sure of it. Charlotte starts to type her number into my birth mother's phone, but the bedroom light floods the drive and she snatches it back from Charlotte. 'I need that back. Go now. Please.'

I hear a man's voice. It's her husband, my possible father.

'Please, leave,' she yells, followed by more words I don't hear.

We hurry across the road. My heels are killing and I'm

numb to everything except the burning in my throat and the churning of my stomach. As soon as we turn the corner, I throw up the cocktails and shots as Freya holds my wavy hair away from my face.

'We did it,' Charlotte says with a big grin on her face. 'We're meeting her the day after tomorrow.'

I don't feel her joy; in fact I still feel as sick as a dog at the thought of what's to come. I wish I could immerse myself into this investigation of my parentage, or whatever it is we're doing, but I can't. All I could see was fear on my birth mother's face. Finally, her past is coming for her and there's nothing she can do about it. Like me, she's on a journey. Both of us are treading unknown waters and I have yet to tell if one of us will drown because of it. We're about to find out.

FORTY-ONE

My throat is like sandpaper today and all I can do is lie here. At least I'm not dizzy any more. I don't know why I woke up feeling so ill as I threw up most of what I drank last night. My head has this dull thump that gets worse every time I exert myself. Actually, I do know why I feel awful and it's not just the drink. It's the look on my birth mother's face as we stood outside her door last night, the fear of her husband coming down the stairs and finding out her little secret. That leads me to believe he's not my father.

Lying on my mother's childhood bed with the blanket of squares pulled up to my waist, I twiddle the daffodil between my finger and thumb, then I smell it. I tried to go into Jean's room but as soon as I pushed the bedroom door open, I couldn't breathe. It was as if she was trying to kill me but she wasn't. Jean is dead. The dead cannot hurt me. The only person who can hurt me now is Leah Jones. She doesn't want the truth to come out and I wonder what she'll do to save herself.

Tomorrow, we get to meet her again. This time she knows that her daughter is trying to make contact, but she doesn't know I'm her daughter. I lay my finger on her bedside table and wonder what she used to keep on it. Did she have snacks in the drawers just like I do? Did my father used to sneak into her room? I mean, she was only sixteen and I don't think Jean would have allowed a boy in her daughter's bedroom. Were they in love? She wanted to kill me. That sours the notion of her being in love. Maybe it was because my father abandoned her on hearing the news. I shake those horrible thoughts away. No. They met and were in love until their parents drove them apart. They sent him away, and she couldn't contact him. Her heart pined for him and she was so sad, she couldn't bear to be reminded of him, which is why she... I can't say it in my head. I like this story though. It's better than the horrible ones which whir around my head that Jean planted there.

I wonder if my birth mother was lonely living in the sticks on this gloomy street. I can't see anything fun to get involved in around here. She would have lain here, like I am now, wondering if there was more to life. I smell the blanket and it smells musty, not like my baby blanket made out of the same yarns. My mother has hand washed that numerous times over the years, but this one still throws up dust when I shake it.

A breeze rattles the window and I wonder if it's a sign from Jean, telling me I should leave. It's cold in here and once again, I hear pattering coming from the ceiling. The rats scurry above me, and my heart bangs away. A key is turned in the front door lock.

Gasping, I jump up, tidy the blanket and drop the daffodil on the bed while I listen. I catch a reflection in the stained glass. My birth mother is here. I don't know what to do. I'm stuck. Each stair creaks. If I try to leave, she'll hear me. I'm not ready to confront Leah, not alone. I wish I'd brought Charlotte with me. She'd know what to do. I creep across the landing and nudge open the bathroom door as I hear my birth mother opening a filing cabinet. There's a huge cupboard. I open it and there are only a few towels folded up in it. I squeeze my body into the bottom and pull the door closed as I listen to her going about her business.

I don't know how much time has passed but it feels like forever. Slipping my phone out of my pocket, I turn it to silent and clutch it against my chest. A part of me wonders what would happen if she found me. Maybe she still wants her secret to stay a secret. Would she finally get to bury me under the daffodils? I try to swallow but my mouth is dry and all I want to do is cough. She's coming upstairs. I don't know where she is, but she's close. My heart is hammering so loud, it's all I can hear. That's when the yell cuts through the air followed by her running down the stairs and out of the house.

Hurrying out of the cupboard, I head to her old bedroom, wondering why she yelled. Then, I see the daffodil on the bed. She knows someone has been here. I snatch it and take each step carefully, just in case she runs back into the house. I'm safe because her car has just pulled away. I glance through the netting at the study window. Mrs Pearson is standing outside her own front door. There's no way I can go out the front with her there. I run to the French doors, unlock them and leave. After stepping out, I lock the doors from the outside. I have the daffodil and it looks like no one was here. As I fall over the fence onto the horse track, I sit and try to control my racing heart. I'm safe and no one saw me. Clutching the daffodil closely, I make my way around the house and I can see that Mrs Pearson has gone. I throw the flower away and sprint towards the bus stop, where I watch the police pull up. I wasn't expecting that to happen today. I glance back up the road and see that Mrs Pearson has come back out and her gaze meets mine. I am in so much trouble.

FORTY-TWO

I don't know why I'm here but the urge won. There was no way I could get to sleep anyway. The early hours always give me a chill. I know I'm seeing my birth mother later at the Hibiscus Café, but I wanted some time alone to work through my feelings and what better place to do that. I'm sitting on the kerb twiddling another damn daffodil, at the end of Carraway Road, where my birth mother lives, and I can just about make out Leah's bedroom. I saw her closing the curtains earlier. She looked out as if she was expecting someone to be there but she didn't see me, not in my black leggings and black coat with the hood up. I blend into this dark corner. It feels odd, me being here, alone; like I'm a stalker. I'm not. I'm merely lost and, really, I don't know what I'm doing and why. I just want to know more about the woman who's denying ever giving birth to me.

The breeze has picked up and a chill hits my neck. I pull the drawstrings of my hoodie, tightening the material to keep me warm. I'm just grateful there is no rain. Every time a gust whooshes past me, the trees go from the sound of a gently caressing whisper to a terrifying roar. Again, I feel it is Jean telling me to go home as I'm not safe. Branch shadows reach across the road like bony fingers and I feel the urge to run away from them as they try to grab me.

Once again, the baby cries and the dog barks. I find those sounds reassuring. Someone else is awake at this hour and it's not only me.

I freeze as the sound of footsteps get louder. As the breeze retreats, I can tell they're coming from the wooded area opposite. Leah appears at her bedroom window. I run and hide behind someone's hedge, not wanting to get caught loitering. The last thing I need is for the police to come. Crouching, I peer through the gaps and wait for whoever is out there to emerge. A figure in black, wearing a huge baggy coat and a baseball cap, emerges before standing outside Leah's house and staring at her. I feel as though my heart has stopped. Yesterday was scary but this figure terrifies me. My birth mother steps out of view, and the figure remains for a few minutes, then walks off.

I fall from my crouching position as the baby cries again, sending my heart rate through the roof. My boot scratches the pavement, and the figure darts back through the trees not looking back. Someone is watching her and I don't know what I'm meant to do with that knowledge. If I tell her, I have to tell her everything and I can't do that. I remain still for a moment, frozen with fear. That's when I hear the footsteps again, only this time, they're the other side of the hedge. A tear bounces off my nose just as my phone beeps with a TikTok notification. Why didn't I turn my phone onto silent? Just as the stalker is about to find me, their phone rings. The old-fashioned sound and yodelling on the ringtone is fairly quiet but I do manage to hear a few words. I've never heard this song before but it looks like it saved me. The stalker runs fast as they head into the trees. I hold a hand over my banging heart as I get up and sprint as fast as I can.

FORTY-THREE

'Do you girls need picking up later as I'm finishing work early? I can drop you all home.' Freya's mum has pulled up next to the car park by the river. I get out first and wait for Charlotte and Freya as they faff around with their bags and talk to Freya's mum.

'Maybe. I'll call you,' Freya replies.

'Are you three alright? You all seem a bit... I don't know. Like you're up to something.' Freya's mum raises her eyebrows.

Charlotte clears her throat and puts her phone in her bag. 'No, we're just checking out the summer clothes in the shops.'

I'm still shaking after last night. The thought of my birth mother's stalker being so close to me has hit home. She's in danger. I came within an inch of being caught. If the stalker's phone hadn't rang, I'm sure they would have found me. That song and the yodelling keeps going through my head like an earworm burrowing into my brain. I replay it as I watch a group of people canoeing up the River Severn. A man stands on the bank bellowing instructions at them through a megaphone. I looked the song up when I got home. It's called, 'It's Party Time Again,' by a singer called George Van Dusen, and it definitely

sounded like it came out during its original decade in the nine-
teen thirties.

'Angel.'

I flinch as Charlotte grabs my hand. Freya waves her mum
off. 'Bye,' I call out to her, but she doesn't see me. I check my
phone. We're late.

'Come on, we've got to go.' Charlotte runs and we follow
until we reach the Elgar statue.

That's when I see her through the window, sitting behind
the table at the front of the café. There are also a group of
women with babies and a man holding a pen as he watches
people go by. Before I get a chance to say anything, Charlotte
has led us to the window. She knocks and waves. I hold my
pinafore dress down because it keeps rubbing against my tights
and riding up. I look at Charlotte's sensible jeans and jacket
and I think I should have dressed more comfortably. My legs
wobble as we open the café door, the bell ringing as we enter.
Freya has her head buried in her phone as she texts her
boyfriend. Charlotte heads to the counter and orders three cans
of cola. I didn't want a drink, I feel sick, but it looks like I have
no choice. My birth mother's gaze lands on me and she looks
me up and down while furrowing her brows. Does she see
herself in me? Has she clicked that Charlotte is not her
daughter?

I grab a chair from another table and sit with the others.

'I was hoping we'd be able to talk alone,' my birth mother
says.

Charlotte twists a wooden stirrer between her fingers. I
wish she'd stop. I'm finding her, and Freya tapping on her
phone, distracting.

'We're best friends so we look out for each other.' Charlotte
finishes what she was saying, and I nod in agreement. We don't
know this woman and Jean warned me about her.

Charlotte starts to tell her things, things that she's making

up on the spot. 'I grew up in Bromsgrove. We're all from Bromsgrove so we had to get the bus, but it isn't far.'

That's a lie. None of us grew up in Bromsgrove. We live in
and around Droitwich, which is a stone's throw away from
Worcester and not too far from Jean's house. Charlotte is
pretending to be me and doing a terrible job of it.

'Why do you think I'm your mother?' she asks.

I want to yell, *because Jean, my grandmother, told me everything. She told me how you hated me and wanted me dead*, but I
bite my tongue. If I even go to speak my words will come out all
gobbledegook.

'Because you are.' Charlotte starts to tap her feet on the
floor. It's rare I see my brave friend acting nervously.

I pick up a wooden stirrer and accidentally snap it. All three
of them stare at me. I throw it on the table. 'Sorry.'

'How do you know I'm your mother?'

'Nan told me.' Charlotte sits up straight.

'What did she tell you?'

'She sent me a message one day on Facebook. Of course,
there was no picture and I thought it looked like a weirdo
message. But then she sent another. Again, she said she was my
grandmother and that she also knew who my real mother was.
That's when she told me she was dying. It was a shock to me
too. I had no idea I was adopted.'

Well done, Charlotte, I want to say. At least she got most of
that part right.

'Do you still have these messages?'

My heart begins to pound. I didn't keep the messages on my
Facebook in case my mum saw them, but I took screenshots.
They're saved on a memory stick hidden in my room. Charlotte
doesn't know that, though.

Charlotte glances at me and I can see the panic in her face.
Everything is going wrong. 'No, I deleted them.'

Charlotte continues to say she deleted them because her

mother would be really upset if she saw them, and I breathe an inward sigh of relief. *Well covered, Charlotte.* Charlotte goes on. 'I went to her house a few times. I was even there on the day she died.' I place a hand on her shoulder like a friend might do if Charlotte was telling the truth. 'The nurse let me stay with her. Nan was insistent that she died at home, and she found a nurse who would help her to the end. That's when she told me things. She told me where you lived. She only gave me the name of the road, but I knew your surname. I knew I'd be able to find you. She told me to tell you how sorry she was, that she'd been wrong and that she wished she could have spoken to you one more time, but she didn't have your number. I don't know what happened. I don't know why you gave me up—'

'I didn't give you up. I don't have any children.' Leah frowns and I can see that she's confused by what she's saying.

Freya leaves to answer her phone, and I grab mine and begin scrolling. I need something to hide behind or I'm going to run out of this café like a crazy person and I don't want to make a show of myself.

'Nan wasn't delirious,' Charlotte continues. 'We played cards and she told jokes. We watched films together; she said her favourite was *The Wizard of Oz*; it reminded her of you when you were little. She said you used to watch it together.'

The lump in my throat gets bigger. I actually enjoyed watching that film with Jean, and I imagined what it would have been like to watch it with my birth mother. We sit in uncomfortable silence and I can see that Leah is rooting around for something in her bag.

'I don't know how to ask you this?'

'It's okay, you can ask me anything.' Charlotte tightens her ponytail and sits back. I just want this to be over. I give her a little kick under the table in the hope that she gets the hint that we should leave.

'I think it would be good for both of us if we did this test. It will tell me if I am your mother, for definite.'

No, no, no, this can't be happening. We're busted. I kick Charlotte again. We have to go, now.

'I thought you said you didn't have a child.' Charlotte folds her arms.

My birth mother's eyes begin to water. 'I had a baby once but my baby was born dead. I held my lifeless little girl in my arms. Her name was Sophie.' I'm not sure if she's about to cry. 'All you have to do is brush your cheek with the stick. I'll send it off and very soon, we get the results. We'll both know for sure.' She wipes a meandering tear from her cheek with the back of her hand.

Dead, she thinks I'm dead. My head is spinning and all I hear is my own voice in my head. She's just confirmed what I know. All those tears are a show. She thinks that Jean took care of her little problem and I'm buried under the daffodils. Jean was telling the truth.

Charlotte takes the swab. I want to reach out and bat it out of her hand but I can't move. She rubs the stick on her cheek and hands it back.

'I've got to go.' Charlotte stands and grabs me. 'I have proof by the way. I'll bring it next time, to show you.'

The bell rings as Freya comes back in.

'I should take your number,' Leah calls out.

'I've got to go. I'll come to Nan's tomorrow lunchtime with the proof,' Charlotte says as we all leave. We stand outside.

I grab her, my tense hands pinching her arms. 'Why did you do that? We should have just come clean.'

Charlotte shrugs. 'Well, why didn't you? You could have said that you were her daughter at any time. I didn't know what to say and she just handed me that stick. I had no choice.'

'You always have a choice,' I yell. I glance back and see that my birth mother is checking us out, so I walk away and call the other two over, where we stay out of sight behind a wall. Freya pops a stick of gum in her mouth, watching as we continue to bicker. Freya could at least stick up for me, as we're related.

'Well,' Charlotte continues, 'I guess we have another chance to put things right tomorrow.'

She walks off and heads towards New Look. I clam up and struggle to think of what to say to her. Charlotte walks away when things get tough. That's how we've always been. Freya is the silent observer. She stands there chewing gum, passing no judgement and not being any help at all. I frown as I catch sight of Freya's mum coming out of a pub while chatting to a man. Great, that's all we need. She says bye to the back of whoever she's talking to before feeding her shopping bag over her arm. That's when she spots us and hurries over.

'Mum,' Freya says.

Freya's mum smiles. 'I decided to grab a couple of things and have a snack. Gosh the cravings are bad at the moment and, right now, it's scampi fries. I knew I'd manage to buy them in a pub.' She frowns. 'Are you all okay?'

I know we don't look okay. We look far from okay. My eyes are watery, and Charlotte's neck has gone blotchy. It does that when she gets het up, and Freya looks on awkwardly as she chews the life out of her gum. 'We're fine,' I reply.

That's when I crane my neck to see around the wall. My birth mother in the distance, leaving the café. I watch her as she passes the Edward Elgar statue and glances back, not seeing me.

Freya's mum leans across and follows my sight line. 'Who's that?'

'No one. I have to go.'

I leave them all standing. I don't need Freya's mum interfering and telling my mum anything, but I know the time will come when I'm going to have to have it out with my parents. I can't keep this to myself much longer.

My walk turns into a jog, then into a run. I hear Charlotte

calling me but I'm not going back. I need to be alone to decide what I'm going to do next. Leah's words ring through my head. She held her dead baby in her arms. Did she think I was still-born? If so, why did Jean lie to me? And who was watching my birth mother last night? The look on her face when she said her baby was dead seemed genuine and she seemed upset. Maybe I have it all wrong and she did want me.

That tune warps in my head and I feel dizzy as the chorus and yodelling keep playing. No, she wanted me dead. That's what Jean said. I picture my birth mother smothering me to the sound of that tune, and I sob my heart out. People stare but I don't care one bit. I don't know who to trust. All I know is that I need to be at Leah's house again tonight. I just need to hide better. If the stalker comes back, I will find out who they are and just maybe they will lead me to the truth. My phone beeps and a text from a withheld number flashes up.

Your only way out of this is to say nothing. Stop digging. I say this as someone who cares. Go back to your life. If you don't, there will be consequences. Say a word to anyone, you and your parents will get hurt and it will all be your fault!

FORTY-FOUR

I feel silly heading to Leah's house again, especially as I went home in the early hours scared out of my mind. Truth is, I can't stay away from her because I need to find out more. My mother also noticed me missing in the night, and I had to lie and tell her I was out with Charlotte. She can sense that I'm hiding things from her, and I feel so bad.

After walking through the wooded area, I reach the road. I know I'm going to have to waste money I don't really have on an Uber home later. The front of my birth mother's house is in darkness, and I wonder if I should get a little closer and take a look. I glance at the neighbour's bungalow and she is nowhere to be seen either; and her curtains are closed. It's been a dismal evening, which is good for me as it's darker than normal, although it's cold. I do the top button of my puffer coat up in the hope I'll stay warm. Only one car sits on the drive and it's Leah's. Cain must be out. Once again, I listen to the baby's cries coming from the house opposite. No one is looking at me so I make a mad dash along the side of the house and test the gate. It's locked. I stand on tiptoes and reach over, sliding the lock across. It's open now. What the hell am I doing? I could get into so much trouble by being here, but then again, I guess I've been taking so many risks lately. As I creep alongside the wall in the hope that there are no security lights, my legs begin to tremble. What if her stalker comes back later? I have thought about this and I know where I'm going to hide in a while. There is a huge double garage a little further down. I'm going to hide beside it.

As I near the front of the house, I peer through the edge of the bifold doors. The kitchen shines and it's much bigger than ours, and Leah is standing by the island. Several minutes pass. She keeps looking at her phone. I withdraw into a dark part of the garden. My heart begins to bang as I see a border of daffodils and I wonder if she planted them as a reminder of me. I snatch one up and my first instinct is to crush it in my hands, but I don't. Instead, I gently hold the stem between my fingers, protecting it like my life depends on it. I hold it to my chest and try to hold back the emotion that's building.

I glance up at my birth mother. Her eyes are red rimmed and she's rubbing them. I flinch as she grabs a ramekin and throws it. Brown splodges begin to slide down the white wall, leaving a trail as they slip down the skirting board and onto the floor. I wonder if she has told him, the man I don't think is my father now. Maybe that's why she's upset. She snatches two puddings off the side and hurries out of the kitchen, turning the lights off as she leaves. I think she's going out. I run back towards the gate and listen for her car to start up, but all I hear are her footsteps as she heads to the neighbour's bungalow.

* * *

I'm hiding beside that double garage, concealed by a bramble bush. I've done nothing but stare at the bungalow, wondering when she's going to come out. Every time I hear a noise, I think it's her stalker but, so far, they haven't come. Maybe it was a one off and the stalker won't be back. I hope so. It's all getting a bit scary real now, especially as I had that message. Am I risking my parents by being here? I did wonder, which is why I didn't even tell Charlotte or Freya that I was coming again.

After what feels like an eternity, I gasp as Leah opens the neighbour's door. She says her goodbyes and heads back into her own house. I check my phone and see that no one has messaged me tonight. After our little argument earlier, I think Charlotte is having a bit of time out from me. As for Mum, I think she realises that she needs to give me some space. I did message Charlotte to say I would go to Nan's house tomorrow, but she never replied. I still think she was stupid to take that maternity test. I glance back at Leah's house. Nothing has happened for ages. I'm wasting my time here. The best thing I can do is go home and get some sleep. I go to step out from my hiding place, but the sound of a boot clunking on the pavement stops me. A figure emerges from the trees, and my heart feels as though it's in my mouth. I was right, the stalker is back.

Heart pounding, I step back and sit on the ground, peering through the gaps in the brambles. The figure stands and stares. My birth mother's bedroom light comes on and she appears at the window. Her gaze meets that of the stalker. She opens her window.

'Who are you? What do you want?'

I've never heard someone shout so loud. She roars and bangs her hands on the window ledge, forcing the stalker to run back between the trees. I bow my head as someone opens a window behind me and loud baby cries fill the night air. It's the mother of the baby, she's telling Leah to shut up. Both women slam their windows closed and they draw their curtains. I place a hand over my pounding heart, willing it to calm down. I'm dizzy so I use the garage wall to steady myself. I have to go.

As I run past her house, I drop the daffodil and I don't stop until I reach the bus stop, where I sit on the plastic seat and call an Uber.

* * *

Half an hour later, I'm home and the kitchen light shines through the hall. No one is usually up at this time. Mum is normally in bed at ten, and Dad is usually earlier as he has to be up with the birds. I turn my key in the lock and step in.

'Angel.'

I head through to the kitchen and my mother is sitting at the table, holding the photo I found in my dad's study. The photo of the baby in the incubator who I am certain is not me.

'I found this in your bed drawer.'

I'm livid. Not only does she check my phone, but she is also now going through my things. I have zero privacy in this house.

'Where did you find it?'

'I, err...'

Again, I'm speechless. To tell her would mean talking about Jean and about my investigations into my birth mother and I'm not ready. How do I tell my mother that someone is threatening us because of what I'm doing?

'It was on the floor, by Dad's office.'

A tear falls down my mother's cheek. I know she's been snooping but I love her so much, more than anything. Sitting next to her, I rest my head on her shoulder.

'I had a baby before you.'

I look at the infant in the photo and now it makes sense. This isn't me.

'She was born too early, and she died. Your father and I miss her so much. I'm sorry we never told you but it's still too painful.' She shifts slightly and looks me in the eyes before placing a hand on my cheek. 'You were our little miracle.' Tears now stream down her face, and I feel awful for the things I've been doing.

'I love you, Mum.' I wipe my own eyes.

We sit there for several minutes, her hugging me and crying

and me stroking her hair. I can't imagine what she's been through.

A crash makes me jump away from Mum, and she yelps. We run to the lounge and see a brick sitting amongst glass on the living room floor.

You and your parents will get hurt.

The words in that text are a reminder of the threat, and the brick tells me that the sender isn't bluffing. They're coming for us and I don't know what to do.

It will all be your fault.

I can't breathe as I stare out of the window, looking for the stalker. It has to be them.

FORTY-FIVE

'Charlotte, someone put a brick through our window last night and you saw that message on my phone. It's too dangerous. We shouldn't be here.' I couldn't help but tell Charlotte everything. I told her about the stalker, about the message and that my mother had told me she'd lost a baby before they had me. 'Maybe we've got this all wrong. I think Jean messed up.'

'We've come too far to let this go, Angel. We have a couple of days before that test result comes through, so stop worrying. That brick was probably kids.'

I shake my head. 'How convenient. It wasn't kids. It was the stalker.' I glance around the quiet road that Jean used to live on, and there is no one loitering and there isn't a car out of place. 'And where the hell is Freya? She said she'd be here.'

'She had to work.'

Charlotte walks ahead at speed. I have to run to keep up with her. As we reach Larrison House, I go to grab her, but miss and before I know it, she's already knocked on the door.

'Give me that.' She snatches my bag and pulls the blanket from it. As if a blanket of squares is really absolute proof of who my birth mother is. The more I think about what we're doing or what we've done, the more ridiculous it sounds.

As soon as my *so-called, probably even not, who the hell knows*, birth mother answers, I shut up, struck speechless. She stares at the blanket in Charlotte's hand and tears begin to slide down her cheeks.

'I'm so sorry I doubted you.' She reaches inside a box in her hand and shows us a photo of a baby wrapped in my blanket. It's me. 'I don't know what happened. I'd never have let you go, ever. I thought you'd died.' Leah reaches out and touches Charlotte's cheek, and I hate myself for our lie but I can't speak. I go to say something and a croak comes out. We follow her into the kitchen and sit at the kitchen table.

'Have you got the results back?'

I nudge Charlotte. I may not be able to get my words out but my hands work fine. They talk about our visits to Jean before she died, but all I can do is think about the woman in front of me. I try to take in her eyes and nose as I envisage my own.

'You used to come too?'

I flinch as Charlotte kicks me. I missed what was said so I just nod. Charlotte mouths the word Jean and I click. 'We, err... took it in turns so she wasn't alone all the time. By we, I mean me and Charlotte. Freya didn't come. She spends most of her time with her boyfriend.' Saying that was easy. I go to interrupt and tell my birth mother the truth, but she cuts me off with a question.

'How old are you both?'

I missed my moment – again. Leah and Charlotte continue talking but their words aren't sinking in over my loud thoughts.

She wipes her nose. 'When I held you in my arms you weren't breathing. My mother, Jean, took you from me and that was it. I never saw you again.'

'Where did you think I went?'

'I thought you were dead.' My birth mother stares with her mouth open at the messed up daffodil patch. She definitely thought I was buried. I never got a proper funeral. I chide myself for thinking that. I never got a funeral because I'm alive. 'I spent the first week in my mother's bed battling an infection. I don't remember much. All I remember is weird dreams, and being so hot I thought I was going to die. When I was awake, I couldn't stop shaking. I remember my mother trying to force me to swallow tablets, and...'

'How old were you?' Charlotte asks.

'Sixteen. I was younger than you...' Again, her gaze wanders back to the daffodils, and I wonder how much the stalker knows. 'I'd planned to run away with you in the hope that social services or the council would help... I should have left earlier. Why did I listen to her?'

Right now, I'm thinking the worst. Who wouldn't want the truth to come out? The only people I can think of is my own parents. I force that thought away. There's no way my own mother would send me that threatening message. My dad isn't a stalker, and he wouldn't put a brick through our window. One thing gets to me, though: why didn't Mum call the police last night?

'Nan didn't tell me who my dad was.' From the look on my birth mother's face, I can tell that Charlotte has hit a nerve.

'I can't talk about that.'

'But I need to know.'

Leah stares at Charlotte. 'Why? You have a family who love you. I'd love to get to know you and, in my heart, I've always loved that little baby I held in my arms. As for the man who fathered you, please don't make me go there.' Her phone beeps and I'm glad. I need to get out of here. I'm hot, my chest is prickling and all I want to do is unzip my coat and scratch.

'You have to leave. I'm really sorry to rush you. Don't forget this.' My birth mother throws the baby blanket at Charlotte like it's nothing.

'Angel?'

My hands are trembling. Is she about to ask me outright if it's me who is her daughter?

'What were you doing at the Business Centre on Blake Road the other day?'

'I, err, I was meeting Freya in her lunch break and I got lost. She works close by. Were you there?'

She nods. 'I popped by to see my husband. He was out but I thought it was you.'

I'm relieved that Charlotte grabs me.

'We best hurry. The bus is due any minute, otherwise we'll have to wait an hour for the next one. Text me so I have your number.'

The last thing I want to do is explain to her that she's my mother and I thought that Cain Jones was my father.

As we scarper to the bus stop, Cain drives around the corner. He steps out of his car and stares at us. I see them exchanging a few words and I really want to know what they're saying. Charlotte nudges me.

'What were you doing there?'

'Like I said, I was meeting Freya.'

'So, you stopped off on Blake Road. You'd have to go out your way.'

'We knew where he worked. I was checking him out. I just wanted to see him. Not see him, see him. Just get a closer look. I thought he might be my biological father.'

'And now you don't?'

I shake my head. 'Not after the night we went to the house and she didn't want him to know we were there.' I shrug. 'I don't know anything any more.'

* * *

The bus pulls up. We pay the driver and sit at the back. 'Your mother's story is really sad. She wanted you but you were taken from her. She thought you were dead.'

'Did you see the way she was looking out of the window at the daffodils? All these years she thought I was buried under them and she never said anything.'

'She was scared,' Charlotte replies as the bus hits a pothole. My friend begins to take her make-up bag out and she fishes for her compact. She grabs some concealer and begins to rub a smudge on a spot. Charlotte's phone beeps. She glances at it on the bus seat. 'It's her. We have her number.'

'Forward it to me.'

Charlotte picks her phone up and pings the number across to me. Leah wasn't scared. Charlotte is wrong. I shake my head. She was happily living her life, thinking I was dead and then Jean messaged me, which has inconvenienced her life. I run to the front of the bus.

'Open the doors.'

'You have to wait for the next stop.'

Charlotte is gathering her things up, ready to follow me, but she drops her make-up bag and everything spills out.

I know what will make him pull over. 'I'm going to throw up.'

The driver stops immediately, and I get out and run. Just as Charlotte reaches the doors, the bus pulls off. There is something I have to do and it can't wait. I need to confront her. It takes me an age to run back to Larrison House, but she's not there. I call an Uber. This can't wait.

FORTY-SIX

I can't stop thinking about how Leah felt when I was first born. Leah holding me in her arms, thinking I'm dead or wishing I was dead. Which is it? Me being buried forever would have been the answer to all her problems. I knock on Leah's front door but there is no answer. I glance up and down Carraway Road, wondering if her stalker is watching and then wondering if the stalker is my dad, doing all he can to protect his family. It makes sense. My parents have been looking through my stuff. Although the memory stick was where I left it, in the pocket of a jacket I haven't worn in months, I think they've found it, read what's on it and put it back. They're acting strange all the time. I know Mum found the photo of the baby in the incubator, which means she would have seen the photo of my birth mother with Santa. I am so confused it hurts.

It's no use me standing here at the door getting nowhere while my thoughts run wild. I hurry to the side gate again and slide the lock. I'm sick of everything, yet I still know nothing. I'm sick of Charlotte and her silly ideas. She's created nothing but chaos. I check my phone. She's tried to call me a million times and left so many messages, I wouldn't know where to start listening and reading. My phone lights up again so I turn it off. As I reach the garden, I see those yellow flowers, their heads all pointing my way as if they're mocking me, and I can't stand them. I kick one and snatch another. My stubby fingers squeeze the stem, releasing sap onto my hand which I wipe on my coat. I run to the bifold doors and press my nose on the glass so I can see inside and I can clearly see that there's no one in. I wrench the door handle in a temper and it slides open. Standing in front of it, lips parted, I wonder if I should go in and check her house out. Maybe this is where the truth lies. Then I remind myself that she's been lying to her husband all these years too. Leah doesn't know the meaning of the word truth.

I step in, my footsteps echoing in the tidy kitchen. 'Hello,' I call out. Stupid maybe, but I've done it now. My throat is dry and I think about pouring a glass of water, so I open a cupboard. I go to take a glass but change my mind. My hands are trembling which means I'd probably drop it. I've never broken into a house before. Jean's house doesn't count, as I have keys to get in. The kitchen table seats eight people, not like our tiny table that is always pushed against the back of the kitchen wall. We tend to eat dinner on our laps while watching TV since my dad started using it as an overflow office.

I brush the daffodil against the wall as I head into the wide lounge. They have a television that looks like a cinema it's that big. Actually, they have everything we don't. I nudge the door to the downstairs loo open. A citrus smell hits my nostrils and I sneeze. This place is unbelievably clean. Taking the stairs, one by one, I soon reach the top. There are four doors and only one is closed. I can see a room containing a single bed at the far end, and there is a bathroom ahead of me. The other room contains a computer and a desk. I press the handle to open the closed door and see a king-sized bed. It looks like one of the display beds in expensive department stores, all colour matching cushions and layering throws. I creep in and stare out of the window at the end of the drive. That's where the stalker has been standing. I step back and lie on the bed, and I can't control the emotion building up inside me so I let out a cry and then that cry turns to a huge wet sob. She's not here. I rip the petals from the flower and drop the whole lot on the floor before running back the way I came, sliding the lock on the gate behind me.

I turn my phone on and ignore Charlotte again. I see that Freya has tried to call me too. Instead of replying or putting them out of their misery, I hurry to the bus stop and sit there weeping into my hands, not knowing what to do next. After Jean's death, my life was hell. I was lost and I thought Charlotte was right when she said I had to find out the truth. She was wrong. I should never have done any of this. Once again, I find myself wishing that I'd never heard from Jean Harrison. I know I'm spiralling into something I can't control and it petrifies me. The dark veil has descended and I don't know how to remove it. I grab my phone and punch in the nastiest words I've ever typed and I ping them to my birth mother.

There's nothing like the smell of fresh flowers but they're easily trampled on and some die. Some deserve to die. How can you not see what's right under your nose?

I can't help myself, it's as if someone else is controlling my fingers; and the GIF of the dying weed was too much, I know it was, but I can't take it back now. Although, if she can't see me, she needs to open her eyes. I hurry onto the bus and know I'll be home soon.

My phone beeps. It's a withheld number.

You were warned. You leave me with no choice little Angel. The devil is coming for you. X

It's the stalker, it has to be. Heart pounding, as soon as I get off the bus, I run all the way home. What have I done?

When I turn the last corner, I see that the bonnet of my dad's car is caved in. My parents have been in an accident, and the person who messaged me has hurt them. I open the front door and call out. 'Mum. Dad.' There is no answer. I phone them but all I get are their voicemails. The kitchen is a mess. I stiffen as I see my memory stick on the table. They know everything now and they've been hurt. I run out of the house scared for myself. The last place I want to be is here and given that I think my parents are involved in all this, and not in a good way, I can't call the police. I turn off my phone and pull the SIM card and battery out. I'm sure I can't be traced now. There is only one place I can think of that I'll feel safe at and I must go there, but there's something I need to do first.

FORTY-SEVEN

I know Charlotte and Freya will be looking for me and I hope they haven't gone to my house. It's dark and late so they probably haven't. A part of me wonders if they are in danger too. After all, someone calling themselves the devil wants to shut me up. How far will they go to make sure I don't find out who they are, and what have they done with my parents? My hand brushes my SIM and battery. If they try to contact me, I won't know. I have no choice but to reassemble my phone. My phone lights up with message after message, but no more have come from the stalker and there aren't any messages from my parents, which is why I'm back at Leah's house. It's the only way I can find out who's behind all this. Being behind the garages is too far away. I tuck myself in behind Cain Jones's car and I sit in silence, my bottom numb from not moving and my bones are stiff from the cold that has crept in since midnight passed. They went to bed a while back and nothing. Maybe the stalker isn't coming tonight.

The wind whistles and a cat meows in the distance, then I hear a light tapping of feet on pavement. I've seen people passing with dogs, and the woman next door rode past on her scooter not long ago. A drunken couple came back from the pub and stopped to grope each other, and the woman across the road with the crying baby came out and hugged a woman before they went in the house. I've seen everyone tonight except the stalker. The tapping of feet gets louder, and I stiffen as I tuck myself in between Cain's car and the fence. The person stops at the end of the drive. I gently lean forward and crouch so that I can see the feet under the car. Two heavy black boots face the bedroom window. The stalker has arrived. I shake as the wearer of the boots walks down the path. Their breaths come rapidly. I need to come out from behind this car and confront them, ask them what they've done with my parents, but all I want to do is cry. I close my eyes, hoping they don't hear or spot me. As they get nearer someone is battling to unlock the front door, and the stalker turns to run.

It's now or never. I scuttle on my knees to the end of the car and peer up. Gasping, I can't believe who I'm looking at, and, not only that, but I can't tell whether they're looking at me. All this time, someone I know and trust with my life has been stalking Leah. Why? It's too late for me to ask that question, as they've already run towards the trees and Cain Jones has opened the door. I fall flat onto the gravelly drive and hold my breath. He paces up and down before halting at the other side of the car. My lungs feel as though they may burst, then he turns to the other car. Leaning up, I catch sight of him in one of the mirrors and my heart pounds. This is the best glimpse I've had of him. Only the other day, I saw him and not only that, but I saw him with the stalker.

The woman on the scooter is coming back.

'I want you to leave me alone. Mess with me again and you'll wish you were never born, Zara.'

'Never. I'm watching you all the time.'

'You're just jealous because your life is so shit. You just

want to ruin things for everyone else,' he spits. 'I could just tell Leah. Now that would be hilarious.'

There is a pregnant pause and the woman starts up her scooter and shuts herself into her house. I remain silent, still in shock at who I've seen tonight.

Leah calls him from inside the house and, just as he steps into the hallway, I stand and run as fast as I can. I don't look back, and I run in the opposite direction to the stalker.

My phone buzzes in my pocket. It's Freya. I end the call. Charlotte calls and I end that too. I can't trust anyone right now, so I turn my phone off.

A short while and an Uber ride later, I'm walking along the horse track at the back of Larrison House, terrified by the shuffling foxes and hooting owls. Before climbing over, I peer into the garden to make sure no one is there. I have nowhere else to go. Nowhere is safe and everyone is lying to me. Satisfied that I'm alone, I pull myself over the fence and fall into the back of the garden before letting myself into Jean's kitchen. Leaving the lights off, I hurry upstairs, go into Leah's childhood bedroom. Running to the window, I peer out to see if there's anyone there but I can't see a soul. I push the bookcase in front of the door and get into her bed and lie there, not sleeping a wink. All night I listen and wonder if the stalker saw me.

The devil is coming for you. All I can think of is that message. Now I know who the devil is, everything is harder. A deep sob comes from within. The house is enveloping me in its pain and that yodelling ringtone fills my head. Shadows dance on the wall as the trees shake in the breeze. I pull the blanket over my head fearing that if I keep looking, Jean's ghost will appear, bringing with her the smell of death that I've tried so hard to forget. The rats shuffle in the loft. Is it rats? As hard as I try not to go there, my mind is conjuring up the sound of Leah's pained cries as I came into the world, lifeless. Am I real? Is all this real?

The pillow is soon soaked with my tears, but I can't stop weeping. All I can do is lie here and hide, then I don't know if I can leave. I hope Leah will come soon. After seeing the stalker with my own eyes, Leah is the only person I can trust and I never thought I'd say that.

FORTY-EIGHT

I nibble on another biscuit from the pack I found in the kitchen cupboard. I've waited all day with my phone off in the hope that Leah comes. I'm too scared to leave this house and if I call the police, my parents will be in big trouble. The bookcase is back in its place and darkness is about to fall again. Last night was tough. I didn't sleep at all. My phone is still off and I wonder what's happening in the outside world. Every time I look through the windows, I wonder if I'll be faced with the stalker. How long will it be until they guess I'm here? A part of me thinks I'm being paranoid, thinking the stalker can trace my phone, so I turn it on. I ignore all the missed calls and open the message from the withheld number.

Hello little Angel. You can't hide forever. Come out, come out, wherever you are.

I run back into the bedroom. This isn't happening. It's not real. Another message pings. It's my dad.

Angel. Where are you? I can pick you up. Mum's worried. X

Considering I've been gone all night and something was clearly wrong when I went back to the house, I'm surprised he didn't call. Then again, I get the feeling this message wasn't sent by my dad. My dad hasn't called me Angel, ever. It doesn't matter who's around or where we are, it's Stubby Fingers, Stubby or Stubs. The messenger isn't my dad. I reply.

What happened to the car? How's Mum?

A reply comes back instantly. This is also proof. My dad rarely replies to texts, preferring to call. He's old school like that. He can't be bothered with messaging.

We're fine, it was just a little bump. We're worried about you because you didn't call or come home last night.

I send another message.

You're not my dad.

A reply comes back.

You can end it all, Angel. Just come home now. Come home or people will get hurt.

I have to help Dad but not by going home. He's not there and, if I go home, I know I'll be in danger. Think, Angel, think.

What do I know? I know who's stalking my birth mother. I'm pretty certain Cain isn't my father. It may be more of a feeling, but I believe that Leah didn't know I wasn't buried in the garden, which makes Jean a liar. Did Jean lie about everything? The stalker has a connection to me but what is it? My parents' car is damaged, and they've seen the screenshots of my Facebook messages with Jean. My dad isn't messaging me. The stalker has my dad's phone. Where is my mum?

I imagine my mum holding me, telling me how much she loves me. They may not be my biological parents but they're everything to me and I've let them down. Maybe I do need to go home and face whatever is waiting for me. It's the only way I can help them.

As I walk down the stairs past the stained-glass window, my legs almost buckle. I can't breathe. Gasping for air, I hurry to the back doors and open them. Fresh air doesn't help. In fact, it's making everything worse. The world is swaying and I topple over. It's as if the outdoors are crushing me and this little voice in my head screams for me to go back into the house and get back into the bed, where I'm safe.

I stumble back inside and back up the stairs, where I hide in the bed from the world. If I go home, the stalker might kill me. I need to think about this, to fathom out my next move.

Day turns into night and, once again, the rats scurry above me and I hear my birth mother's screams echoing through the house, and I know I'm destined to be here. I can't leave. The house wants me to stay, at least that's what I'm telling myself. I'm safe here.

With chattering teeth, I pull the blanket over me and find myself drifting.

I wake with a start and rub the sleep from my eyes. Voices come from downstairs but I can't make out who's speaking. The voices are coming from the study. I didn't hear anyone come in. I must have slept like a log. My heart slams against my ribcage. What if they catch me here? I wonder if it's Mrs Pearson and the person who lives with her, or maybe it's Leah. If it is I need to speak to her. But if it is, she's not alone. Is the stalker with her? I wonder if Leah already knows and trusts the stalker; after all I've seen the stalker with Leah's husband, Cain.

I flinch as I hear the French doors flinging open beneath me. Creeping to the window, I peer out of the side in the hope I won't be spotted. I still don't know who else is downstairs. My birth mother is scooping earth out of the ground. What's left of the daffodils has been torn up and flung everywhere. Tears slip down my cheeks. She must have found out that Charlotte is not her daughter and now she's looking for the truth. Like me, she doesn't know who she can trust. I choke on my sobs as I see the pain in her every move. What have I done to her with my lies? It's time for me to be brave and face my fears. Despite who's downstairs, I need to go to her and trust that we can both work out what to do next. She can help me find out what's happened to my parents and I can tell her what I know about her husband. Just as I go to turn, a figure creeps into view and they hit Leah over the head with Jean's stone owl. She topples and, right now, my heart feels as though it's pushing its way up my gullet. I stumble back and once again I can't breathe as anxiety twists my guts. I gasp, I choke on my sobs and my body shakes. Pressing myself into the floor, I sit and hug myself as I cry into my legs. If I don't do something, she will die.

That's when I hear someone stepping into the hallway and a massive thump renders me silent and holding my breath. I activate my phone. I might be making the biggest mistake of my life here but I'm calling the police and an ambulance. She needs me and I won't let her down. I don't know who to trust but I don't want her to die. My phone won't come on. I haven't charged it. I didn't even bring my charger. It's game over.

PART 3

FORTY-NINE

LEAH

'Wakey, wakey.' Leah jolts up as a splash of cold water hits her face. Ouch, her head, it's as sore as hell. She wipes the wet trail running down her face and she holds up her damp hands. The crimson smear and dirt in her nails come into view, that's until her vision blurs again. The text that Cain sent enters her thoughts. *You can't trust Zara.* Her teeth begin to chatter. She loves Zara with all her heart. They are best friends.

The enormity of her situation causes her to gasp as she stares at the hole in the ground. She held one of Sophie's little bones, then someone hit her over the head. She wants nothing more than to lie on the grass and break down but she thinks of Zara. Cain is lying. Zara would never jeopardise their friendship. All he wants is for Leah to go home so that he can have a go at her. Her heart pounds as she glances towards the path that leads down the side passage, but it's pitch black and she can't make anything out. Whoever hit her must have gone for her best friend. She reaches in her pocket for her phone but it's not there.

She needs to hurry before her attacker comes back and sees that she's conscious. Zara – she left her friend in the study. As she tries to stand, the outline of a figure walks from the dark corner of the garden. Slow steps tread down the dewy grass. It's too late to run. She has to stand and fight her attacker. Once on her feet, she sways as a sharp pain flashes through her temples and her vision blurs. Over the stranger's footprints an owl is hooting. 'Zara,' she calls, in the hope that her friend will hear and try to hide.

'It's too late, Leah. It's over. You are over. I will not let you destroy my life with your lies.' The stranger is no longer a stranger. She knows that voice. She scrunches her eyes to get a better look at her attacker, but it's no good, it's like she's opening them underwater. As her attacker comes closer, she brings her arms up to guard her middle and chest. It's her against one other person. She can do this. Leah staggers towards the dark clothed person and stops just before she walks into what looks like the tip of the knife.

Without a thought for her safety, she blocks the arm of her attacker and goes to push the woman over. Then she goes in with a punch but it's no good. The attacker brings up the knife and slices at her. Blood gushes down her forearm. Mouth open, Leah stares, knowing if she gets slashed again, she might die.

'Don't make this harder for yourself.'

Another jabbing pain flashes through her head. That's when the stone owl on the grass comes into view. Her attacker must have hit her with it. She sways but just about manages to hold on to her footing. She raises her arm above her head, knowing that's what a person is meant to do when bleeding, but she doubts it's going to help much given the depth of the gash.

'Why are you doing this to me?' Leah recoils as she inhales the woman's rose scent. All this time, Lady Rose or Rosie was out to kill her.

'Like I said, I won't let you destroy my life.'

Rosie's phone rings in her pocket, and Leah instantly recognises the yodelling tune, and she now knows Rosie's her stalker too. 'I don't want to destroy your life. Let me go and we never need to speak of this again. I need a hospital.' If she survives this ordeal, there is no way Leah will drop everything, not now, and she suspects Rosie isn't stupid enough to think she will.

Rosie walks behind Leah and points the tip of the knife into her back. 'Move.' The woman's quivering hands tell her Rosie is nervous about what she's doing.

Leah is nudged along the side path and out of the garden gate, across the road towards Mrs Pearson's open door. Now she knows who was in Mrs Pearson's house the other day. She couldn't quite see then but now she sees clearly. Rosie and Derren came to her house, they injected themselves into her life through Cain, played with her mind and now they're going to kill her. Why? Because Charlotte came knocking at her door and pretended to be her daughter? Leah's life had been nothing but uneventful for years until Charlotte knocked. It has to be because of that. But Charlotte doesn't share her DNA. The email she opened only a few hours ago told her.

Leah wonders if Derren is in his mother's house, waiting for Rosie to deliver her to him. She now understands Jean's note, the one she found in the pen. Leah thought she was referring to the girls when she wrote: 'I don't trust them'. Really, she meant Rosie, Derren and Mrs Pearson. Her mother knew and she was trying to warn Leah. For once she did the right thing, even though it wasn't clear for Leah to see. She guessed her mother had been close to dying when she wrote it.

'Help me,' Leah attempts to yell, but she knows there is no one close enough to hear her feeble cries. They're at the edge of the village but that doesn't stop Leah hoping. Maybe someone is out walking a dog. She hopes for a car to pass through, maybe dropping someone off after a really late night out. 'Help,' she yells again.

'Shout again and you die now, understand?' The knife pierces the skin on Leah's back. Rosie has already sliced Leah's arm so she knows the woman will hurt her without a second thought. She goes to speak but stops. She has a lot to say but whether it's wise to say it all is another matter. How does she reason with the woman who's holding a knife to her back?

As Rosie nudges Leah over the threshold of the Pearsons' house, Leah's throat starts to close. She's back where it all began and the fear of that night hits her with another blinding head pain. She can smell the crackling fire, and her heart beats like it's about to fly out of her mouth. Her legs are leaden. She passes through the hallway, glancing up the stairs, and then stands by the door to the snug, right where Harry Pearson watched his son rape her all those years ago. Pleading with her eyes, Leah had begged him to help her but he ignored her, allowing Derren to finish assaulting her before throwing her out like she was trash. She can't breathe. No way can she enter that room with its nightmare shadows that dance on the walls.

'I can't go in there. Please, anywhere but there.'

'Okay, okay. This is where the lie began but I guess you don't want to be reminded of that. Go in, your friend is waiting for you.'

Sobs spill from Leah's mouth. Poor, lovely Zara. How could anyone hurt her? There was no way she'd let Cain try to tell her that she couldn't trust Zara. She trusts her more than anyone. Cain is the liar.

Zara is slumped in the far corner, wedged between a sofa and a chair, her limbs seemingly entangled in her sticks. She's still and Leah can't even tell if she's breathing.

'Zara, please talk to me, Zara.'

Her friend doesn't respond. Leah pushes back, resisting entering the room, but the knife jabbing her back tells her she has no choice, plus she needs to help Zara. That's if she can help herself. She's not sure she can. Blood still drips down her arm and onto the blue rug. As soon as she sees that rug, her body stiffens, just like it had on that night all those years ago.

Leah's shaky legs lead the way as she moves on autopilot. A chair has been placed in the middle of the room, facing the inglenook fireplace. Just like years ago, the same ornaments decorate the top. There are two china houses and a large carriage clock taking centre place. She remembers back then, the tick, tick, tick of the clock as she lay there waiting for Derren to free her from his hefty weight. The burgundy settee is still along the back wall and there is a chair next to it. The other chair sits under the window. It was the chair Mr Pearson always sat in. What Leah doesn't see in the room is Mrs Pearson or Derren. Is it just the three of them?

'What have you done to Zara? How could you hurt her?'

Rosie lets out a nervous laugh. 'It was a pain to get her over here but her poor legs managed it with those sticks. What a struggle she had but I guess that's the least of her problems. She should be out for the count, I hit her hard enough. That's what she got for trying to fight back. Besides, why do you care? She deceived you.'

'No, Zara would never hurt me.' Rosie is trying to hurt her when she's at her lowest, just like Cain is. Everyone is trying to make her believe she's losing it, but she's not.

Rosie shrugs. 'Believe what you like.'

Leah spots the charred metal poker lying on the floor.

'Don't even think about it.' Rosie jabs the knife at her.

Rosie must have hurt Zara with the poker. She glances back at her friend. Zara isn't bleeding, thankfully. The only person bleeding in the room is her.

'Sit.'

Leah falls on the wooden chair. Within seconds, Rosie has yanked her arms back and her hands are bound with a thin rope behind her back. The room begins to sway. Leah closes her eyes, and she focuses on the sound of the spitting fire to ground herself. Her legs start to burn under her jeans. Any closer, she might ignite, taking the whole house with them. The idea of burning alive and being tied to a chair brings a fresh wave of fear. All she can do is hope that talking will help her out of this situation. She tucks her legs under the chair and tries to shuffle it back slightly. On opening her eyes again, she flinches as a huge lump of wood drops onto the grate as it chars around the edges.

That tune with the yodelling cuts through the atmosphere again. Rosie grabs her ringing phone and cuts the call. 'The joys of running a party business. Every day is a party and today is no exception. Today is the day we deal with you, once and for all. Why didn't you just tell the girls to go away when they contacted you? It would have been so easy.'

Leah hiccups a sob. She thought Charlotte was her child. She had yearned to build a relationship with her, yet it was all a lie. It feels as though her heart is twisting in her ribcage. One minute her daughter was back and had been looking for her, the next, all that love and hope for the future was snatched away. Charlotte lied to her. That's why she'd been arguing with her friends outside the café. They knew taking the DNA test had been a mistake and that their lie would get exposed. And now this, the woman she thought was having an affair with her husband is about to kill her.

'You don't know what it's been like for me. I thought there was a chance that my baby lived. I wanted to believe—'

'Well look where belief got you and you saw for yourself, your revolting garden is full of bones. Your baby didn't make it. It's sad but you know the truth now.'

Leah turns away, trying not to give Rosie the satisfaction of seeing her pain. Sophie died though Leah had hoped it wasn't true.

'You don't have to do this. Please let me and Zara go.'

'I do. You've left me no choice. Derren knows. Your stupid mother couldn't keep her mouth shut on her deathbed, and you know the worst thing, she just couldn't resist trying to ruin everything for me and Derren, and now we have you and the girls digging things up that should stay buried. It's over for you, Leah.'

'Why would my mother do that? For all her faults, why would she contact Charlotte and claim she was my daughter?'

'The woman was senile.'

Her mother was anything but senile from what the nurse had told her. Rosie is lying. It is evident that Charlotte isn't her daughter. Leah bursts into tears, the confusion swimming in her head. A few days ago, she thought that no one else in the world knew about Sophie.

A bang comes from above, followed by footsteps slowly coming down the stairs, one slow step at a time until the person enters the room. She doesn't even need to turn around to know that Derren is behind her and that she's trapped. Panic rises in her chest. She can't run from him and she can't hide. Whatever they have planned for her, it's all happening now. She closes her eyes and braces herself for what's about to happen, then she whispers under her breath as she thinks of poor Zara: 'I'm so sorry.'

FIFTY

ANGEL

It seems like forever but now they've all left Larrison House, I get off the bedroom floor and run downstairs and into the garden. I know why Leah was digging: she was looking for me and I'm not there. She knows I'm alive and she knows I'm hers. Then Freya's mum, Rosie, hit her and took her. Shaking, I step onto the grass and hurry towards the hole. I need to see what's in it for myself. Maybe Jean left something in there for me to find. I reach the hole and peer in. There's so much dirt but what I do see is a dirty cream-coloured stick. Reaching in, I prod it, then recoil as I lift it up. It looks like a really old bone so I drop it. I press my fingers into the earth and find more. Some small, some a little bigger, and I hold my breath. Bones. No, I have this all wrong, so wrong. Leah's baby is buried here.

How could I doubt the parents I love so much? They're missing because of me. I can't call the police, my phone is dead and, as for Leah, she may not be my mother but she had a knife to her back a few minutes ago. Up until now, I almost hated her at times for what I thought she did to me, for not wanting me, but the way she was digging, she looked like she was suffering and heartbroken.

Standing, I pace up and down. I need to help her and I need to find my parents. I run back into the kitchen and grab a pair of scissors from the first drawer I open. As I hurry out of Larrison House, I notice the orange glow coming from one of the front rooms in the house across the road. I look left and right. Maybe I could run to the village and try to get help.

A cry comes from the house. I don't have time, not when Leah is in such immediate danger. As I jog across the road, I almost trip over my own feet more than once. I go to nudge the front door then stop. The last thing I should do is walk straight into danger. Against my better judgement, I hold my breath and gently push the door, but it's locked. I exhale and take another deep breath.

I scurry around to the side gate, which is unlocked, then I run alongside the house into an overgrown garden. Stingers brush my ankles, instantly irritating my skin. I let out a tiny cry as I rub my skin. There is a cleared section at the one side of the back garden, and my blood runs cold when I see the huge grave and a pile of earth next to it. I stand there staring and gasping for a few seconds, knowing I need to turn back.

The kitchen is in darkness. I almost faint with fear as a fox dodges past me and disappears into the stingers. Heart pounding, I know Leah needs help but I really can't do this alone. Rosie looked like she wanted to kill her and if I get in the way, she might kill me too. I've never seen her looking that scary before, or scared. Maybe her fear makes her more dangerous. I feel a quiver running through me. Whatever secret she's trying to hide involves me. It has to. If it didn't, why would I get those messages and why would Mum and Dad be missing? The police need to be involved. I can't face this alone.

As I turn to go back out of the garden, I hear a murmuring voice.

'Mum?' I glance up and see an open upstairs window. She must be in the room above where I stand.

The murmur comes again but it isn't any louder. It sounds like she's trying to call for help. I just want to find Mum and Dad and tell them how much I love them and how sorry I am for getting them into all this. If I go to get help, might Rosie hurt them before I get back? I won't be able to live with myself if something happens to them and I could have helped. Taking a deep breath, I know I have to be braver than I've ever been in my life. The scissors shake in my hand. I don't know if I could even defend myself with them. I couldn't stab a person and I couldn't hurt anyone. I'm scared of blood. The very thought of seeing a massacre in there sends me weak at the knees.

'Mum, I'm coming,' I call in a loud whisper, hoping that no one in Mrs Pearson's house hears me. I nudge the back door, but it's locked. There has to be a way in. That's when I spot the old wooden ladders against the other fence.

I battle through the bushes and drag them along with half a trailing branch until the ladders are underneath the open window. Snatching the branch, I fling it in the grave. The moon escapes through the clouds and I can now clearly see that there are missing rungs and they're mossy. A flashing thought of me slipping off them from the top makes me wince. They're definitely not safe but I am going to do this. Just as I step onto the bottom rung, the kitchen light flashes on. I crouch and press my back against the cold wall, ready to run if I'm spotted.

Cups clatter like they're being dropped into a washing-up bowl that is full. The shadow cast from the kitchen gets larger as the figure comes closer to the door. I'm going to faint. My vision prickles. I gasp for air while trying to silently hold back my tears. That's when I hear the key turning in the lock. I clasp a hand over my mouth to muffle the sobs just as they open the door.

FIFTY-ONE

ANGEL

A tied-up bin bag lands with a thud on the other side of the door and whoever is in the kitchen has gone back in and locked it again. I wait until the light goes off. Kicking the bag, I wonder if there is a body in it. It doesn't feel dense enough, thankfully. I reach across and prod the bag until it tears. A great big melded lump of teabags mixed with rotten food spills out, and the disgusting smell hits the back of my throat. There's a white cloth mingled in with it. I give it a tug and hold it away from me. There is a large dark smear in the middle of it. It's blood. I drop it and wipe my hand in a panic on my coat. The knife wasn't just an empty threat: someone in there is bleeding and it could be Mum or Dad, Leah, or even Leah's neighbour. I heard Leah's neighbour crying as Rosie forced her out of Larrison House. After a few minutes, I went to help Leah but Freya's mum came back. I've never felt so helpless or terrified, and now I feel worse. I could have run from danger but I'm stepping right back into it.

I place my feet on the bottom rung of the ladder and it complains with a creak. The next rung is missing so I take a larger step and I'm further up. I take one at a time, gripping as hard as I can and not looking down as I near the window. My foot slips and I let out a shriek and grip the rung above. After taking a few breaths, I find the rung again with my foot and keep going. Mrs Pearson's house is tall, just like Larrison House, but I've almost made it to the top of the ladder which only reaches the middle of the upstairs window.

Peering through, I can't see a thing. The window is covered in a dusty film and thick lacy netting. For a second, it feels like I'm being watched. Head dizzy as I look down, the fox peers up at me. It's okay, it's just me and the curious creature and I feel comforted by its presence. At least I know the fox doesn't want to hurt me. It begins to lick at the tea bags. I take the last step and flinch as a splinter embeds itself into my hand. Nudging the open window, I listen for my mum's voice again but all I hear is another slight murmur and a cough. I pull at the larger window to my left in the hope that it'll open, but the only open window is the tiny one at the top. I know it's going to be a squeeze but it's also my only way in. I'm not going to fit through it with my coat on though. Why didn't I think of that while I was on the ground?

I place the scissors in the pocket of my jeans and flap around, one arm at a time until I've released my coat. It floats down and rests on the slabs below, sending the fox back into the darkness of the bushes. Reaching up, I hold on to the open window frame and step onto the ledge, where I'm willing my shaky legs not to let me fall to my death. A huge, thick-bodied spider darts from a crevice. It creeps over my hand and I want to cry. This is a complete nightmare. I have to get off this ledge from hell. Before I know it, I've wedged my head through the top window. I reach in, grab the netting and tug it hard in the hope I'll get a better view. Now I can almost see in. I place my nose against the cobweb-covered glass and peer into the dark room. There are two lumps on the bed.

'Mum.'

'Ange...' The gruff voice is unmistakably Mum's.

She's trying to talk to me. She sounds like she's really drunk or maybe she's been drugged. I almost lose my footing again as a door slams downstairs. A chunk of moss lands on the pavement, and my heart bangs like mad. I've never been so close to death. After waiting a moment, I feel sure that no one is coming up. I push my head through the gap and follow that with my middle. The scissors dig into my thigh. I reach ahead for something to grab or steady myself with and there's a unit or a chest of drawers right underneath the window. I swipe away a collection of objects which scatter onto the carpet. Hands down, I wiggle through the gap and my body follows, then I tumble off the drawers and land with a thud onto what feels like a hairbrush. My eyes adjust to the room and the outlines get clearer. My dad isn't making a sound, and my mum is stirring. Just as I go to hug Mum, footsteps bang up the stairs.

'Stay quiet, Mum.'

I lie across the floor against the bed base and hope that I'm not spotted. Then I see the torn netting hanging from the window. Whoever is about to come in the room will know my mum and dad aren't alone.

FIFTY-TWO

LEAH

'Where is he?' Leah shouts as Rosie comes back into the room. She was so sure that Derren had been behind her.

'By he, I gather you mean Derren.' Rosie shrugs. 'He doesn't even know I'm here, does he, Elisabeth? I left him at home sleeping of the excesses of your dinner party. He did wake up and he's tried to call a couple of times but I guess he went back to sleep. For some reason, he feels sorry for you and I can't have him being the weak link in all this. That brandy was good stuff.' Her phone rings again with the party song, and Rosie cuts the call.

Mrs Pearson clutches her shiny bag. 'We have to protect him. He's my boy. I can't let you hurt him, Leah. I told you to go and not come back, but would you listen? Those things you said about him were wrong. You and Derren were friends and when girls like you make things up like that, it damages lives. You could get him into a lot of trouble. My husband saw it all. That's how we all know you were lying.'

'And we can't have that, can we?' Rosie places a hand on her stomach. 'We all have so much to look forward to. Do you get what I mean? My baby isn't going to lose her father to your lies.'

Rosie's bottom lip quivers and she relaxes the arm holding the knife. Leah watches how she rubs her belly.

That's why Rosie didn't drink at the dinner party. It wasn't just because she was driving: she's pregnant.

Rosie shakes her head. 'Even your own mother didn't believe you, did she? Why, because you're a liar. You can't lie about things like rape. Derren is the gentlest and most loving man I know.'

Tears run down Leah's face. She had told her mother she was raped but it had been brushed over and now she knows why: Mrs Pearson had come over to tell her everything that Mr Pearson had told her. After all, he caught Leah and Derren in the act of consensual sex, or so he made out, all to protect his rapist son. That was his version and he'd lied to protect Derren.

'I didn't lie. Believe what you like but I told him to stop. I said stop while Mr Pearson stood in that doorway behind me and watched the whole thing.' Leah pauses and watches a tear glistening down Rosie's cheek. 'The truth hurts, doesn't it?'

Mrs Pearson opens her bag and pulls a photo out. She holds it to her mouth and kisses it before showing it to Leah. It's a photo of Mr Pearson in his younger days. 'You are the liar. How dare you speak ill of the dead. He isn't here to defend your slanderous claim, young lady. Look at him.'

Leah turns her head.

'I keep him with me at all times. I know he's here with me in spirit, and he tells me you need to go, that you're dangerous and you'll ruin our lives. I still talk to him, you know. He looks out for me and Derren. Back then, he did tell me he saw you, Leah. He interrupted you both being disgusting on this very rug under our feet, and you were writhing like some sort of nymphomaniac. My husband was so horrified that he had to gather your clothes up and tell you to leave, after all the kindness we'd extended to you. Then to save the shame of it all, we had to send our Derren away to another school. You caused that. You took him from us! Then poor Jean comes over a few months later all in a fluster, telling me that you were close to giving birth with Derren's child. We talked for days about what to do with you and your little problem. Jean said it was too late for an abortion but you know me, dear, I don't believe one should kill children just because stupid girls who can't keep their legs shut make a mistake. I also didn't believe that Derren should know. You would have ruined his life. He needed to concentrate on his A levels and prepare for university.' She licked her lips and sighed. 'He wouldn't have known until you and the girls started digging. I couldn't hold the truth about the baby back from him any longer. Rosie has been such a support in all this.' Mrs Pearson places a hand on her daughter-in-law's arm and smiles.

'What did you and Jean do to me and my baby?' Leah trembles. She wonders how much blood she's lost from her arm and head. Every time Mrs Pearson moves, her face looks slightly blurry and Leah's head throbs.

'I was a midwife. I did what midwife's do. From Jean's landing, I made sure you safely gave birth. Your mother cut the cord. She helped you deliver the afterbirth. After all the nasty things you said about Derren, and given the heartache I was going through when he moved away, I still helped you and, without me, you'd be dead. Without me, you would have died of that infection. After all, we couldn't take you to a hospital, could we?'

'Really?' Leah manages to stutter. She's tired now and her arms are dead after losing circulation. 'Without you, I could have been taken to hospital and given birth there. Sophie would have lived and I wouldn't have been infected.'

'We had plans for your baby and going to hospital would have ruined it all. We planned to save your reputation, dear.'

'And my baby died so I ruined your plans, or was that the plan?' She imagines holding and cuddling Sophie. She'd have given anything to kiss her delicate baby skin and feed her.

Despite what Derren did, she would have been the best mother ever. That baby would have been hers and hers alone. She could have left the village and never let Sophie's monster of a father anywhere near them. She let out a yell. 'You both killed my baby. You killed her. You murderer.' Leah yells as loud as she can. 'Murderer.'

'You're wrong. An angel came from heaven, that's why I know I did the right thing.'

Just as Mrs Pearson is about to continue, a loud thud comes from above. Both she and Rosie turn to face the door.

'You're crazy. You're both crazy. Let me go,' Leah shouts.

Rosie turns and slaps Leah, the veins running across her temples twitching. 'Watch her. There's clearly someone I need to deal with.' Rosie points to Leah, and Mrs Pearson sits in the armchair by the window.

Rosie heads out of the room, pulling the door closed as she leaves. Someone else is in the house. Leah glances around at Zara whose eye twitches. She wants to shout and rouse her friend, but doing so could render her with the fire poker in her face, especially now that Mrs Pearson has picked it up.

FIFTY-THREE

ANGEL

My heart still pounds like mad. Someone stopped outside the bedroom door and waited for ages, listening outside before going back downstairs. I tried to get Mum to stand but she dropped like a dead weight onto the floor. 'Mum, get up. We have to get you out of here.' The scissors came in handy. I've cut the binds that held her hands behind her back but it doesn't seem to help. She can barely function. There is a trail of dried-up blood on my mother's forehead, and there is also blood matted into Dad's hair.

Mum and I have kept our voices down but they're coming back. I hear footsteps climbing the stairs.

'Hide.' That is all Mum manages to say.

Just as the door bursts open, I crouch and roll under the bed. Mum still lies at the end of the bed on the floor. I don't know what I was thinking moving her like that. It's clear I can't save Mum and Dad on my own. Mum kept muttering something about a tablet, but I couldn't see any pills around. I know my parents have been drugged though.

The room lights up and I see Freya's mum, Rosie's, muddy boots. Mum squints and tries to hide from the stark main light.

Her hands are behind her back, like she's still tied up, and I'm hoping Freya's mum doesn't see that she's free. The knife comes down with a bang as the woman stabs the floor. I try to wriggle a little so I can reach the knife. If I get the weapon from her, I might be able to fight back.

'You've made a bit of a mess here. Trying to escape, were you?'

Freya's mum grabs the netting and throws it in a pile over all the trinkets and the hairbrush. If she gets any closer to the window she might see the tip of the ladder, then she'll know that Mum didn't make that mess and I'll be busted. 'I truly am sorry you're here like this but Angel has left me with no choice. It'll all be over soon.' She goes on. 'I didn't plan for any of this to happen but I love my life and I want to keep it that way. You know exactly why this has to happen. I mean this secret has to be kept, which means you all must vanish forever?' My mum whimpers. 'I know. We both hoped the truth wouldn't get out for all of our sakes. Given all that's happened, I know it's on the verge of escaping unless I step in. I don't want to hurt you or Leah or anyone but there really is no other way.' Freya's mum stops before she goes on. 'You know, I don't like doing this. I don't like hurting people.' She tuts. 'But as mothers, we'll do anything to protect our families. I mean anything. You know how that feels.'

What is my mum hiding from me? I've spent ages thinking I was illegally adopted by my parents, but I saw the baby's bones so what has that got to do with my mum? Whatever it is, I forgive her, I don't blame her, I just want us all to get out of this and live. Maybe we can pretend none of this happened and start again. I don't even want to question what all this is about.

'What are...?'

I know my mum is trying to ask what Freya's mum is going to do with her, but she can't manage the whole sentence. It hurts to see my mum like this. I want to reach out and save her, and hug her, but I can't. It pains me to see someone threatening her and hurting her like this. I pull the scissors from my pocket and wonder if I can use them. Maybe I can stab her in the ankles and hope she doesn't have time to catch me with her knife. My hands shake that badly I fear that the scissors are going to clatter against the floor at any moment, so I place them back into my pocket. Besides, the very thought of seeing spurting blood makes me feel like heaving.

'Here.' Freya's mum bends down and forces a pill into my mother's mouth and then she rams a water bottle between her lips. 'Drink.'

Tears run down my mother's face as she chokes and tries to spit the pill out. Freya's mum clamps her mouth shut and grabs the knife again. I see Mum swallow and I know the pill is gone.

'There. Go to sleep.'

The room is silent as my mum stares at me from the floor with watery eyes. I know they'll close soon. I fear my banging heart is so loud, Freya's mum will hear and who knows what she'll do to me? She takes a step closer to the bed, and I go to grip the scissors again. Just as I psych myself up to use them, she turns and leaves. After she slams the door shut, I tear up and lie there until I hear her going downstairs.

I drag my body along the floor until I'm clear of the bed. Dad is still fast asleep, and Mum hasn't moved. I run over and snip his binds, then I kneel and press my face next to Mum's. She half smiles and spits the pill onto the floor. I want to yell with delight. Mum didn't swallow the pill. I lean over to help her up. She has no strength at all, but after a few attempts, we manage to get her back onto the bed, where she slumps back with her head on the pillow. She gasps, exhausted from that small amount of movement. The pills she had earlier are still in her system.

'Mum, I'm going to get us out of this.' I don't know how but I will. 'I'll be back okay.'

As I go to stand, she loosely grips my arm and begins to sob. 'Please, just get out of here. Leave us,' she mutters.

'I am not leaving you, Mum.'

'I'm sorry... We wanted...' she says half coughing and whispering. 'Wanted a baby so badly. We love you.'

'No, I'm yours.' I can't stop my own tears. I know I'm not Leah's. If I'm not Mum and Dad's and I'm not Leah's, whose am I?

'I love you. Please forgive me. I...' she gasps. 'I don't want to lose you.'

I hold her hand on my heart and realise nothing else matters. Mum and Dad are everything to me. I shake my head. 'Never going to happen, Mum.' I pause, then go on, 'I have to go down there. I need to find a phone.'

Mum shakes her head and looks at the window. 'No. Save yourself.'

No, I have no phone. It's the middle of the night and as soon as I leave someone will get killed. I hold the scissors up and I know what I have to do. I have to make all this right again. It's my fault. I believed Jean. Over and over again, I keep thinking, if only I'd blocked her and ignored her message. If I had, this wouldn't be happening. I started it so I have to finish it.

I open the door and shut Mum and Dad in, ignoring Mum's almost silent pleas for me to escape.

FIFTY-FOUR

LEAH

'I don't think we'll be bothered again this evening.' Rosie smirks as she sits in the chair by the window.

Leah can't hear anything from above now. Someone else is up there and now they've gone quiet. She looks at the woman beside her and wonders what she's capable of. Or maybe Derren is up there. But why would he hide upstairs and not come down?

'Rosie, Zara hasn't done anything. All she did was drive me here tonight. Your problem is with me, not her. Maybe you could just take her to A&E. You don't have to say who you are. Please help her.'

'And let her tell the authorities. No, Leah. I am not risking losing my baby and going to prison, just like I am not risking letting you blab your lies. It's gone too far for me to go back now. There is no other way. When I said you'd be buried under the daffodils, I lied. This back garden is like a jungle. You, Zara, and anyone else who tries to ruin my life is going to end up there.'

'Please, you don't have to do this. All so you can protect Derren. What's the point?' Leah wonders if she can reason with Rosie. 'How about this: I'll go along with your story and never mention that he raped me, and I'll pretend that Mr Pearson didn't lie and we can all go back to our lives. I'll also never say that you brought me here. You're desperate and I don't want to ruin you or your child's life. I know Zara won't say anything if I speak to her. Please let us go. Nothing can bring my baby back.' I swallow my sadness down. 'Yes. I had hope in my heart but that hope has gone. It's gone...' Leah looks down and wonders if she cares what happens to her any more. All she cares about is Zara, which is why she needs to keep talking.

Rosie swallows, and Leah can see that the reality of what she's planned is kicking in. A tear drizzles down her cheek, but all Mrs Pearson does is put the poker down and grip that shiny bag containing her precious photo.

'If only it were that simple.' Rosie blows out a breath and places a hand on her stomach.

'It is that simple.'

Mrs Pearson struggles to get out of the chair. 'But it's not.'

'Shh, please, Elisabeth,' Rosie says. 'Can I talk to Leah alone for a minute?'

Mrs Pearson is thoughtful. 'Yes, but don't believe her lies.'

For some reason, Leah is more scared of being left alone with Rosie. Is something about to happen? She pictures the knife plunging through her top and piercing her skin. The cut on her arm stings and the rope rubs against it, making her yelp.

'You've led a bland life, haven't you, Leah? Pregnant at sixteen, when you lost your baby, you moved out of Larrison House—'

'I didn't move out. I was told to leave. Jean rented me a flat in Worcester and told me it was best that I go away for a while. I know it's hard for you to believe that the man you love raped me, but he did.'

'This again.' Rosie shakes her head and tuts. Leah has lost her. 'Have you ever wondered if everything bad happens because of you? Derren is not a rapist, and you were a little drunk whore from what I've heard.' Rosie goes on, 'It's you who's screwed up. You left home or were told to leave. Whatever. Then you met Cain at eighteen and that's it, you lived with him and then you got married. I've seen the way you and him are when you're together, and he was happy to tell me all about how jealous you were when he met me. You know he even thought it was funny. Sad little Leah thought I was sleeping with her husband, when all that time, he'd slept with your best little friend over there.'

No, it couldn't be true. Leah stared open-mouthed as she pictured Cain and Zara together. Zara was stunning with her honey blonde hair and her bubbly personality, everything Leah wasn't. The pain she felt right now made the knife wound pale into comparison.

'You're lying. Zara wouldn't do that.' Rosie was just trying to upset her by saying horrible things that weren't true. No, Zara would not have slept with Cain.

'Whatever, Leah. Believe whatever the hell you like. I don't care. I can't say it's been a pleasure but I enjoyed toying with you. It was quite fun.'

'Why were you stalking me?' The ringtone had given Rosie away.

Rosie lets out a huff and shrugs. 'I didn't enjoy that. I wanted to see the liar for myself. I wanted to see the world she lived in. Derren said not to; he said just to give you a warning to keep out of our lives and shut up. He thought it would be over after the dinner party, but Elisabeth and I knew it was only the start of things.'

Leah doesn't get it. All this to stop Leah going to the police about Derren raping her. She's spent days getting confused by the girls, too. 'Did you tell Charlotte to say she was my daughter, to hurt me?'

'Why would I do that?'

'All this, it's not just about me accusing Derren, is it?'

'Well, that would just be silly, wouldn't it? The police wouldn't believe you anyway. I mean you accuse your husband of this and that. You think you're being stalked. Clearly, you're having some sort of breakdown. And you allowed your baby to be buried in the garden all those years ago. Do you know what the police would do with that?' Rosie's bottom lip trembles slightly. However, cruel she's being, Leah senses that she isn't finding any of this easy.

Leah knows there is more and the butterflies turning in her stomach wonder what else is going to come out. 'What aren't you telling me?'

'Let's talk about you. I'll give you something, just for fun.' Rosie swallows and takes a moment, then goes on. 'While I was in a meeting with the lovely Cain, he went outside and answered his phone to a woman called Alison, and he said he was going to meet her at The Hollybush. He was telling her all the things he wanted to do to her and boy it was racy. I think I even blushed at one point and it takes a lot to make me blush. He couldn't see me listening in the beer garden at the pub. We always met at pubs, which I don't think is great for business. It's not professional really, is it? Anyway, I'm assuming Alison has far more about her than you do.'

Zara had been right. 'You're not doing all this because my husband is having an affair.' Leah thought that news might have hurt a lot more, but compared to the situation she's in, it is a relief to get some truth out of it. She only hopes what Rosie said about Zara isn't true and that the woman had only said it to hurt her.

Rosie stares and her brow furrows. Leah can tell she's aware that she's said too much. 'No, I can't say any more. I won't say any more. It doesn't matter either.'

The yodelling ringtone starts again. Rosie answers this time and leaves the room. Leah can't hear what she's saying but she can tell that Rosie's words are coming out fast.

'Zara, can you hear me?'

'Mm. My head.'

Leah turns as far as she can but her neck is stiff. She can just about catch a glimpse of Zara moving.

Rosie storms back in. 'We have to do it now,' she shouts.

Mrs Pearson hurries back in. 'There's a ladder at the wall outside.'

'What?' Rosie frowns.

'There's someone in the house.'

'But I went up there. Everything was okay.'

A loud roar comes from behind and it doesn't belong to Mrs Pearson or Rosie. Leah is knocked to the floor in the struggle. Wiggling, she tries to loosen the binds but they're tight and the rope scrapes her cut and it begins to gush again.

'Let her go and let my parents go.' The girl's voice is meek and barely loud enough to hear.

That's when Leah sees Angel holding a pair of scissors in front of her face. The girl is trembling, and Leah wonders what else can happen tonight.

'Angel?' she gently says, feeling sorry that the innocent girl has ended up in this mess too.

'Angel, put the scissors down,' Rosie says.

'Put the knife down,' Angel says to Rosie.

Leah lies on her side, still bound to the wooden chair. She can see the fear in Angel's face. The girl shakes and she's sweating.

'Angel, get out while you can. Run.' Leah wants the girl to be safe.

'I can't just run and leave them,' Angel says with a sob.' I'm not leaving without my parents and you, Leah.'

Rosie tilts her head and holds the knife beside her. 'Angel, I do a lot for you girls. I give you all lifts and I know your mother. I'm doing all this to protect you and her. She'll see that in the end, when I explain to her and your dad why I did all this.'

'Really? Why do you have my mum and dad drugged and tied up upstairs? And you sent me those horrible messages. It was you who put the brick through our window.'

Rosie sighs. 'I just needed you to leave all this alone, but you wouldn't. It was just meant to scare you, but you left me no choice. I don't want to hurt you.'

Zara groans in pain as her legs begin to spasm.

'Let us go, and her?' Angel points at Zara.

'Not going to happen.' Rosie lunges towards the girl to grab the scissors, but Angel dodges out the way. Leah thinks of the moment her baby lay in her arms and she can't even cry any more. She's cried everything she has. Then Mrs Pearson's words hit her like a flash of lightning: *An angel came from heaven, that's why I know I did the right thing.* An Angel? This is all about Angel. Angel's parents are upstairs too. But who is in the grave under the daffodils? Whose bones were buried? 'Mrs Pearson, who is the angel from heaven?'

Rosie runs at Angel again, and Leah can see the look of horror on Mrs Pearson's face.

'Stop.'

She didn't know Mrs Pearson could shout that loud. The old woman steps between Rosie and Angel, using her shiny bag to protect herself from the knife.

Zara brings one of her sticks from underneath her and jabs it with a grunt into Rosie's knee. Rosie screams and falls to the ground, sending the knife hurtling into the rug. Zara grabs the weapon and places it under her body. 'Got you.'

'You touch a hair on my granddaughter's head and I will kill you myself.' Mrs Pearson tuts at Rosie.

Leah thinks she hears a car pulling up, then it leaves. There's no escape from this.

Angel runs over to Leah and cuts the rope from around her wrists and, under the dim light of the fireplace, Leah can see herself in Angel, just at that angle. The way her round face looks heart-shaped when she tilts her head, and the shape of her eyes; they are the same as Leah's. She recognises Angel's nose. It's a little longer than hers, more like Derren's. 'Mrs Pearson. No more lies. Who is buried in my mother's garden?'

Derren walks into the room. 'Mum, what's going on?' His gaze meets Leah's, and she gasps.

Leah sits up and shakes the binds away. Angel grabs a small blanket that is hung over the side of a chair and passes it to Leah. She wraps it around her bleeding arm.

'It's game over, Derren.'

FIFTY-FIVE
ANGEL

No, no and no. Why is this woman claiming to be my grandmother? First Jean, then all this, and now Freya's stepdad, Derren, has turned up and Mrs Pearson is his mother. How, why? I'm so confused I could fall over and watch the room spin as I try to make sense of everything. Derren is my mum's second or third cousin, I'm not totally sure which. I've met him a handful of times in my life, mostly when I've called for Freya. My earliest memory of him is at a family barbecue, that's when I friended Freya. We were about seven or eight. I wonder if Freya knew what was going on? I don't believe she did, but who knows?

Derren fully steps into the room. 'Can I have the scissors, please?' I can smell alcohol on his breath, and his hair sticks up at the one side like he's just woke up.

I shake my head. There's no way I'm handing them to him when Freya's mum just went ballistic. 'Let Mum and Dad go,' I stutter.

'Mum, go up and see if Lance and Cheryl are okay.' He looks at Mrs Pearson. 'What the hell is going on? Rosie?'

Mrs Pearson blows out a breath and leaves the room.

'I couldn't let it all come out. I thought this is what you wanted. She lied about you and I... I just wanted to protect you.'

I don't know what to think. 'If Mrs Pearson is my grandmother...'

Leah stumbles across the room and helps Zara up and they both sit on the settee before she speaks. 'He's your father. I'm your birth mother.'

Zara puts the knife under the settee cushion, out of the way.

'What...' I can't speak. I want to ask what happened and how it happened. It's no good, right now, I need my voice. I have questions that need answering. I take a deep breath and psych myself up for it.

Mrs Pearson comes back in. 'They're still sleepy. I think it'll be a while longer before they can come down. Cheryl tried to walk but she fell back onto the bed.'

'Mrs Pearson. What happened? Tell me who I am.' Tears slide down my face. Jean was telling the truth, and it's about time the rest of it came out now.

The old woman slumps on the chair under the window, exhausted and massaging her temples.

I wait for her to speak and I can tell Leah needs to hear this too. She's tensely holding Zara's hand. Zara doesn't look well. Her muscles stiffen and she winces. We can all see she's in pain, but no one dares to leave the room. She secures her sticks between her legs and sits back into the settee, yawning and rubbing her eyes.

Mrs Pearson clears her throat. 'Derren, you know that Lance and Cheryl lost their baby after they'd been trying for so many years?'

He nods.

'I begged Jean to let them have Angel. We both knew that Leah wouldn't be able to cope. She'd kept most of the pregnancy to herself and she'd withdrawn. Jean told us that she couldn't even take care of herself. It is true that you withdrew,

Leah, like you were having a breakdown?' Mrs Pearson glances at Leah, but Leah shakes her head. One of her knuckles is clenched. 'We both knew it would be bad for you and Leah, Derren. You were both so young and stupid and you still had your whole lives to live.'

'I was not too young,' Leah shouts. 'You stole my baby, and he raped me. I hate you both. I wanted my baby. I wanted to keep her and you let me think she was dead.'

'And I'm not proud of that but sometimes a person needs to do what's right. You were a kid and you were throwing accusations around. I understand, the shame got too much.'

I gasp. Not only did they steal me from Leah, but I was the product of something horrific. I can't help but cry and however hard I try I can't stop crying. Leah pulls me over to her, and I sit beside her. She draws my head to her chest, and I bury myself in her as I think of the pain she's been through.

Derren shakes his head. 'It's not true, Angel. I did not do that. Leah, how could you say things like that? I knew you'd be a bitch about things. We were young, we were drunk and one thing led to another.'

I hear Leah's heart booming in her chest through my right ear. She sits forward, and I am nudged into an upright position. She grips my hand. 'No, that's not what happened. All evening while your parents were out, you kept topping my glass up. The others had gone home and I told you I was going home too. I fell over, onto this rug.' She points at the blue rug. 'Instead of helping me up, you pushed me back and lay down next to me. I was so drunk I couldn't push you off as you kissed me. We'd never kissed before. We were friends, just friends.'

'That's not what happened and you know it. Such a lying bitch.' He punches the wall, and Mrs Pearson frowns at him.

'Then you grabbed at my underwear. I tried to make a joke of it and told you to stop and that I really wanted to go home. Then you almost crushed me with your weight, and while I kept telling you to stop, your disgusting pervert father was watching from that door, and he did nothing to help me. From that, I found out I was pregnant. Yes, I spent all day in my room. I didn't take my exams and I felt this life growing inside me. I denied it was happening, then I wished it wasn't...'

I pull away and cry into my hands. It hurts to hear all this but I don't want her to stop. I don't want any of them to stop talking however horrible it is to hear.

'This is horseshit!'

'No, Derren. You know I'm telling the truth and you have to live with who you are and what you did. Deny it all you like.' Leah pauses before continuing. 'Going into labour was the scariest moment of my life. After hours, I pushed this tiny baby girl out and I named her Sophie. She wasn't breathing. I barely had a minute of holding her in my arms before my mother snatched her from me. You'd know that, wouldn't you, Elisabeth? You were there. Go on, Elisabeth. What happened next?'

Rosie sits on the floor, hugging her legs as she keeps her head down and cries. 'You've ruined my life. You've ruined my baby's life.'

I see Rosie for the selfish human being that she is, and when I see the way Derren looks at Leah with a slight snarl on his lips, I can tell she's telling the truth. She's scared of him. My life is going from bad to worse. I really want to hear what my parents have to say. When they wake up, we'll be having a long talk.

'It's all about you, isn't it, Leah? I could tell when I first saw you.' Rosie spits as she talks.

'Seriously?' Zara says. 'That woman there stole her baby and gave it to someone else. You had a knife at me and forced me on my sticks across the road, even though you could see it was agony for me. You whacked me with a poker and now it's poor you! Stop bloody well victim blaming. And you, you prick, you raped her.' Derren goes to speak, but Zara doesn't let him get a word in. 'I lay there for ages and listened to everything while my head's been throbbing like a train has crashed into it. What you've all done to Leah and Angel is unforgivable.' Zara yells as another spasm stiffens one of her legs. She places a hand on her head. 'Now, the only person who matters in all this is Angel. Forget your selfish selves. It's about this poor girl and what you all did to her, except you.' She presses her cheek against Leah's cheek. 'Mrs Pearson, talk.'

I love Zara right now. She's the only one who's really putting me and Leah first in all this. We're the victims of their lies. 'Mrs Pearson, just tell us all what happened on the day of my birth?'

The old woman slumps back and nods. 'This has got out of hand.' I wait for her to talk. 'I knew what was happening. It was an acute hypoxic event following your prolonged labour. Angel became tired and unable to cope with the contractions and that resulted in her not getting enough oxygen, that's why Jean snatched her away almost immediately. I worried that without my immediate intervention, we might lose her. As soon as Angel was handed to me, I sealed my mouth over her nose and mouth and blew air into her lungs; she was revived as my first breath entered her. She let out the tiniest of cries when we got her downstairs then I took her to my house and continued caring for her. Jean and I had already spoken to Lance and Cheryl. Their baby girl was so premature, she didn't make it. They were heartbroken. It was worse because they'd been trying for what felt like a lifetime and that baby was already their miracle baby. There was little to no chance of them conceiving again.' Mrs Pearson blinks away a tear, and we wait for her to continue. I just want to bawl my eyes out as I think of how wanted I was by them. But then I think my birth mother wanted me too. Far from not being wanted, I was more than wanted by everyone. Mrs Pearson wipes her tears away and continues. 'I contacted them and told them about the situation. They weren't sure to begin with but I told them that the baby was going up for adoption anyway and that it might be their only opportunity to have a baby. When Angel was born not breathing, we thought it would be easier for you to accept she was gone, so we let you believe that's what happened,' she said to Leah. 'The alternative would have been us telling you that we'd arranged an adoption and hoping that you saw sense. Anyway, Lance and Cheryl decided to go ahead. They moved overnight from up north and rented down here. Cheryl came down wearing a fake bump and when we presented you to her, she was so happy. She removed the bump and everyone thought she'd given birth. No questions asked. They soon fit in to the community. We did have to obtain a couple of fake documents to get you into school. They love you a lot, Angel.'

Derren walks in front of the fire. 'How about me, Mum? I only found out about Angel after Jean's death. You lied to me, too.'

I glance at everyone and see the weight of the secret they've all been keeping.

'What about you?' Zara piped up. 'I think had Leah kept Angel, the best thing she could have done would be to run away with her and never come back.'

Derren kicks the door and storms out.

'I didn't tell him because—'

'You knew, didn't you, Elisabeth? You couldn't tell him because you knew what your son did.' Zara pursed her lips in disgust. 'The lies need to stop now. Look what they've done to everyone here, most of all, Angel.'

The old woman sobs. 'You're right. My husband told me he saw Leah saying no and that he didn't know what to do. We saw Derren's future getting ruined for one silly drunken mistake.'

'How can you say that. Elisabeth?' Rosie gets off the floor and sobs loudly as she chases after Derren. I hear shouting in the back garden as they argue.

Zara lays her head on Leah's shoulder and yawns again. 'So,

what now, Leah? I'd say it's your call. Do you want to go to the police?'

My heart races again. I pull away from Leah. 'No, no, no. You can't go to the police. My mum and dad will end up in prison. I can't lose them...'

Leah places a hand over my shoulder. 'She's right. Angel has to come first.'

'But that animal raped you.' Zara puts her sticks to the side of her and painfully sits up. She takes a few breaths.

'I know, Zara.' Leah turns to glance at me, and I see her welling up. 'I thought my baby was dead and she's right here in front of me. I want to get to know her, I want to be a part of her life and I hope she wants the same. We can't change the past, and it sounds like my mother and Elisabeth lied to Cheryl and Lance too, while they were at their most vulnerable. I think everyone has suffered enough. Maybe even Rosie will have the sense to leave Derren after what she's heard.'

I'm literally sobbing now. I want to be in Leah's life too.

Zara shakes her head. 'We were threatened with a knife, and there are two people upstairs who have been drugged and hurt. They dug a hole in the garden to bury us in.'

Leah wipes her eyes. 'I know and I'm sorry I dragged you into this, Zara. I'm sure Angel's adoptive parents won't want the police involved either. We have to find a way forward and what I want is my daughter in my life. That is all I want. Please say you'll support me, Zara. You're my best friend.'

I bite what bit of nail I have as I wait for her answer.

Zara shakes her head and sighs. 'Of course I will. But I need to go home and sleep. I need my MS tablets and I'm sure this will all look different in the morning. And you need to get your arm looked at, and my bloody head hurts because that homicidal bitch outside hit me with the poker.'

Leah moves away from me to hug her friend. Just as I breathe a sigh of relief, my mum staggers through the door.

Leah nods to me. I run over to her and hug her like I never want to let her go. I'm sure she's been listening to everything as she grips me harder than she's ever gripped me in her life. Mrs Pearson leaves the room, and I let her. I don't want to see her again, ever. I don't want to see Rosie and Derren again, but Freya is my friend. The truth is out and as Leah said, we all have to find a way forward. It's over.

Leah stands. 'Let's get you home, Zara.' She turns to Mrs Pearson, who is only just shedding a tear. 'Who is buried in my mother's garden?'

We all got so caught up in what was going on, the bones slipped my mind. My stomach begins to churn as I think of the daffodil patch.

Mrs Pearson frowns and shakes her head. 'What bones?' She looks genuinely confused by that question.

PART 4

TWO WEEKS LATER

FIFTY-SIX

LEAH

Leah eventually got back from A&E about seven in the morning, after having twelve stitches. Zara just about managed to drive and, all day, her pains were excruciating. Leah spent the day looking after her.

Leah knows she'll need to give Angel some space to talk things through with Cheryl and Lance. The anger hasn't subsided, and the pain of what had happened isn't any lesser, but the truth did provide some comfort: she has a daughter and she is going to get to know her. A smile beams across her face. After all the heartache, something good is emerging. As for Cain, he'd heard her come back and stumbled down the stairs bleary-eyed. She hasn't told him anything; in fact she doesn't want to speak to him again after he'd tried to poison her and Zara's friendship with that text message, telling her she couldn't trust Zara. Alison is welcome to him. He's been nothing but horrible to her and she deserves more, not a man who speaks to her like she's rubbish and cheats on her. She told him there and then that she was moving out. Of course, he would eventually blame her for losing him the contract that never was.

After grabbing a few essentials, Leah drives to Larrison

House, her new home. It had been passed down to her and, when she dies, it will be passed down to Angel.

The past couple of weeks have been up and down. Leah refilled the hole in the garden. A bit more exploration told Angel and Leah that the bones belonged to an animal. On piecing them together, they looked like a baby deer. It makes sense. Jean always shovelled up the roadkill and she must have happened upon a dead animal around the time of Angel's birth. She must have thought that if Leah ever doubted her story, she would dig up the grave and find bones. As for the clues, Jean left them as she wanted the truth to come out. Jean had written her a letter, and Leah knew that Jean had wanted to see her so that she could tell her the truth about Angel. She'd regretted what she had done, and she did want to meet her granddaughter before she died.

Leah enters the password into Jean's laptop. She sheds a tear as she thinks about *The Wizard of Oz*. She doesn't have many pleasant memories of Jean but they shared a love of this film. After a bit of clicking and scrolling, she comes across a file marked *Leah*. It contains a single Word document. Leah hesitates for a moment, wondering if she's sure she wants to venture into Jean's world. What she's already been through is painful enough.

Then she clicks it open. In about half an hour Zara and Molly will be coming over for lunch. Angel is due to arrive a short while after. The sun beams through the study window as she starts reading.

> *Leah,*
>
> *I'm keeping this short as I simply don't have the energy for much, not any more. I wrote to you in the hope that you would come and see me but you didn't reply and I understand why. Instead, I'm hoping that you find this letter when I'm gone.*
>
> *The cancer is ravaging me and I can barely breathe.*

Anyway, I'm not writing this to garner any sympathy. I'm not writing this to offer an apology. I did what I thought was right at the time and what's right now is that I get to know Angel and she learns of your existence. Larrison House has been in the family for a long time and if you're reading this, you are now its keeper. One day I know you will leave it to Angel.

What I did back then might seem cruel but you shocked me. One minute I find out you're pregnant, the next we have a baby. I had to think fast and Elisabeth came up with a solution. When the baby came out silent and still, I took her off you and passed her to Elisabeth who managed to revive her. I can tell you that was a tense moment. Telling you she was dead had seemed the kindest solution at the time. It allowed you to move on.

Over the years I watched Angel from afar. Sometimes I'd sit outside her adoptive parents' house and wait for them to bring her out. They looked so happy. They worshipped her and it reassured me that I'd done the right thing. I sense you're disagreeing with me right now and that is your prerogative. I'd do the same again.

I'm not writing this letter because of the past, I'm writing it because of what's happening now. Ever since I contacted Angel, Elisabeth has become quite threatening. She keeps going on at me, saying that I was slanderous because I mentioned what you said about Derren, that he raped you. Her daughter-in-law even whispered to me that she ought to smother me with a pillow, before I could do any more damage. I made the mistake of giving her a key early on in my illness so she keeps coming to visit and she sits there with her daughter-in-law, holding that red pillow of mine. They're dangerous. Don't trust them and Derren is back in the picture. He knows too, and from what they say, he wants to intimidate you, to shut you up and show that he can mess your life up if you say anything. Don't trust any of them.

I hope you get this letter before it's too late.
Jean

She didn't even type the word, Mum, at the bottom of her letter. A fat tear plops into Leah's lap, and she wipes her eyes. Someone rings the doorbell, and she hears Molly barking outside. As Leah no longer lives with Cain, Molly can come in. She can tread mucky footprints on the floor if she wants, and she can lie on the couch. Leah wants a new start for Larrison House. Mrs Pearson has put her house up for sale and soon she'll be gone. She knows the memories will always be there but she's stronger now. That house no longer scares her, and the ghosts of Larrison House have been put to rest, too. It's the start of a new chapter.

A few minutes later, Zara is sitting at the kitchen table in front of the huge Victoria sponge that Leah made, and she swipes a bit of cream with her finger and licks it. Molly lies at her feet, and her sticks are up against the wall, next to the dresser. 'This cake is so good and this place finally looks homely. I miss you as my neighbour though but at least you're not far away. Did you know that the prick you left has put your old house up for sale?'

Leah nods. 'He told me he needs a fresh start, but I'm guessing he's moving in with her. I don't care any more.' She glances out at the few daffodils that made it, and all the other flowers in the garden that are starting to open. It is a beautiful garden and it's hers.

Zara sighs. 'I have a confession. I've done something I'm not proud of and I don't want you to hate me.'

'Zara, I could never hate you. Ever.'

'You haven't heard what I've got to say yet.' She begins twiddling with the end of her ponytail that drapes over one of her shoulders. 'I guess that all the lies are out now so I want to come clean.'

Leah's stomach begins to churn as the scent of the cream cake coats her nostrils. 'Okay.'

'You know you mentioned that Cain had some really horrible messages, really nasty ones?'

Nodding, Leah waits for Zara to continue and she thinks she knows what Zara is going to say.

'I sent them. I was so angry with the way he was treating you; I couldn't help myself. I just let it all out. I should have told you when you mentioned them to me. It felt rotten not to say anything. It was stupid and immature and I'm an idiot.'

Leaning over, Leah bursts into fits of laughter and hugs Zara. 'You're the best friend ever.'

'So, you don't hate me?'

Grabbing a knife, Leah begins cutting a slice of cake and places it on a side plate in front of Zara. 'Hate you, don't be silly. I love you to bits.' Molly lets out a little yelp. 'And you too, Molly.' Leah reaches down and strokes the dog's head. 'Zara, I have to ask you something.' It was now or never and, although Leah didn't believe a word that Rosie had said, she had to clear it up.

Zara pushes the cake aside, as if she knows what's coming, and that tells Leah a lot. She wishes she'd never asked now because before Zara even answers her, she knows what she's about to say.

'I know what you're going to say. I was lying there listening that night and I hoped that I'd dreamt it. I'm sorry, Leah. I should have told you when we became friends.'

'Rosie wasn't lying about you sleeping with Cain?'

'It was once.'

Leah can't swallow all of a sudden, and she clenches her fists. Everyone has let her down but it hurts more that Zara has.

'Wait, before you hate me, let me tell you everything. I didn't even know you, I'd just moved in.'

'So that made it okay?' Leah wipes her damp eyes.

'No, nothing makes it okay,' Zara says. 'Alison and I were friends, not close or anything but I'd meet her for the odd coffee out. We met at a salsa dance class believe it or not.' Zara runs a hand through her fringe. 'She mentioned that she was selling her bungalow. I told her that I'd just received my MS diagnosis and I was after a bungalow, so we rushed the sale through. I sold my house and moved in. I'd been living there for several months and I came home really drunk. My diagnosis hit me like a train. I wasn't in a good place.' Zara's chest heaves and she lets out a sob. 'The depression had me sinking fast and I'd been drinking when I shouldn't have been, not with my tablets. Cain helped me into my house and he sat in the kitchen with me. He made a few jokes while we shared a bottle of wine. Before I knew it, he'd made a move and I didn't stop him. I thought my life was over at the time and I didn't know you. Later on, I spoke to Alison again and she then fell out with me for sleeping with him. Apparently, before you, he'd told her that she was his world and they were going to move in together, but then he moved you in. She was heartbroken, Leah. She thought you'd taken him from her. She saw you as the person he'd cheated on her with.'

Leah feels her breaths quicken.

'I contacted her recently to tell her to leave Cain alone, as it was hurting you. You couldn't find her on Facebook because she blocked you. The truth is, despite him stringing her along before you moved in, she's always loved him and she'll do anything for him. I think it's mad and I told her how much it had hurt you, but it didn't seem to matter to her. Cain must have told Rosie that he slept with me at some point, and I wouldn't be surprised if he had been hitting on her when Derren wasn't around. I'm sorry, Leah. I love you so much and I've hated myself for years. I made a vow to be the best friend ever to you and I hope you'll allow me to stay in your life because I don't know what I'll do without you.' Zara bursts into tears.

Leah leans over and hugs her friend. Right now, she is going to blame the one person who deserves it all, and that's Cain. She could get angrier over Alison but right now, she thinks that the woman is welcome to him. Most of all, Leah hopes she'll come to her senses one day. She's seen the depth of Zara's suffering over the years as her body has failed her physically and the mental impact has floored her. Zara would have been vulnerable at the time of her diagnosis, and Cain had taken advantage of that. Besides, Zara had nearly been killed because of her. Leah had so much making up to do. 'You'll never be without me, Zara, but no more secrets, okay?'

Zara blows her nose and smiles. 'No secrets, ever. None.' They both take a deep breath and compose themselves, ready for Angel's visit.

Molly barks at the doorbell. Leah can't wait to open it and see Angel again. She's seen her since but things are starting to feel a bit more normal between them after that weird night. She runs to the door to see her daughter's smiling face. Her new life has begun and she's embracing it with all she has.

FIFTY-SEVEN

ANGEL

I wish I could say how happy I am right now but something is niggling inside me, something I can't let go. I try to ignore it for now and relish the happy scene before me.

The cake looks delicious and Zara seems genuinely happy to see me. They look watery eyed but I guess it's been an emotional time. She tells me how much she can see Leah in me and what a lovely girl I am. I love her dog. Molly is so cute, I just want to cuddle her. Mum and Dad talked to me for hours about the past and what happened. I believed them when they said that they genuinely thought I was going up for adoption anyway. They had panicked, knowing they'd have to wait years for a baby if they went down that route and they felt they were already getting on in age a bit. Mrs Pearson had put up such a good argument. They trusted her. She is family; and Mum said the moment she held me in her arms, it was the happiest day of her life. At first, they were really worried that I'd disown them when the truth came out, but Leah has been really supportive too and I trust Zara to keep our secrets. Leah says all she wants is for me to be happy and that they are obviously good loving parents. I don't know how she can be so forgiving. If someone took my baby, not that I'm planning on having one for many years, I'd hate them forever. She literally is a saint and she's so kind.

As for Freya, when she heard what had happened, she left her house; and Mum said she could stay with us for as long as she needs to. She's sharing my room. It's a bit cramped but she needs time to cool down. It's obvious she didn't know. Also, her mum threw Derren out and she's going to bring up the baby alone. Freya has said that she'll have to move back in when the baby is born because her mother will need help, but she's just too mad at her at the moment.

'Would you like some cake?' Leah smiles at me.

I nod. 'I'd love some. Did you make it yourself?'

'Yes, when I knew that the two most special people in my life were coming for lunch, I knew I had to make an effort. I've made sandwiches too, they're in the fridge. I've also done up my old room, just in case you ever want to stay over. You don't have to but I want you to know that you're always welcome here, anytime, even if it's the middle of the night. You have a key, don't you?'

'Yes, and thank you.' I reach over and hug her. Zara mutters some joke about us all getting a bit soppy, but she too wipes a tear from the corner of her eye. This is the start of me getting to know Leah and I couldn't be happier. I'm not losing my parents; I'm gaining another mother. I am wanted and loved. I know now that we're all going to be okay.

I think back to my last moments with Jean. She'd gone on one of her rants, telling me how Leah never wanted or loved me. I believed her and I did all manner of horrible things to Leah. Thank goodness she's never mentioned that horrible message I sent with the wilting weed emoji. I let myself into her house too. I'm sure she'd forgive me if I told her but there's no need, like there's no need to tell her that in my anger, I smothered Jean with that red pillow she used to lean her arm on. Her game-playing and her nastiness – it all got too much and I snapped.

'Angel, are you okay? You look deep in thought.'

I smile. 'I'm fine, it's just lovely to be here. I'm glad we found each other.'

Leah tilts her head, and I've never seen her looking happier. 'Me too.'

My heart is bursting with love for this woman who gave birth to me and then thought I was dead. I'm not going to mess this up by confessing to getting rid of the person who started this whole chain of events off by giving me away. Jean deserved everything she got. Actually, she didn't start the whole chain of events off. That is down to someone else. I take a bite of the cake, and Leah smiles. 'This is amazing.' And it is. This whole day is amazing and I never want to forget it.

There's only one more thing I have to do. I have to make sure Leah never gets hurt again. It feels like my fault and I have to fix things. It's not right that someone should get away with rape, and I don't care that he's my biological father. He's scum and I will make him pay. I won't use a knife though; I really hate blood. Accidents happen when you least expect them to.

A LETTER FROM CARLA

Dear Reader,

I'm so thankful that you chose to read *On a Quiet Street*. Writing this standalone was totally different to writing my series books. I got to create a whole new set of characters and build them up from scratch, which felt exciting to do. I really enjoyed playing with the setting of Leah's childhood home.

I hope you enjoyed Leah and Angel's story. At times, it was heartbreaking to write and I can't ever imagine going through what Leah went through.

If you would like to keep up-to-date with all my latest releases, just sign up at the following link. Your email address will never be shared and you can unsubscribe at any time.

www.bookouture.com/carla-kovach

Whether you are a reader, tweeter, blogger, Facebooker, TikTok user or reviewer, I really am grateful of all that you do and as a writer, this is where I hope you'll leave me a review.

Again, thank you so much.

Carla Kovach

KEEP IN TOUCH WITH CARLA

facebook.com/CKovachAuthor

x.com/CKovachAuthor

instagram.com/carla_kovach

ACKNOWLEDGEMENTS

I'd like to say a huge thank you to everyone who has helped *On a Quiet Street* come to life. Editors, cover designers, people working in every aspect of publishing from administration to management are all a part of this large team.

A big special thank you goes to Helen Jenner, my fabulous editor. I couldn't do all this without her. She helped me so much with this book from the idea up and I'm super happy with what we've achieved.

Thank you again to Jo Thomson for the cover design. I love it!

The Bookouture publicity team are phenomenal. Noelle Holten, Kim Nash, Jess Readett and Sarah Hardy make publication days fun. Many thanks for everything.

I need to thank the generous blogger and reviewer community. I'm always grateful to anyone who chose my book out of the many brilliant books out there.

Mahoosive thanks to the Fiction Cafe Book Club. They are so supportive towards authors, giving up their time to shout about our work.

I'm also in awe of the Bookouture author family. Many thanks, they're amazing. My other author friends are fabulous too. Authors are the best!

My beta readers, Derek Coleman, Su Biela, Jamie-Lee Brooke, Anna Wallace, Abigail Osborne and Vanessa Morgan, are all lovely and I'm grateful that they read my work before publication. Further thanks to Jamie-Lee Brooke, Julia Sutton and Abigail Osborne. Our author support group keeps me happy and motivated.

I'd like to give special thanks to expert, Christine Eddy, who kindly answered my midwifery questions. I barely know anything about babies, let alone midwifery – hehe.

Lastly, thank you to my husband, Nigel Buckley, for the coffees and being supportive throughout the whole process.

PUBLISHING TEAM

Turning a manuscript into a book requires the efforts of many people. The publishing team at Bookouture would like to acknowledge everyone who contributed to this publication.

Audio
Alba Proko
Sinead O'Connor
Melissa Tran

Commercial
Lauren Morrissette
Jil Thielen
Imogen Allport

Cover design
Jo Thomson

Data and analysis
Mark Alder
Mohamed Bussuri

Editorial
Helen Jenner
Ria Clare

Copyeditor
Janette Currie

Proofreader
Liz Hurst

Marketing
Alex Crow
Melanie Price
Occy Carr
Cíara Rosney

Operations and distribution
Marina Valles
Stephanie Straub

Production
Hannah Snetsinger
Mandy Kullar
Jen Shannon

Publicity
Kim Nash
Noelle Holten
Myrto Kalavrezou
Jess Readett
Sarah Hardy

Rights and contracts
Peta Nightingale
Richard King
Saidah Graham

Milton Keynes UK
Ingram Content Group UK Ltd.
UKHW010727110124
435856UK00004B/138